DEATH OF A U.S. MARSHAL

Billy continued to hesitate. "Besides, that teller was goin' for a gun behind the counter. I shot him in self-defense."

"There weren't no gun behind that counter," Malone said. "You just flat-out murdered him." His hand tightened on the handle of his Colt. "I ain't gonna tell you again, Billy. Now let me see those hands on the table. We got a long ride back to Fort Smith."

"All right, Malone, you win. I don't wanna cause no trouble. You want 'em on the table, here they are." He brought them out from under the table, but one of them held a Smith & Wesson .44 revolver. The silence that had descended upon the tiny barroom was suddenly shattered by the harsh report of the handgun as Billy fired two shots into Malone's gut. The surprised deputy staggered backward, grasping for a chair back or table for support while trying to draw his weapon from its holster. Another shot from Billy's pistol struck him in the chest, and he crumpled to the floor.

BLACK HORSE CREEK

Charles G. West

A SIGNET BOOK

SIGNET
Published by New American Library, a division of
Penguin Group (USA) Inc., 375 Hudson Street, New York, New York 10014, USA
Penguin Group (Canada), 90 Eglinton Avenue East, Suite 700, Toronto,
Ontario M4P 2Y3, Canada (a division of Pearson Penguin Canada Inc.)
Penguin Books Ltd., 80 Strand, London WC2R 0RL, England
Penguin Ireland, 25 St. Stephen's Green, Dublin 2,
Ireland (a division of Penguin Books Ltd.)
Penguin Group (Australia), 250 Camberwell Road, Camberwell, Victoria 3124,
Australia (a division of Pearson Australia Group Pty. Ltd.)
Penguin Books India Pvt. Ltd., 11 Community Centre, Panchsheel Park,
New Delhi - 110 017, India
Penguin Group (NZ), 67 Apollo Drive, Rosedale, Auckland 0632,
New Zealand (a division of Pearson New Zealand Ltd.)
Penguin Books (South Africa) (Pty.) Ltd., 24 Sturdee Avenue,
Rosebank, Johannesburg 2196, South Africa

Penguin Books Ltd., Registered Offices:
80 Strand, London WC2R 0RL, England

First published by Signet, an imprint of New American Library,
a division of Penguin Group (USA) Inc.

First Printing, December 2012
10 9 8 7 6 5 4 3 2 1

PUBLISHER'S NOTE
This is a work of fiction. Names, characters, places, and incidents either are the
product of the author's imagination or are used fictitiously, and any resemblance
to actual persons, living or dead, business establishments, events, or locales is
entirely coincidental.
    The publisher does not have any control over and does not assume any
responsibility for author or third-party Web sites or their content.

For Ronda

the player seated to his left to see if he was going to call or fold, he realized that everyone else's attention was focused on something behind him. Looking back at Billy, he saw the cocky smile spreading across the young man's face that usually meant trouble for someone, so he quickly turned in his chair to discover the deputy marshal within several steps. He knew it was Billy the lawman was probably looking for, so he didn't hesitate to push his chair back and get out of the way.

Deputy Marshal Thomas Malone took a cautious look at the three men playing cards with Billy, his hand resting on the handle of the Colt .44 holstered at his side. Abruptly leaving their chairs, the three joined the small crowd of spectators, obviously wanting no part in what was about to happen. Still, Billy sat, smiling, with no apparent sense of alarm. "I'm fixin' to take you back to Fort Smith, Billy," Malone said. "That bank teller died, but not before he identified you as the person who shot him. So let me see your hands on the table before you get up, and we'll make this as easy as we can."

Billy didn't respond right away, continuing to sit calmly with his hands in his lap. "Deputy Thomas Malone," he finally announced grandly. "I was wonderin' if you'd be the one comin' after me. That damnfool bank teller might still be alive if he hadda got down on the floor when I told him to." His smile broadened when he saw Malone's look of impatience. "I gotta give you credit, though. You got sand, walkin' in here to arrest me, 'cause folks around this part of the river ain't got much use for lawmen." He continued to hesitate. "Besides, that teller was goin' for a gun behind the counter. I shot him in self-defense."

"There weren't no gun behind that counter," Malone said. "You just flat-out murdered him." His hand tightened on the handle of his Colt. "I ain't gonna tell you again, Billy. Now let me see those hands on the table. We got a long ride back to Fort Smith."

"All right, Malone, you win. I don't wanna cause no trouble. You want 'em on the table, here they are." He brought them out from under the table, but one of them held a Smith & Wesson .44 revolver. The silence that had descended upon the tiny barroom was suddenly shattered by the harsh report of the handgun as Billy fired two shots into Malone's gut. The surprised deputy staggered backward, grasping for a chair back or table for support while trying to draw his weapon from its holster. Another shot from Billy's pistol struck him in the chest, and he crumpled to the floor.

His revolver cocked again, Billy scanned the faces of the startled spectators, alert for the possibility that Malone might have brought a posse man along for support. After a moment, when it appeared that the deputy had acted alone, Billy released the hammer, holstered the weapon, and laughed. "Did you see the look on that bastard's face when he saw my .44 come out from under the table?" Then he cocked an eye toward the Choctaw blacksmith. "I reckon I oughta thank you for givin' me the jump on that son of a bitch. That gun was in my lap 'cause I was fixin' to shoot your ass if you drew one more card off the bottom of the deck."

Concerned now for his own neck, the Choctaw stammered nervously in defense. "Ah, hell no, Billy. I know better'n to cheat on you. I swear I wasn't even thinkin' about bottom dealin'. I just had a little streak of luck, that's all."

"Yeah, well that little streak was fixin' to end," Billy threatened as he bent over the deputy's body to relieve it of anything of value. He then straightened up and looked around at the circle of spectators, some of whom were heading for the door, the Choctaw among them. "He took a helluva long ride from Fort Smith just to get shot, didn't he? Somebody drag his carcass outta here." He paused when another thought occurred to him. "And don't nobody get no ideas about the horse he rode in on."

Ed Lenta, the owner of the little trading post that served as a watering hole for more than a few out-laws hiding out in Indian Territory, stepped forward to grab one of Malone's ankles. "Gimme a hand, Charley," he said to the man standing closest to him. Turning to Billy while Charley took hold of Malone's other ankle, he complained, "Damn, Billy, I wish you'da took care of this before you led 'em to my door. I sure as hell don't need a bunch of marshals comin' for a visit."

"Ah, quit your bellyachin', Ed," Billy responded. "I spent a helluva lot of money in this dump you call a saloon."

It galled Ed to put up with Billy's obvious lack of concern for his actions. Had it been anyone other than Billy, Ed would most likely have thrown him out the door and warned him never to come back. *Snot-nosed kid*, Ed thought. Billy wasn't but eighteen, but he was the youngest son of Jacob Blanchard. And that was the reason everybody tolerated the obnoxious young gunman. His father cast a big shadow, even down here in Indian Territory. In spite of the fact that

Billy was spending a lot of the bank's money in Ed's place, he had wished he would move on after holing up in his back room for the last three days. Now he was left with a body to hide, hoping no one in Fort Smith knew where the deputy had gone to look for Billy. Thanks to the young hothead, many of Ed's regular customers would most likely shun his place for a good while, for fear of encountering a marshal's posse. And Ed would have to hide his stock of illegal whiskey under the floorboards behind his bar in case of a surprise visit. He had been lucky so far because the U.S. marshal service in Fort Smith had not found his tiny trading post on the south bank of the Canadian River, deep in The Nations.

While Ed and Charley dragged the body out the front door, Billy stood casually reloading his pistol. Looking around him again, he demanded, "Where the hell did that damned Injun go?" Motioning toward the table, he told the other two card players, "Let's get back to the game. I'm too deep in the hole to quit. Maybe with that damn cheatin' Injun gone, somebody else can win a hand."

"Not me," one of the men said. "I don't need to hang around till the law shows up." He turned to leave, wasting no time to get out the door in case Billy was still in a killing mood.

"That goes for me, too," the other poker player said and followed right on his heels. He didn't know if the Indian had been cheating or not, but Billy might get the same idea about anyone else who had a lucky streak.

"What the hell's your hurry?" Billy called after them. "Malone was by hisself. And it took him four days to track me to this hole. Ain't nobody else likely to come nosin' around here."

"Maybe so," one of the departing men muttered almost under his breath, "but he tracked you here. There might be another'n comin' along behind him."

"Shit," Billy exclaimed in disgust. "He'd get the same as ol' Malone did." Although boastful in his comments, the possibility of another deputy, and maybe a posse, following him was reason enough to give him second thoughts. No need to take a chance, he decided, so he holstered his pistol and announced, "Looks like everybody's gone chicken-livered around here. I'm tired of the place, myself." He walked to the open door and called out to Ed Lenta, who was halfway across the bare yard, dragging the deputy's corpse. "Ed, send one of your boys to get my horse saddled up. I'm leavin' this damn flea nest of yours."

Saddle your damn horse yourself, Ed thought, and he and Charley continued dragging the body toward the edge of the clearing. In answer to Billy's call, however, he responded over his shoulder, "Sure thing, Billy. I'll take care of it." He looked at Charley and shook his head impatiently. "We'll all hate to see you go," he muttered sarcastically, only loud enough for Charley to hear.

Back in the store/saloon combination Ed called a trading post, Billy entered the back room he had inhabited for the last few days to collect his saddlebags and the few articles of clothing he had dropped on the floor. He paused to reconsider when he looked at the clock in the corner of the store. It was a good two and a half days' ride to his father's ranch on the Cimarron River, and this day was already half gone. Remembering that he had gained a new horse for himself when he shot Tom Malone, he dropped his saddlebags on the cot again. *There ain't no marshal within a hundred miles of here,* he told himself. *I might as well hang around for another night and start out in the morning.* That decided, he went out to the hitching rail to inspect the horse and saddle he had just claimed.

A common characteristic for the average deputy marshal was the fine horse he rode. So Billy expected to find a sturdy mount tied at Ed Lenta's hitching rail, and he was not disappointed. He made a thorough inspection of the blue roan that Malone had ridden, and grinned his satisfaction. While he looked the horse over, a boy that appeared to be close to his age came from the ring of trees beyond the clearing. When he approached Billy, he said, "Ed said for me to go saddle your horse. Which one is it?"

"Never mind that," Billy told him. "Just take this one and put him in the corral with the other'n. I'll take the rifle outta that saddle sling, though." He raised the rifle to his shoulder, dropped it to waist high, then raised it again, as if sighting in on a target. He repeated this several times; then he inspected the weapon, pleased with the acquisition of the 'seventy-three model Winchester, caliber .44, the same as the Colt handgun he took from the body.

Jacob Blanchard was a hard man to live with. His late wife would attest to that fact had she been able to. After bearing him three sons and miscarrying another, and years of doing his bidding, which required waiting on him hand and foot, she succumbed to pneumonia and departed this world. Some might say she had no desire to recover from the illness and made no effort to get well, even when her husband ordered her to get up out of her bed to resume her chores. Jacob was long accustomed to being obeyed whenever he gave an order. So when his wife died one frigid winter night, he was furious, seeing it as another act of disobedience on her part. No longer able to punish her in the usual way, since it would give him no satisfaction to whip an unfeeling corpse, he took his revenge in the form of carnal knowledge of the Creek woman he had hired as a cook—while his wife lay on her deathbed in the next room.

He was a big man, bigger than any of his three sons, a fact he blamed on the tiny woman he married. With shoulders that appeared to be two axe handles in width and arms that resembled small tree trunks, Jacob Blanchard was accustomed to forcing his will on most everyone he met. And although his silver-white mane and mustache were evidence of his years, there was no hint of decline in his physical dominance. A hard, unfeeling man, certainly, but he possessed some soft spots in his granitelike drive for power. One such soft spot was his affection for his youngest son. He could not help but admire Billy's natural penchant for doing what pleased him, and devil take the consequences. The fact that Billy not only had no respect for the law, but flamboyantly displayed it, gave his father genuine amusement. He understood his rambunctious young criminal son's need to have power over weaker people. As far as Jacob was concerned, it wouldn't hurt if Billy's older brothers were more like his youngest. The two older boys were cut from the same cruel stock as their father, but they did not seem to crave the power that had driven him to his present position. For Jacob saw himself as king of the vast cattle empire he had built around the settlement of Black Horse Creek.

He had welcomed settlers to stake out claims along the wide creek that emptied into the Cimarron River, and eventually a town was built, with a general store, two saloons, a blacksmith, stables, and a rooming house, all beholden to the largess of Jacob Blanchard. And most of the citizens of Black Horse Creek gave little thought to the fact that all their businesses and farms were surrounded by thousands of acres of prairie owned by their benefactor. With young families of limited means and prospects beyond finding a few acres to scratch out a living, Jacob's generous offer to stake out a couple hundred acres of "his" land for a modest yearly payment seemed an ideal solution to their needs. The town itself was built by Blanchard, streets laid out, stores and shops constructed with every merchant leasing their space. It was not long before the merchants and service providers realized that they were little more than bond slaves due to the agreements they had signed.

Jacob had no fondness for the town or the town folk, but it served his purposes in his plans to become the most powerful man in the territory. He was smart enough to know that settlers would continue to come and would eventually cause the government to become involved in staking land lots, territorial districts, and all other curses of civilization. It would inevitably lead to putting a limit on how much land one man could own. In anticipation of that day, Jacob reasoned that it would be more difficult for the government to deal with an entire town, and would most likely leave the business of land lots and claims to the citizens and their elected officials. Since he owned the town *and* the citizens, he figured it a safe hedge against any interference in his plans for conquest.

Black Horse Creek had no official mayor, since no one presumed to question the policies of Jacob Blanchard. A few of the citizens, Louis Reiner in particular, had approached Blanchard about the possibility of establishing a town council, but Jacob rejected the idea as unnecessary. The town was not without authority figures, however, in the form of a sheriff and deputy sheriff. The positions were filled by Slate and Troy Blanchard respectively, and it was commonly accepted that these were not posts filled by the election process. There were folks in the town who had concerns about the feudal arrangement they had sold themselves into, but chose not to discuss them openly for fear they might lose all they had invested.

It was early afternoon when Billy rode across the narrow bridge that his father had built over the creek at the lower end of town. Riding easily, he walked his horse up the street, leading the blue roan behind him. He reined up briefly in front of the sheriff's office, and after seeing no sign of anyone around, continued on toward the Black Horse Saloon. He needed a drink after riding since early morning, and he figured that was the most likely place to find his brothers as well. Tying his horses up to the rail, he paused to look up and down the street to see if anyone had noticed his arrival. Somewhat disappointed when it appeared that no one had, he stepped up on the short stoop and took a look inside the saloon before pushing through the swinging doors. As he had suspected, his two

brothers were sitting at a table in the back corner of
the saloon, enjoying a glass of beer. He stood in the
doorway a few moments longer, but when his presence still went unnoticed, he pulled his .44 from the
holster and fired a round into the floor. It had the
desired effect.

Both Slate and Troy jumped to their feet, sending
beer glasses skidding across the table to land on the
floor. Pistols drawn, they faced the door, ready to
return fire, only to find their younger brother standing there, laughing at them. "That's a damn good
way to get yourself shot," Troy told him, not at all
amused by Billy's idea of a joke. His comment served
to add to Billy's amusement.

"Why, brother Troy," Billy mocked, "you don't
seem glad to see me, and after I've been gone for so
many weeks, too."

Slate, the eldest brother, simply shook his head and
holstered his pistol. He had learned long ago that this
type of behavior was to be expected from Billy and
might as well be tolerated, because there was no way
his youngest brother would likely change. "Where you
been, Billy?" he asked. "You're all Pa talks about lately—
where's Billy? Wouldn't hurt if you let the old man
know from time to time that ain't nobody shot you."

"Where the hell *have* you been?" Troy echoed
Slate's question. "Me and Slate coulda used some
help keepin' the nesters from movin' in upriver." One
of the primary functions of the sheriff and his
deputy was to keep settlers from infringing on Jacob
Blanchard's empire. No one was permitted to settle
on the vast acreage upstream on the Cimarron. Jacob
intended to take no chances that someone above his
ranch might control the water that his cattle and his

town needed. Consequently, he charged his sons with the responsibility for making sure no free-range cattlemen or sheepherders decided to settle on that land. The fact that it was not legally his, or anyone else's, did not enter into it. He planned to eventually own it. In the meantime, he made it clear to his sons that any means to protect that land was justified and acceptable.

"Hell," Billy said as he pulled a chair back from the table and signaled for Roy, who had dived behind the bar when the shot was fired, to bring him a glass, "you don't need no help runnin' off a bunch of sheepherders. I had more important things to tend to."

"Like what?" Troy wanted to know.

Billy grinned, self-satisfied. "Oh, I don't know—there was a lot of ladies that needed tendin' to, and there ain't nobody that can take care of 'em like I can—makin' sure the banks ain't holdin' too much money, and the law ain't got too many deputies—things like that."

His brothers were not as impressed as he thought they would be. "Why, you damn-fool idiot," Slate questioned. "You ain't shot a marshal, have you?"

"Just as dead as hell," Billy replied smugly, "and a teller, too." His lips spread in a wide smile of self-satisfaction. "That hard-assed deputy, Tom Malone, ain't gonna be hasslin' nobody no more."

"And now you led the law straight back to Black Horse Creek," Slate responded.

"Don't nobody know where I went," Billy claimed. "Besides, that was in The Nations, Injun Territory. Black Horse Creek is in Kansas. Ain't no lawman gonna wanna ride this far lookin' for me."

Slate and Troy exchanged impatient glances. It was

useless to try to talk sense to Billy. They both knew it, and it was a source of resentment for the two, because their father favored the young hellion, taking pride in Billy's disregard for rules. "One of these days you're gonna run into somebody who don't back down to you," Slate said.

"If I do, I'll shoot the son of a bitch, just like I did with that damn deputy marshal," Billy replied.

The Creek woman, Rachel, who cooked Jacob Blanchard's meals and took care of his house—and responded to any of his other needs, some reluctantly—was in the process of setting the table for supper when Jacob got up from his chair on the porch. The hint of a smile tugged at the corners of his mouth as he watched the three riders approaching the barn. He walked to the door and called in to Rachel, "Set an extra place at the table. Billy's home."

Billy's face lit up with a wide smile when he saw his father striding from the house to meet them. "Looks like you boys picked up a stray in town," Jacob called out, his face reflecting Billy's smile.

"Yeah," Slate replied. "I reckon we ain't strict enough on who we let ride into our town."

"Howdy, Pa," Billy greeted his father, dismounted, and handed the reins to a young hired hand who worked in the barn. "Reckon a feller could get a good meal around here?" Billy asked.

"Maybe," Jacob said, "if he's got the price. Feller's gotta work for his chuck on this ranch. Ain't that right, Jimmy?"

The young man, waiting to take the reins from Slate and Troy, grinned in response and replied, "That's a fact, Mr. Blanchard."

Jacob stepped back to give Jimmy room as he led the horses toward the corral. "I see you got yourself a new horse," he said when the blue roan was led by. "Came with a saddle, too."

"Yes, sir," Billy said. "I got him at a good price."

"The price of a couple of cartridges," Troy interjected. "And I expect there'll be somebody showin' up around here lookin' for the rest of the price. That's Tom Malone's horse."

"Not likely, Pa," Billy quickly responded. "I got this horse down in Injun Territory, three or four days ride from here. Ain't nobody knows which way I headed."

Jacob preferred not to hear details of what Billy was up to when he rode off to cater to his wild impulses. He knew his son had no concern for right and wrong, the same as himself, but he did wish that Billy was a little smarter about it. "You shot a marshal?" he exclaimed. "What in hell did you do a dumb thing like that for?"

"It was him or me, Pa. I just did what I thought you'da done."

"No way you coulda got around it?"

"No, sir. He was fixin' to arrest me and take me back to Fort Smith to hang."

"Well, what's done is done," Jacob said. "You're sure nobody is on your tail?"

"I'm sure, Pa. I wouldn'ta led nobody back here," Billy said. Troy looked at Slate and rolled his eyes upward. Billy could tell their father that he'd shot Christ, Himself, and Jacob would pass it off as a boyish prank. All of the Blanchard men had innocent blood on their hands. It was easier to kill and steal what other men had worked for, than to work for it themselves, but Billy delighted in flaunting his superiority with his six-gun at every opportunity.

"I don't know what else you've been into," Jacob said. "And I don't wanna know, but your brother's right—there may be somebody showin' up in Kansas lookin' for you. It'd be a good idea for you to ride up to stay in the line camp at Rabbit Creek for a while."

"Ah, Pa," Billy protested, "I just got home. I don't wanna lay around that damned old shack."

"I ain't sendin' you up there to lay around," Jacob informed him. "Won't hurt you to shoulder some of the work around here. I expect you to look after our strays up there, and make sure there ain't no nesters tryin' to move in on our land." He then softened his tone and added, "You can stay here at the house a couple of days before you go, but first I wanna know the truth. Is there a lawman on your trail?"

"No, sir, not no more." He could not suppress the smile that spread across his face again.

The implication carried by his smug reply was not lost on his father. There was no taming Billy Blanchard. Jacob glanced at Slate for confirmation and his eldest shook his head in disgusted response. "Yeah, he killed him," Slate said.

"Damn," Jacob uttered softly as he considered the possible problems that may have followed Billy home. After a moment, he concluded, "Yeah, it's best you hide out in the line camp till we make sure you didn't bring home no lice with you." The tone of finality in his voice was enough to prevent any further protests from Billy. "And take that damn horse with you,

Chapter 2

"I got word you wanted to talk to me," the tall, somber man said as he walked into the office of U.S. Marshal John Council.

Council looked up from his desk to greet his visitor. "Grayson," he said in greeting, and closed the expense ledger he had been making entries in. "I see Rufus found you."

"I wasn't hard to find," Grayson replied. "I've been back in Fort Smith for about a week." He unbuttoned the dark woolen morning coat he wore and let it fall open. "It's hot as hell in here," he commented abruptly and cast an eye toward the little iron stove in the corner of the room, the belly of which had acquired a dull rosy glow. "What are you gonna do when winter really gets here?"

"Get a bigger stove," Council replied in response to Grayson's thinly veiled sarcasm. He knew it was the humorless man's way of chiding him for getting off a horse and mounting a desk.

Grayson grunted his version of a laugh. Thinking that was enough small talk between two old acquaintances, he got down to business, as was his custom. "What did you wanna talk to me about?"

"I thought you might be interested in a little hunting expedition," Council said. "It would damn-well be worth your time."

"I'm listenin'," Grayson replied with no real show of interest. Council didn't expect any. He had known Grayson for more than ten years, and their relationship had always been on a strictly business basis. Council doubted the stoic man had any friends. Not many people could say they really knew Grayson. Council was aware that Grayson had at one time ridden with the Texas Rangers, and for a few years he rode for the U.S. marshal service out of Omaha. Something had happened, Council never learned the details, but whatever it was, it caused Grayson to resign his job as a deputy marshal. Since that time, Grayson had operated more or less as a bounty hunter, seemingly whenever it suited him to do so.

"I lost Tom Malone a couple of weeks ago," Council said, "my best deputy, a man I can't afford to lose, shot down in a dingy little trading post on the Canadian River."

"I heard," Grayson said. "Tom was a good man."

"The best," Council replied, "and I'm sorely gonna miss him, because I don't have anybody else with his experience." He paused to cast a wry smile at Grayson. "I don't suppose you'd be interested in going back to work in the service."

"Reckon not," Grayson said.

"I didn't think so, but you might be interested in

doing a little job for me. Tom was gunned down while attempting to arrest Billy Blanchard on a murder charge."

"I heard that, too," Grayson deadpanned. "He let Billy get the jump on him, was the way I heard it."

"Well, I guess you could say that," Council conceded, reluctant to believe that a deputy with Tom Malone's experience could have been less than careful. "I sent Bob Aaron over there to check it out, but that fellow that owns the trading post where it happened suddenly lost his memory. He said he ain't even sure it was Billy that fired the shots, that he thought it mighta been a stranger just passing through."

"Ed Lenta," Grayson remarked. "I'm not surprised."

"Yeah, that's the man," Council continued. "Anyway, Lenta said he didn't know which way Billy went when he left his store, and he didn't notice which direction the stranger was heading, either. Bob looked around the place, but he couldn't turn up anything to help, so he came on back."

"Might as well forget about the stranger," Grayson said. "I doubt he exists. Billy was the one done the killin'."

"Well, that's what I figure, too," Council was quick to say. "But like I said, Bob didn't have any idea which way he ran."

It was not difficult to figure out why Council had sent for him, so Grayson got down to business. "Billy's most likely gone home to his daddy's place up on the Cimarron, and since that's over the line in Kansas, you don't want to send a deputy out of The Nations to look for him." He paused, but Council said nothing. Grayson continued. "So you want me to go up there and find Billy for you." He paused again before asking, "How much is it worth?"

"My superiors want justice to be served on this one for sure," Council emphasized. "You know, yourself, how many deputies have been killed in this territory in the last ten years. My boss wants to set an example with Tom Malone's death and show these murdering outlaws that they're not going to get away with killing a U.S. deputy marshal. He wants to have a public hanging with all the newspapers covering it." He paused to make sure his next statement had the desired effect. "My superiors have authorized me to offer a one-thousand-dollar reward for the capture of Billy Blanchard." He nodded to confirm it when he saw Grayson's surprised look. It was a lot of money for a low-life piece of trash like Billy Blanchard, so Council went on to justify the amount. "Like I said, we want Billy brought back alive to stand trial for the murder before we hang him."

"Things don't always work out that way," Grayson said. "You know that."

"If at all possible, we want him alive to stand up before the judge. But if there's no way to avoid killing him, I can't take your word that he's dead. Judge Parker wants proof in the form of Billy's body. So if you have to kill him, you're gonna have to produce his body to collect the reward—his guns, his horse ain't enough evidence—we've got to have the body." He waited a moment to make sure Grayson understood the terms. "This ain't going out on a regular wanted poster, because we don't want some wild, half-drunk cowboy taking a shot at Billy and sending him into hiding. We're just giving you the opportunity to slip over into Kansas and bring him out before anybody knows about it. I've got a paper signed by the governor of Arkansas that authorizes you to act on the state's behalf as a representative of the U.S. marshal service. So whaddaya say? You want the job?"

"I reckon," Grayson replied dryly. "It ain't always easy to bring 'em back settin' upright in the saddle, though." He felt he needed to emphasize that fact. "And that's a helluva long way to escort a prisoner, and that's providin' he ain't run off to Montana or somewhere else."

"One thousand dollars," Council said. "That's the reason the reward is that much."

"You tellin' me that if Billy gets his hands on a gun the day before I get him back to Fort Smith, and I have to shoot him to keep him from killin' me, you ain't gonna pay me the money?"

"No," Council replied. "I ain't saying that. I'm saying do everything you can to bring him back alive, but you'll get your money dead or alive. But not without Billy's body. Dammit, we're going to hang him up for everybody to see what happens to people who shoot deputy marshals."

"Just wanted to be clear on that," Grayson said. "I'll go get him for you." He got up to leave, but hesitated before the door. "I'm gonna have to buy cartridges and other supplies."

Council stopped him before he went further. "Damn, Grayson, we don't ever pay bounty hunters' expenses. You know that."

"Just thought I'd ask." He took hold of the doorknob. Nodding toward the stove in the corner again, he suggested, "Woulda been a good idea to have a coffeepot on that stove if you're gonna keep a fire goin' in it."

* * *

There had to be a pretty thick film of dust and dirt on the floor before Ed Lenta could be motivated to sweep. The store having reached that condition several days before, Ed procrastinated no longer, and put his broom to work. A small dirty cloud of dust formed over the back step of the building as Ed swept it through the door. Taking wide sweeps with the broom in an effort to send the dirt as far out in the yard as possible, he suddenly paused when he thought he heard something. Not certain that he had, he turned back toward the front door. "Damn!" he blurted in surprise to find the imposing figure standing between him and the bar, casually holding a rifle in one hand. "Grayson," he remarked. "You ought not sneak up on a man like that. You coulda gave me a heart attack." Still holding on to his broom, he walked over behind the bar. He had seen the notorious hunter of men several times before, and it seemed like a person never heard him coming. Even the gray gelding he rode seemed to tiptoe.

"Hello, Ed," Grayson replied. "You looked awful busy there. I didn't wanna disturb you."

Ed knew full well why Grayson was there, but he planned on playing dumb. His livelihood depended almost exclusively upon outlaws that sought refuge in The Nations, and his business would soon dry up if it became known that he had cooperated with the law. Grayson was no longer officially a representative of the law, but he may as well be, for he did their work for them. "What brings you out this way?" he asked.

"I came over from Fort Smith just because I was curious to see if you've got your memory back."

"My memory?" Ed replied, confused. "Whaddaya

talkin' about? If you're talkin' about that deputy that got shot a while back, there ain't nothin' to remember. Another deputy's already been here and took care of that."

Grayson favored the nervous storekeeper with a knowing smile. "Is that a fact? The way I heard it, you told that deputy that you weren't sure who shot who. To tell you the truth, Ed, you ain't the smartest fellow in the territory, but you ain't so dumb that you can't remember Billy Blanchard shootin' Tom Malone down right here in your store." He shook his head impatiently, keeping his intense gaze locked on Ed's eyes. "Now you oughta know the law ain't gonna let Billy get away with that. Did you think they'd just say, 'Too bad. Some stranger musta done it, but he got away'?"

"I never said Billy done it," Ed quickly reminded him. Seeing the expression of amusement on Grayson's face, he insisted, "There's lots of strangers come in my place. I can't remember all of 'em."

"I doubt there's that many," Grayson said. The smile disappeared from his face and the steely gaze intensified, signaling an end to the meaningless banter. "Billy shot that deputy. You know it, and I know it. You ain't in any trouble so far. All I want outta you is to make sure I don't waste any more of my time. I'm thinkin' Billy more'n likely headed straight back to his daddy's place up near Black Horse Creek. I'm also thinkin' he mighta said somethin' about it before he left, unless he was of a mind to take off for someplace else." He paused to observe Ed's reaction to that suggestion. There was none. "Here's the thing, Ed. It's gonna rile me somethin' awful if I ride all the way to Black Horse Creek and find out that Billy didn't go that way, that he headed in some other direction when he left here. You see where this is leadin'? I'm not a patient man, and I know damn well you know which way he rode outta here."

Not positive there was a definite threat behind Grayson's rambling talk, but suspecting there might be, Ed sang out, "Billy didn't say anythin' about headin' anywhere else in The Nations. I can't say he was headin' for Kansas, but he didn't say he was goin' anywhere else."

Grayson studied the uncomfortable storekeeper's face a few moments longer before deciding Billy had gone home, just as he had speculated. It may have been a waste of his time, sparring verbally with Ed Lenta, but he had thought to pick up a clue in case he had been wrong about second guessing Billy. *Hell*, he thought, *it's on the way to Black Horse Creek, anyway.*

Ed walked outside and watched the solemn bounty hunter as he made his way across to the opposite bank of the river, just as he had watched Billy Blanchard depart from his store. He told himself that he could be proud of the fact that he had not told Grayson that Billy casually mentioned going home to lay up for a while. Another part of him hoped Grayson would catch up with the insolent young gunman. *I sure as hell wouldn't want that mountain lion after me*, he thought.

Two days in the saddle brought him to the point where the Crooked River flowed into the Cimarron. He didn't know exactly where the territorial line between the Oklahoma Outlet and Kansas was, but he knew he was close to it. He made his camp at the confluence of the two rivers, planning to follow the Cimarron on into Kansas in the morning, and figuring to reach Black Horse Creek sometime in the early afternoon. It had been a while since he had traveled this part of the territory, but from what he had heard, a sizable town had grown up on the river and he was curious to see what kind of folks had settled on the flat, grassy plains. It seemed odd to him that Jacob Blanchard had allowed settlers on the thousands of acres he held reign over. The land seemed most suitable for raising cattle, and if memory served him, the town couldn't be much more than fifty miles from Dodge City and the railroad. Jacob Blanchard was as cruel an outlaw as had ever strapped on a six-gun, responsible for no telling how many murders and robberies. The trouble was that no one had been able to prove it. He didn't normally leave witnesses. So why would he permit a town to grow up on land he considered his? Stranger things had happened, Grayson figured.

"Don't recall seein' him before," Troy Blanchard remarked as he stood gazing out the window of the sheriff's office.

Curious, Sheriff Slate Blanchard got up from his chair and walked over to the window to see for himself. Leading a pack horse, a stranger leisurely rode a gray gelding down the middle of the street. "Me either," Slate said in response to his brother's remark. They continued to watch the stranger's progress down the street until he pulled over to tie up at the rail in front of Louis Reiner's store, next to the Black Horse Saloon. It was easy to see by his dress that he was not a cowboy, drifting from one job to another. Instead of going into Reiner's store, the stranger pulled his rifle from the saddle scabbard, walked back a dozen yards and entered the saloon. "Why'd he tie up at Reiner's if he was goin' to the saloon?" Slate asked. The simple act qualified the stranger as suspicious in Slate's mind, remembering his father charging him with the responsibility for knowing everybody's business who entered his town. "I expect we'd better go down to the Black Horse and see who this feller is," Slate said.

Grayson was working on a glass of beer and talking to Roy, the bartender, when the two lawmen walked in. He took a quick glance in their direction before turning his attention back to the glass before him on the bar. Though brief, it was enough to enable him to size up the two. The one leading was a powerfully built man, heavyset through the shoulders while the man following was of a slender frame, lean and wiry. Of the two, Grayson decided that the heavyset one would be the one to deal with first in the event of a confrontation.

"You won't be needin' that in here," Slate informed him and pointed to the Winchester propped against the bar beside Grayson's leg.

Grayson responded with a thin smile as he took note of the badge on each of the men's vests. "Well, I wasn't figurin' on robbin' the place. Just a habit I reckon I picked up, Sheriff. It ain't against the law, is it?"

"It is in this town," Troy answered, making no attempt to disguise his frank appraisal of the stranger.

"Feller's just havin' a beer," Roy said. Then, turning to Grayson, he introduced the lawmen. "This is Sheriff Blanchard and Deputy Sheriff Blanchard."

The hint of a smile returned to Grayson's face. There was no need for further speculation on the accuracy of rumors he had heard about Jacob Blanchard's cattle empire. If he owned the law, he owned the town. "Blanchard," he said. "Now, why does that name sound familiar?"

"Never mind that," Slate replied. "What brings you to Black Horse Creek? You got business here?"

"I'm just passin' through on my way to Dodge City," Grayson answered. "I'd heard about your little town here and thought I'd take a look at it—maybe pick up a few things at the store next door."

"You got a name?" Troy asked.

"Grayson," was the short reply.

"Well, Mr. Grayson," Slate said, "enjoy your visit, but we don't allow weapons in the saloons in this town. Roy shoulda told you that." He cast an accusing glance in the bartender's direction.

"I think he was just fixin' to when you fellows walked in," Grayson said, "but I'll take it back outside right away. I wouldn't want to get on the wrong side of the law. All right if I finish my beer first—if I promise not to shoot anybody?"

Slate shot a quick glance at Troy, not sure if he was the victim of sarcasm or not. It was met with a blank expression. "I reckon that'll be all right. Just remember next time," he mumbled. There was something ominous in the man's smile that made Slate uneasy.

"You fellows have the same last name," Grayson commented. "Are you cousins, or brothers, or somethin'?"

"Brothers," Troy replied.

"I heard of another Blanchard that owns a big cattle outfit near here. How 'bout him? Is he kin of yours?"

"Mister, you ask a helluva lot of questions," Slate replied. "You just finish your beer and be on your way, unless you can tell me you've got some business in Black Horse Creek." He turned to leave. "Come on, Troy, I'm gettin' about ready for my dinner."

"Me, too," Grayson volunteered. "Where's a good place to buy a meal in town?"

The two brothers ignored his question as they walked out the door. Roy, who had said very little during the confrontation, commented to Grayson after they had gone. "They'll go over to the hotel to eat. That's the best food in town. If I was you, though, I might think about gettin' somethin' to eat somewhere else. I think you rubbed the sheriff and his deputy the wrong way."

"I 'preciate the advice," Grayson said and then drained the last of his beer. "Those two, are they Jacob Blanchard's sons?"

"That's a fact," Roy replied.

"He's got another son, hasn't he?" Roy didn't answer. He just shrugged. Grayson continued. "Have you seen him around lately?"

"Mister," Roy replied, "the sheriff's right—you ask a helluva lot of questions."

"Just a natural curiosity, I reckon," Grayson said with a shrug of his shoulders. "Has he been in town in the last week or so?"

Roy didn't care for the direction of the stranger's questions, so he attempted to end the conversation. "I don't pay no attention to the Blanchards's comin's and goin's," he declared. "Billy's been gone for a spell, and I don't know whether he's back or not."

"Suppose I was of a mind to ride out and visit Jacob Blanchard," Grayson asked, "how would I find his place?"

"The minute you ride out of town, you'll be on

his land," Roy said. "But if you're talkin' about ridin'
up to the ranch house, you take the road at the end of
the street and follow it up the river till you get to
another road that forks off to the north. That'll take
you right up to Mr. Blanchard's door. It's about fifteen
miles."

"Much obliged," Grayson said and slid his empty
beer glass across the counter to Roy. "Now I reckon
I'd best get on my way before I get arrested for bringin' my rifle in here."

"Take care of yourself," Roy advised in farewell.
He wasn't sure what prompted him to offer words of
caution. There was something about the stranger that
suggested a familiarity with trouble, and Blanchard's
ranch was not a wise place to go looking for it.

Leaving the saloon, Grayson walked next door to
Reiner's Dry Goods. Before going inside, he glanced
back up the street to see both the sheriff and his deputy standing out in front of the office, watching him
he presumed. *I thought you were going to go to dinner,* he
said to himself as he reached for the knob and opened
the door. There was no one in the store but the proprietor, Louis Reiner, and he stood waiting for Grayson,
having watched for him ever since he tied his horse
out front. "Afternoon," Reiner greeted him. "What
can I help you with?"

"Afternoon," Grayson returned. "I need a couple
of things: some bacon, some coffee, some salt, and
maybe some sugar."

"Yes, sir," Reiner replied politely, and jumped to
accommodate his customer, more so than Grayson
would normally have expected.

"Ain't many folks in town," Grayson remarked.
"Looks like business is a little slow."

Reiner smiled. "You can say that again," he said. "We're a little bit off the beaten path. Not many folks pass through Black Horse Creek. Businessmen like me depend pretty much on the folks that live around the town." He paused as he reached under the counter for a sack. "If it wasn't for Mr. Blanchard and his crew, we probably wouldn't make it at all."

"Looks to me like there's a helluva lot of land along the river," Grayson commented. "I'm surprised there ain't more folks movin' in on it."

"Mr. Blanchard owns all of it, and he doesn't let anybody settle on it," Reiner said, his voice taking on a cautious air, as if afraid someone might overhear. "He says he needs it all for his cattle."

Grayson frowned. "He must be plannin' on one helluva big cattle operation. Ever think about pullin' up stakes and headin' for someplace else?"

Reiner shrugged. "Oh, I've thought about it, I reckon, but I've got too much invested in my store here, and I couldn't pay Mr. Blanchard off for what I owe him."

Grayson nodded, understanding. It was further evidence of the extent to which Blanchard owned the town. He guessed that the other businesses were in the same fix as Reiner. "Well, I wish I could give you a little more business, but I reckon that'll do it for now." He counted out his money and laid it on the counter. "This fellow, Blanchard, he's got three sons. Ain't that right?"

"That's right," Reiner replied. "You just met two of 'em in the saloon, didn't you?"

"Yeah, the sheriff and his deputy, but I didn't meet the other one. Is he a lawman, too?"

"Not hardly," Reiner answered after taking a

precautionary look toward the door. "You won't see Billy around here very much."

"Billy," Grayson repeated. "I ain't sure, but I think I saw him when I first rode in—kind of a tall, heavy-set fellow ridin' a sorrel horse."

"Nah," Reiner replied. "That wasn't Billy. I don't know who that was, coulda been one of Mr. Blanchard's hands, but Billy doesn't look anything like that. He doesn't look like his brothers. I reckon he's about average height, he's slim, but I wouldn't call him skinny— got curly black hair. And he doesn't ride a sorrel, unless he just traded, which I doubt, 'cause he's mighty fond of that Appaloosa he usually rides."

"Well, I reckon I was mistaken," Grayson said as he gathered up his purchases. One of the problems he'd had until then was the fact that he hadn't known how to identify Billy Blanchard. So now, thanks to Louis Reiner's willingness to chat, he had a general description. Adding that to what he *did* know before today, that Deputy Tom Malone had ridden a blue roan that may still be in Billy's possession, he felt he had a lot more to go on. "He most likely ain't been around here for quite a spell," Grayson remarked.

"Oh, he's been around—next door, anyway," Reiner started, then abruptly held his tongue when it suddenly occurred to him that he might be telling a stranger too much. It was too late, for he had already told Grayson what he wanted to know.

"Much obliged," Grayson said. "I'll be on my way now."

While he packed his supplies on his packhorse, he stole a quick glance back up the street toward the sheriff's office. *Roy must have gotten nervous and gone to report our conversation to the sheriff,* he thought, for the bartender was at that moment talking to Slate and Troy Blanchard. *They're either going to come back after me right now, or go tell Daddy there's a stranger in town asking questions.* So he stepped quickly up in the saddle and rode away, preferring the latter.

Watching him from his Harness Shop across the street, Shep Barnhill put aside a bridle he had been in the process of repairing, and walked over to question Louis Reiner. "Don't recall seeing that fellow around here before," he commented to Louis.

"He said he was just passing through," Louis replied, fully aware of the reason for Shep's curiosity. "He said this is the first time he's been in Black Horse Creek."

"Don't reckon he said where he came from?" Shep asked.

"No, he didn't, but he was asking a lot of questions about the Blanchards." He knew what Shep was hoping he could tell him, that the stranger had come from the capital in Topeka, but he doubted that to be the case. Shep, like a few of the other men in town belonged to a covert organization of merchants that met occasionally to discuss the possibility of seeking government help to create a town charter and free them from the dictatorial rule of Jacob Blanchard. It had been over two months since they sent Henry Farmer's son, Bob, to Topeka to inform them of the town's problems. Bob had not been heard from since. Maybe he had simply given up on his mission to gain audience with the new governor, George T. Anthony, and gone instead to join his father in Arkansas, or maybe Blanchard had somehow gotten wind of the boy's mission. It had been long enough to get some response from the governor if Bob had, in fact,

completed the trip. It looked, however, as if something had happened to prevent it, and Louis was
afraid the town was destined to be forever beneath
Jacob Blanchard's iron thumb.

Down at the end of the street, past the blacksmith
shop, Grayson came to the wagon road Roy had
directed him to. He turned his horse up the road and
followed it as it held close to the river. The gelding
had already carried him half a day before arriving in
Black Horse Creek, so he considered whether to push
the horse for another fifteen miles. There was no
doubt that the gray was up to it, but he decided it best
to rest him. He estimated that he had ridden about
three miles before coming to a sharp bend in the river
that formed a pocket of trees, several of which hung
over the bank. Figuring this gave him as much con-
cealment as could be found on the flat, endless, tall-
grass prairie, he guided the gray off the road and into
the pocket formed by the river bend. Once his horses
were watered and unsaddled, he found himself a place
in the trees where he could watch the road. With
his back up against a cottonwood trunk, he settled
himself to wait while he chewed on a piece of beef
jerky.

After a short while he spotted a rider on the road
coming from Black Horse Creek at a lively walk. *Well,
looks like they ain't coming after me*, he thought. *Going to
tell Daddy instead.* He leaned forward, his eyes focused
on an opening in the tree branches that would give
him a window for a good look at the rider when he
passed. Once the rider was opposite him, he was easily identified as Troy Blanchard. *Right on schedule*,
Grayson thought, and got up to go saddle his horse. It

was not yet dark enough to follow Troy too closely, so he was in no hurry. He knew where Troy was heading, anyway. His only purpose in lying in wait for him was to determine if the two Blanchard brothers were coming after him, or sending someone to warn Jacob. Now there were two new possibilities: Billy was holed up at his father's ranch, or he was hiding out somewhere else. And if the latter was the case, there was a good chance that someone would be sent to warn him. This was the situation Grayson preferred, because he was not too keen on the idea of wading into Blanchard's stronghold to serve arrest papers on Billy. The odds were against coming out alive. With that in mind, his plan was to find someplace where he could watch the comings and goings at the ranch house, and hope for an opportunity to catch Billy alone.

Chapter 3

The heavy gray brows that lay like small storm clouds over Jacob Blanchard's deep-set eyes arched in an angry frown as he listened to Troy's report. "Did this nosy stranger have a name?" the old man asked.

"I think he said it was Grayson," Troy answered.

"Grayson!" Jacob responded heatedly, for he was familiar with the name. "He's a damn bounty hunter, and a dangerous one. He's come lookin' for Billy. There ain't no doubt about it. Where is he now? Still in town?"

"I don't know for sure," Troy replied. "Roy Brown said he was askin' how to get out here to the house, but I didn't pass him on the way out from town. So maybe he just rode on to Dodge City like he told me and Slate."

"Not likely," Jacob fumed. "He came to Black Horse Creek for a reason, and that reason is Billy." He paused for a moment, thinking about what Troy had just said. "I wish to hell he *would* come out here. I'd be glad to talk to him, and he wouldn't be botherin' nobody else after that."

"Whaddaya reckon we oughta do, Pa?" Troy asked.

Still fuming over the situation, one that he felt should not have gotten this far, he said, "You shoulda never let that bastard get outta your sight, and he shoulda had an accident on his way out here to my house. Damn bounty hunter. He used to be a deputy marshal, but he ain't no more, so nobody would miss him, and they sure as hell wouldn't care what happened to him. But that can't be helped now, dammit. First thing is to ride up to the line camp and tell Billy to stay put and keep his eyes open. And tell him not to get any ideas about riding into town to raise hell. He's been up at that line camp long enough to get rutty and itchin' to go stir up some trouble. It don't take but a few days for Billy."

"That's the truth," Troy said. "You want me to ride up there in the mornin'?"

"I want you to ride up there tonight before he decides he's gotta go let off some steam somewhere," his father told him.

"Damn, Pa," Troy complained. "That shack's a good eight miles. That'll take me half the night, and I told Slate I'd sleep in the jail tonight so he could take a night off."

"What's he need a night off for?" Jacob wanted to know.

"So he can go see that little Mexican gal that works in the hotel," Troy answered with a grin.

"Hellfire," Jacob responded in disgust, then had a change of heart. "All right, I'll send Stump up there to tell Billy. Go on down to the bunkhouse and get him."

The stubby little man they called Stump made no complaint when Troy told him he was going to ride up to the northern boundary of Blanchard's ranch that night. It was all the same to him, spend the night in the bunkhouse, or spend it on a mule, as long as he was able to fill his belly with a good meal—and he had already done that. Stump was not very bright. Some claimed he was kicked in the head by a horse when he was a boy, and that accounted for his preference for mules over horses. Others had it that he had been very ill with a high fever when still a baby, and it cooked half of his brain. Of the two explanations, the latter was probably closer to the truth. He was a cousin of Yancey Brooks, Jacob's foreman, so that was the main reason he was on the payroll. He was not much of a cowhand, but he shone in doing odd chores around the ranch and the house, like the job he was given this night. Jacob knew he could be depended upon.

Jacob stood beside Stump's stirrup while he gave him instructions. "You remember what you gotta tell Billy, now, don'tcha?" Stump repeated Jacob's message, word for word. "All right," Jacob said, "you'd best get started." Stump started to turn his mule toward the gate, but Jacob stopped him for one last reminder. "And, Stump, you make sure you tell Billy that I said he don't wanna mess with this damn Grayson. It's best to stay holed up in that cabin."

"Yes, sir, Mr. Blanchard," Stump replied and started for the gate.

"He'll take all night to get up there on that damn slow-walkin' mule," Troy commented as he prepared to step up in the saddle. "I'd best get on back to town. Slate's probably already gettin' itchy."

"You keep your eyes open," his father reminded him. "That damn Grayson might still be hangin' around town." He grabbed Troy's elbow to make sure his son understood his instructions. "And, Troy, if he does show his face in my town again, I want him to have an accident. Understand?"

"Yes, sir, I understand."

Grayson got to his feet when he saw two riders leaving the ranch house at almost the same time. Standing close beside a tree trunk in the faint evening light, he could see clearly enough to recognize the figure of Troy Blanchard as he turned his horse back toward town. That was enough for Grayson to turn his attention to the other rider, mounted on a mule, and heading in the opposite direction. Knowing this was the man most likely to lead him to Billy, he watched for only a few moments more before walking back to his horse and climbing in the saddle. "Let's go, boy, we gotta go to work."

As he expected, the pace was leisurely and he let Stump get out about a quarter of a mile ahead of him in the fading light. As darkness came on, Grayson closed up the gap between them to keep the mule and rider in sight. They continued on until a half-moon climbed up from the horizon behind Grayson's right shoulder, causing him to rein his horse back again in case Stump decided to watch the trail behind him. On they rode through the night until the moon had traveled across the sky to a position above a line of hills to the west. Weary from spending so many hours in the saddle since the day before, Grayson began to wonder if the stubby man on the mule was going to stop before they rode all the way to Canada.

Suddenly, he had to rein his horse back hard when he realized that the mule had stopped before crossing what appeared to be a creek.

Stump let the mule drink; then, instead of crossing over, he turned the mule to follow the creek back to the west. Grayson nudged the gray to tighten the gap between him and the mule, and when he reached the creek, he was able to see a rough shack by the edge of the water, about fifty yards from where he now sat his horse. He dismounted at once, for fear of casting an obvious image in the pre-dawn light. Reprimanding himself for almost riding right up Stump's back, he looked hurriedly around for a place to hide his horses and himself before it got any lighter. The best he could find were some scraggly trees along the banks of the creek with patches of berry bushes in between, but it appeared to be sufficient—as long as no one in the shack was concentrating on it. By the time he had his horses safely hidden, he could hear the mule rider hailing the cabin.

"Hey-oh, Billy!" Stump called several times. "Billy, it's me, Stump," he called again. "You in there? You awake?"

"Well, I am now, you damn fool." A shadow separated from the back corner of the rough cabin and walked to meet the man still aboard the mule. There was not enough light to determine the man's features, and he had nothing on but his long johns. He was wary, as evidenced by the fact that he had gone out the back window of the shack when called out, his pistol in his hand. Grayson moved along the bank of the creek, getting closer to the cabin, close enough to better hear the conversation between the two men.

"Stump," Billy blurted, "what in the hell are you doin' up here?"

"Mr. Blanchard sent me to warn you. There's a bounty hunter in town lookin' for you, and your daddy said to tell you not to leave this camp," Stump reported dutifully. "He said this feller's as dangerous as a rattlesnake, and you'd best stay hid till he's gone somewhere else."

Billy released the hammer on his .44 Smith & Wesson revolver and put it back in the holster on the belt he was carrying in his hand. "Is that a fact?" he asked, while thinking that his father had been right about sending him up to the line camp. It irritated him sometimes that his father was always right. "You know what I do with rattlesnakes, Stump? I skin 'em and eat 'em—the same as I do with deputy marshals."

Stump was immediately concerned, afraid he had not delivered Jacob Blanchard's message as instructed to do. "Your daddy don't want you to tangle with this feller. He told me to tell you that."

"All right, you told me, but I'll do what I damn-well please, and it riles me to have a stinkin' bounty hunter think he can come after me."

"Ah, Billy," Stump moaned, "don't go doin' nothin' your daddy don't want you to."

Knowing the main thing that was worrying the simpleminded cousin of his father's foreman was the fear that he had failed to deliver the message as instructed, Billy changed the subject. "You might as well get down off that mule and we'll see 'bout some breakfast. You bring any grub with you?"

Stump slid off his mule. "No, they didn't tell me to."

"They didn't, huh," Billy replied sarcastically. "If

they didn't tell you to take a shit, I reckon you'd just hold it till you blew up." Stump, obviously confused by the comment, did not reply. "Well, get some of that wood on the pile yonder and build up that fire." He pointed toward the ashes of a fire beside the shack where most of the cooking was done. When the weather dictated it, the little stove inside was used to do the job. "I've still got plenty of bacon and coffee. We'll have us a little breakfast." He started to go inside the cabin, but paused when an idea struck him. "I'm gettin' damn sick and tired of bacon and beans. Tell you what, before you start back to the house, you can help me do a little butcherin'. Pa told me to round up strays up here. Well, I rounded a few of 'em up before I said to hell with it. We'll cut out a nice young calf and eat some beef for a change." Stump didn't have to say anything. Billy knew what the simple man was thinking. "Don't worry about it, Stump. I'm the one callin' the shots. Pa don't ever have to know about it."

"If you say so, Billy." The idea of some fresh roasted beef appealed to him.

For the man hiding in the clump of berry bushes, Billy's decision was good news, because it meant the young outlaw did not plan to go anywhere that day. Having had no sleep during the night just passing, Grayson saw an opportunity to catch some while Billy and Stump were slaughtering one of Jacob Blanchard's cattle. His horses could use the rest as well. He would wait to make his move on Billy later in the day after he and Stump had filled their bellies. The task at hand now was to find a place to hide, for with the rapidly approaching morning light, it would soon be fairly easy to spot a man trying to hide in a bunch of serviceberry bushes. So as quietly as he could manage, he backed slowly away.

He led his horses back for about fifty yards before stepping up in the saddle and continuing for another quarter of a mile when he felt it safe to leave the cover of the creek. The vantage point he sought was the hill behind the shack, which would give him the best view of the cabin as well as the small corral on one side. Because of the open prairie, it would be necessary to make a wide circle to come up from behind the ridge. He decided to rest his horses and himself right where he was, by the creek, where the horses could drink and graze. There was plenty of time, for he was confident that Billy wasn't going anywhere, at least until after the butchering and the feast. He was not sure what complications Stump might cause, so he preferred to deal with Billy alone. By waiting to arrest Billy, he hoped that Stump would be on his way back home, none the wiser, and no one would know that Billy had been captured before he was halfway across The Nations.

It was past noon when he awoke, at once concerned that he had slept longer than he had planned. He hurriedly climbed the bank of the creek to look back toward the line shack, and was relieved to see a thin brown string of smoke wafting up in that direction. Admonishing himself for his carelessness, he saddled the gray, loaded his packhorse, and started out on a wide circle to eventually come up behind the low ridge backing the shack. Within half an hour, he was in a position above the rough building, his horses tied in the brush below him. *Damn*, he thought, for the first thing he noticed were the two horses and one mule in the tiny corral, which meant that Stump was still there. At least Billy's Appaloosa, and the blue roan that had belonged to Tom Malone, were there. That was the main thing that concerned him, since he had allowed himself to oversleep.

Moving along the ridge, he made his way to a point where he could see the fire and the two men. Some several dozen yards below him, Billy sat eating a chunk of roasted beef while Stump was tending a haunch on a spit that he had fashioned from a green willow limb. Grayson could smell the aroma of the roasting beef as it drifted up from below. It reminded him that he had had nothing but cold jerky. Sitting in the coals on one side of the fire was a coffeepot, which added to his envy and made him resolve to share in the feast. It didn't appear that Stump was going to depart anytime soon. Grayson decided he might as well make his move and deal with the two of them, still with no idea if Stump was going to fight or run.

Looking about him, he decided his best approach to the party was by way of a shallow gully that ran down the ridge to a point behind the cabin. He estimated it to be no more than a dozen yards behind the man lolling with his back up against the shack, eating his fill of fresh meat. Grayson carefully looked the situation over. Billy was still wearing nothing but his long underwear; his gun belt was hanging on the corner of the open cabin door, perhaps ten or twelve feet from him. Shifting his gaze back to Stump, he was satisfied to see that the simple man tending the meat was also without a sidearm. His pistol and belt were lying on his saddle, which had been dropped beside the corral. With his rifle in hand, and a couple of coils of rope on his shoulder, Grayson crawled over into the gully and started working his way slowly down it, taking care not to disturb the loose rocks along the sides.

"I swear that sure beats the hell outta salt pork," Billy exclaimed as he set his plate down on the ground beside him. "I've had a hankerin' for some fresh beef ever since I got up here. I was thinkin' about butcherin' one of them cows, but I'm glad you came along to do it for me. I couldn'ta done it as good as you."

Dumb enough to believe he was receiving an honest compliment, Stump broke out a wide grin, and turned to show it to Billy. His face froze and he stopped dead still, causing Billy to ask him if he'd seen a ghost. Stump didn't answer, but pointed to the corner of the shack behind Billy with the fork he had been tending the meat with. Still puzzled by Stump's strange behavior, Billy turned to see what Stump was pointing to. His reactions were swift as he rolled immediately away from the shack, but his pistol was too far away, and the grim stranger's reflexes were just as quick as his. Firing and cocking in rapid succession, Grayson sent two shots ripping into the dirt inches before Billy's boots, causing him to jump back to avoid being hit. "The next one's goin' in the side of your head," he warned, stopping Billy dead in his tracks with only the scowl on his face with which to defend himself. Glancing quickly back at Stump, who had not moved from the paralyzed crouch at his first sight of the somber avenger, Grayson said, "Sit down right there and don't move till I tell you to." The confused man did as he was told.

Unable to hold his tongue or his temper for very

long, Billy snarled in defiance. "Are you Grayson?" he demanded.

"I'm Grayson," he answered calmly.

"You're makin' one helluva mistake," Billy blurted, his anger barely under control. "You might as well take that rifle and shoot yourself in the head with it, because you'll never live to collect any reward for takin' me in."

"I reckon you're the one that made the mistake when you killed that deputy back at Ed Lenta's place on the Canadian," Grayson said.

"You ain't no lawman," Billy exclaimed. "You're a damn egg-suckin' bounty hunter. You can't arrest me."

"As a matter of fact, I can," Grayson said. "I just happen to have papers that say I can, but it doesn't really make any difference. I'm takin' you back to Fort Smith so you can get a proper hangin', papers or not. The only thing you have to decide is how you're gonna travel—sittin' in the saddle or lying across it—'cause it's all the same to me."

Desperate now, Billy yelled at Stump. "Help me, Stump! He can't take both of us if we jump on him at the same time." Stump, his eyes wide with uncertainty, looked back and forth from Billy to the man with the rifle.

"That's bad advice, Stump," Grayson told him. "He's lookin' to get you shot and hopin' he has enough time to get to his gun while I'm doin' it. You just use your brains and sit right where you are. I didn't come after you. Billy's the one done the killin'. I got no reason to do you any harm unless you force me to."

"By God, Stump," Billy threatened, "you'd best

remember who you work for. Pa will have your hide if you don't help me. I'm tellin' you, he ain't no lawman." Totally confused now, Stump was wavering between saving his own neck and acting to help the son of his employer.

The indecision was clearly evident upon the perplexed man's face, so Grayson cautioned him. "You'd be makin' a mistake, Stump." It was too late; Stump's fear of Jacob Blanchard's wrath was the determining factor. He let out a howl like that of a wolf and charged Grayson. As soon as Stump howled, Billy lunged to his feet and sprinted for his pistol hanging on the door. Already anticipating something of the sort, Grayson deftly sidestepped Stump's clumsy charge and felled him with a sharp blow to his skull with the butt of his rifle. Then without pause, he leveled the rifle again in time to fire a round that struck Billy in the thigh seconds before Billy's outstretched hand could reach the pistol.

Billy screamed out in pain as he spun around and fell to the ground. "You shot me, you son of a bitch!" he wailed as he grabbed his leg.

"That I did," Grayson replied with no hint of concern. He glanced down at Stump, who showed no signs of getting up. Then he walked over to the door, took the gun and holster, and tossed them over to the other side of the fire. He paused to take a look at Billy, who was writhing in pain, his full attention captured by the necessity of stopping the flow of blood oozing from the bullet hole in his leg. Deciding he was occupied for the moment, Grayson turned his attention back to Stump. Shaking a coil of rope from his shoulder, he laid his rifle down and rolled Stump over on his back. Working quickly before the stunned man had time to think about resisting, he bound his hands and ankles securely. Satisfied that Stump was taken care of for the time being, he moved to incapacitate Billy.

"Whaddaya doin'?" Billy complained when Grayson turned him over roughly and proceeded to tie his hands behind his back. "I'm shot! I need to tend to my wound!"

Grayson finished tying him up before replying, "I'll take care of your wound. Quit your cryin'." He preferred to have Billy's hands tied behind him while he wrapped a cloth around his leg. "Now sit there while I find somethin' to bind that leg." He went to the door of the shack and peered inside to see if he could spot anything to use for a bandage. Seeing a couple of shirts hanging on a chair back, he decided one would do the job. So he looked back to make sure his prisoner was sitting where he had left him, then hurried inside to fetch one of the shirts. Even though only seconds, it was time enough for Billy to struggle to his feet and limp over on the other side of the fire where Grayson had thrown his gun and holster. He was sitting on the ground with his back to the pistol, trying to find it with his bound hands, when Grayson walked casually over to kick the weapon away. "You're lucky you couldn't get your hands on that pistol," the imperturbable man told him. "You'da probably shot yourself." He then tore Billy's spare shirt into strips and bandaged Billy's thigh.

"I need to see a doctor," Billy whined. "I'm gonna bleed to death if I don't."

"I'm fixin' to take you to one," Grayson replied, "in Fort Smith."

"Ah, hell no," Billy protested. "I can't go that far."

Grayson paused to give his prisoner an inquisitive stare. "Have you got it in your head somehow that you're the one callin' the shots here? That little ol' bullet hole in your leg can wait till we get to Fort Smith. The only decision you've got to make right now is whether you wanna ride all that way in your underwear, or do you want your clothes on?"

"Damn you," Billy cursed, "let me put my clothes on."

"All right, but here's the way it's gonna work. We'll play a little game. You like games, don't you, Billy? I heard you were in a card game when you cut Tom Malone down. Well, here's how you play this game. I'll put your clothes in front of you and untie your hands. Then I'll stand there and hold my rifle on you while you pull your clothes on. And every time you make a move that don't look right to me, I put another bullet hole in you—arm, leg, shoulder, I get to pick. So the only way you can win the game is to end up with your clothes on and no more bullet holes in your hide."

The message was received and understood by the prisoner, so Billy got his clothes on with no problems beyond the discomfort of his wound. Once that was accomplished, Grayson secured his prisoners, one to each corner post of the small porch, while he took time out to enjoy the freshly roasted beef the two had prepared, and washed it down with hot coffee. When that was done, he saddled Billy's horse and Stump's mule, then packed everything useful he found in the cabin on Tom Malone's blue roan. "Well, boys," he announced when he had finished, "I reckon we'd best get started." After taking a check to make sure each man's binds were secure, he hurried back up the gully behind the cabin to fetch his horses.

Still dazed by the blow on his head, Stump was left in a state of confusion and uncertainty, wondering what was to become of him. Grayson had told him that he had not come after him, but what now, since he'd made an attempt to help Billy? He was soon to find his answer when Grayson untied Billy's feet and helped him up in the saddle, after which he tied the horse's reins to the porch post and turned his attention to Stump.

He untied the stubby man's feet, but left his hands tied together in front of his body. "I told you before that I had nothin' against you, but I can't let you go runnin' back to Black Horse Creek to tell Jacob Blanchard where his son is, so I'm gonna take a little head start." He turned to point toward a low line of hills in the distance. "You see those hills yonder? I'm gonna head straight for that notch between the two farthest right." He pulled Stump's knife from a scabbard on the stocky man's gun belt. "You start walkin' toward that gap in the hills, 'cause I'm gonna leave your mule tied to a tree there. You understand?" Stump nodded, but still looked confused, so Grayson spelled it out for him. "You're gonna be in for a good walk till you get to that tree. Then you just ride on back home. Now do you understand?"

Stump nodded again, this time with the light of understanding in his eyes. "You're wantin' to make sure I can't catch up, right?"

"That's right," Grayson answered and stepped up in the saddle. "Now hold your hands up here and I'll cut you loose. I wouldn't leave you out here without a weapon, so I'll drop your gun belt on the ground a little piece ahead." He cut Stump's ropes.

"Much obliged," the simple man said as Grayson rode away, leading the horses and his mule.

"You tell Pa!" Billy shouted after them. "You tell Pa he's plannin' on takin' me all the way to Fort Smith!" Strictly for Grayson's benefit, he added, "It's a helluva long way from here to Fort Smith. There's plenty of time to catch up with us."

It's longer than you think, Grayson thought, *because I'm going to take the long way back.* He fully realized the possibility of pursuit, and deemed it safer to take a not so direct road to Fort Smith. He estimated that it would take almost two weeks to ride to Fort Smith, and he wondered if he could stand Billy Blanchard for that long. It would be so much simpler, and sensible, to take his prisoner to Fort Dodge and hand him over to the military there. From where he now started out, Fort Dodge was no more than a long day's ride. John Council was adamant about delivering Billy to the court in Fort Smith, however, for the specific purpose of making an example for those lawless individuals who were attracted to The Nations. Council knew it was a long way to escort a prisoner, and that was the reason such a high bounty was approved. It was going to be one hell of a ride, but he shrugged it off as just a dirty job, and one with a big payday to justify the trouble.

Chapter 4

When he finally approached the gap in the low hills that he had pointed out to Stump, he realized the walk was going to be longer than he had guessed. *All the better*, he thought to himself as he looked around to determine the best place to leave Stump's mule. A small stream cut through the gap with a scrubby growth of trees scattered along its path. Deciding on one that leaned out over the water, he tied the mule there, with enough slack to nibble the grass and water to drink. *If he follows the line I pointed out to him, he can hardly miss his mule. And if he doesn't take too long to walk it, he'll be back on his way home, providing a stray Indian doesn't come along and beat him to it.* He didn't really think there was much chance of it. So he stepped up in the saddle again and led a sullen Billy, followed by the late deputy's blue roan and his own packhorse, through the gap to the other side. The brief exposure he had had to Stump left him with the impression that he had little to worry about as far as being followed. He figured Stump would wear his mule out in his haste to report Billy's capture to his father. With that thought in mind, he changed his course directly eastward on the far side of the hills. "Where the hell are you goin'?" Billy promptly piped up. "You sure you know which way Fort Smith is?" When Grayson failed to respond, he continued to rail against his treatment. "My leg's gettin' worse. I ain't gonna be able to stay on this horse much longer if we don't stop to let me rest. If you'd untie my hands, I could at least tend to it to stop some of the bleedin'."

"Damn," Grayson said, sarcastically, "why didn't I think of that?" He made no move to grant the request, however. They continued on through the unassigned lands of the Cherokee Outlet for the rest of that day. Billy's frustration with the stoic bounty hunter's stony lack of sympathy gave way to constant threats regarding Grayson's fate when Billy's father caught up with them. When this was also ignored by Grayson, Billy eventually gave up and silently endured his capture, counting on the probability that there may be a few opportunities for escape.

Their supper that night was more of the beef that Stump had slaughtered that morning. Afraid the meat might turn, Grayson cooked up all that he had brought with them. It would do for their second night on their journey, but then it would be back to salt pork, which he planned to resupply when they reached a trading post on the Beaver River that he hoped would still be there. He could not be sure. It had been over a year since he had been in this part of the country, but Earl Johnson, the owner, had always gotten along with the Indians in the area, and they often traded at his store.

Grayson was glad to see the log buildings clustered on the bank of the river at the end of a long day's ride along the Beaver River. It was hard to see if the store was open, due to the lack of windows, but there was lamplight in the windows of the house built on to the back of the store where Earl lived with his wife and daughter. There were a couple of horses in the corral next to a small barn. It sure looked like Earl was still in business, so he was no longer concerned about running out of supplies before reaching Fort Smith. Earl's dog announced their arrival as they approached the store and a few minutes later, the door was cracked ajar, just enough for someone to look out. After a few more minutes, the door opened wider and Earl poked his head out, straining to see in the fading light. "Is that you, Grayson?" he asked.

"Yeah, it's me," Grayson replied. "You open for business? I need some things."

"Hell, yeah, I'm always open for business." He propped the shotgun he had been holding against the inside door frame and stepped outside on the porch. "Who's that you got with you?" he asked.

"This here is Mr. Billy Blanchard," Grayson said, "and I'd like to find him a good secure place for the night, someplace where he won't be disturbed. I'm thinkin' about that smokehouse of yours. Have you got a padlock for that door?"

"If I didn't have, I'da been cleaned outta salt pork a long time ago," Earl answered. He walked out in the yard to get a better look. "You gone back to bein' a lawman?" he asked when he saw that Billy was sitting in the saddle with his hands tied behind him.

"Nope," Grayson answered as he stepped down. "I'm just doin' a job for the marshal over in Fort Smith."

Still peering intensely at a sullen Billy Blanchard, Earl asked, "What did he do?"

Grayson looked back up at Billy when he answered. "Billy's specialty is killin' deputy marshals and bank tellers, although he has a sideline of robbery and stealin' horses. Ain't that right, Billy?" Billy declined to answer.

Earl continued to stare at the prisoner as if studying his face. "Blanchard, did you say?" When Grayson nodded, Earl asked, "One of them Blanchards that run that outfit up on the Cimarron?"

"Yep, he's Jacob Blanchard's son."

A deep frown appeared upon Earl's face. "I expect old man Blanchard ain't too happy about you havin' his boy, is he?"

Holding his tongue until then, Billy blurted, "That's a fact, mister, and my pa will be comin' after him and every son of a bitch that helps him."

Grayson could see that the insolent outlaw's threat had a sobering effect upon Earl, so he thought to assure him. "That's another thing Billy specializes in, shooting his mouth off. There ain't much to worry about as far as you're concerned. His gang don't even know which way we went. If they do try to cut us off, I expect they'll figure we headed straight down through The Nations and the unassigned lands, trying to get back as soon as possible. And I figure they're two days behind us at that."

"I need a doctor," Billy complained. "I'm bleedin'

bad and this son of a bitch don't care if I bleed to death."

Earl looked at Grayson, questioning, obviously uncomfortable with the situation and already wishing that the ex-lawman had chosen another route to Fort Smith. He had a wife and a thirteen-year-old daughter to be concerned about. Aware of his concern, Grayson sought to ease his mind. "He took one bullet in his leg. It ain't nothin'. I wrapped a bandage around it, and the doctor can take a look at it when I get him back to Fort Smith. I need to buy some supplies from you; then I'll be on my way in the mornin'. You'd be doin' me one helluva favor if you'd let me lock Billy in your smokehouse for the night. I'll lay my blanket right outside the door, and we'll all get a good night's sleep. Whaddaya say?"

"I reckon it'd be all right," Earl replied with some hesitation. "I just don't wanna get crossways with that Blanchard crowd, you know, with Mae and my daughter to worry about."

"There won't be anybody to tell 'em I came this way," Grayson told him. "And we'll be gone in the mornin'." Earl shrugged, still not comfortable with it. Mae, his wife, was full blood Osage, and one of the reasons he never had much trouble with the Indians, but that wouldn't do him much good if a gang of Blanchard's men came looking for Billy. "I reckon it couldn't hurt nothin'," Earl decided reluctantly, "long as you'll be on your way in the mornin'."

"I 'preciate it, Earl. You suppose I could buy some supper for me and Billy?" Grayson asked. "You still got that Osage woman doin' the cookin' for you?"

"Yeah," Earl replied. "That's Mae, my wife." He felt it important to stress that fact as a precaution, although

Grayson had never demonstrated any interest in his wife. Unless the somber bounty hunter had changed since he had last seen him, he would not be thinking about anything beyond the job he had set out to do. "I expect so," he replied to Grayson's question about supper. "We'd already et when you showed up, but I reckon she can rustle up enough to keep the sides of your belly from rubbin' a blister. Lemme go get the key to the smokehouse, and I'll tell Mae to see what she can scare up."

"Much obliged," Grayson said. "Tell her not to go to too much trouble. A biscuit and a cup of coffee would do. Me and Billy ain't particular. Are we Billy?"

"I need some decent food," Billy complained. "I've lost a lot of blood, and I'm still hurtin' somethin' fierce."

When Grayson ignored his prisoner's pleas, Earl hesitated before going inside. Looking at Grayson, he asked, "You want me to have Mae look at that boy's wound? She's pretty good at healin'. You know, in case he's really sufferin'." It had occurred to him that it might go in his favor if Jacob Blanchard found out that he had offered to tend to Billy's wound.

"His leg ain't that bad," Grayson replied, "not near so bad as he lets on. But what the hell? Maybe it would stop some of his whinin'. If she don't mind, it couldn't hurt to let her make sure it ain't gonna fester." The thought struck him that if Billy's simple wound did happen to turn bad, it might give him just one more problem to contend with before he made it back to Fort Smith.

"I'll tell Mae," Earl said. "Bring him on in the store and set him down on that chair by the stove." He left Grayson to pull Billy off his horse.

Amid curses and complaints, Grayson tied Billy's bound hands to the porch post while he unsaddled the horses and turned them out in the corral with Earl's two. Finding a sack of oats in the barn, he gave a portion to each of the horses—something else to add to his bill. When the horses were taken care of, he returned to the front porch to find Billy straining on the rope holding him against the post. His efforts had been so frantic that the ropes had brought blood to his wrists. When he saw Grayson, he let his body slide down the post until he was sitting on his heels. Grayson paused to look at him a moment before shaking his head patiently. Then without saying a word, he went to his packs, which were still lying on the ground beside the saddles, and pulled out a bottle of whiskey. Pulling the cork with his teeth, he walked over beside Billy and poured a generous amount of the whiskey over Billy's abrasions, causing the startled outlaw to yelp with the sudden pain. "A waste of good whiskey," Grayson muttered and replaced the cork.

"Gimme a drink of that bottle," Billy said. "You owe me a drink after haulin' me all day with my hands tied behind me. My shoulders are gonna be so stove up I won't be able to move 'em."

"Fair enough," Grayson said. "I figure I owe you one drink after such a long day in the saddle." He nodded toward Billy's hands. "You just had it, and you ain't gettin' but one, so think about that tomorrow and decide how you want that drink, in your belly, or on your hands."

"You go to hell," Billy shot back.

"In time," Grayson replied. "You just behave yourself while I put the saddles in the barn. Then I'll take you inside to let Earl's woman take a look at that leg."

* * *

"Who'd you say he was?" Mae asked.

"He's Jacob Blanchard's youngest son," Earl answered, "and Grayson's takin' him all the way back to Fort Smith."

"What did he do?" Cassie whispered as she peeked through the crack of the door leading to the store.

"Grayson said he shot a deputy marshal," her father answered.

"He doesn't look much older than me," Cassie said, still whispering. "Is he hurt bad?"

"I don't think so," Earl replied. "Your mama's gonna look at him. You stay here in the house."

"Mama might want me to help her," Cassie said. The young man didn't look like he was as dangerous as her father and Grayson seemed to think. She had certainly heard of Jacob Blanchard—everyone within three days' ride of Black Horse Creek had. She couldn't help but be curious about the notorious family of men that seemed to own all of the state of Kansas on the other side of the Oklahoma line.

"I don't expect your mama needs any help in seein' to that young hellion's leg," Earl told her. "You'd best just stay put right here in the house."

"You go ahead and make up them biscuits," her mother said. "Since your pa said we'd feed 'em, I reckon we're gonna have to cook something." When Earl reminded her that Grayson expected to pay for the food, she hesitated. "I reckon we could give 'em something besides coffee and biscuits," she said, having a change of heart. "Before you start them biscuits, Cassie, go out to the smokehouse and cut off some ham. That oughta do for 'em."

"Be quick about it, Cassie," Earl said. "He's wantin' to lock that boy up in the smokehouse."

Cassie went back to the kitchen to fetch a butcher knife and a pan, then hurried out the back door to the smokehouse where Earl had several salt-cured hams hanging. When she returned, her mother was already cleaning the wound on Billy's leg. Cassie pushed the door ajar, just enough to peek through. "You want me to get the bullet out?" she heard her mother ask.

"If it ain't too much trouble," Grayson replied. "If you think you can get to it pretty easy, go ahead and dig it outta him. If it's in too deep, just leave it in there. He wouldn't be the first one walkin' around with lead in his leg."

"I'll get it out," Mae decided.

"Thank you, ma'am," Billy said, surprising Grayson with the polite expression of appreciation, one that was certainly not typical of the usual ungrateful ranting of the young outlaw. He didn't have to think about it very long, however, before figuring Billy was just smart enough not to antagonize one who was about to carve into his leg with a knife.

"I'll do my best not to hurt you too much," Mae replied.

The young girl watching from the other room was struck by the meek attitude shown by the prisoner. With his hands still tied behind his back, he didn't look to be the wanton murderer that Grayson had said. She shifted her gaze to the formidable bounty hunter standing beside the slender young man, his rifle ready to fire at the first hint of trouble. He looked to be twice the size of his prisoner with his broad shoulders and the steely eyes of a predator peering out from under heavy black eyebrows that, along with his dark mustache, made him the image of cruel justice. Looking again at the young man gritting his teeth with the pain of her mother's probing knife, she immediately felt compassion for him. No longer wishing to witness the operation, she closed the door and busied herself preparing the biscuits and ham. *At least I can give him something to eat*, she told herself. She paused to picture him again. He looked hungry, she decided, and wondered if Grayson had given him anything to eat before reaching her father's store.

When the bullet was successfully removed from Billy's thigh, Mae applied a new bandage. She stepped back to take a look at her final work. Satisfied that it was a good job, she said, "I'll go see about your supper."

"Billy will have his in the smokehouse," Grayson said. He took Billy by the arms and lifted him to his feet. "I'll untie your hands in the smokehouse so you can eat." He motioned toward the door with his head, the rifle pointed at him, and Billy went quietly, limping noticeably.

In less than thirty minutes, Cassie came out to the smokehouse carrying two plates of food. Her mother was behind her with two cups of coffee. "I reckon you coulda had yours inside at the table," Mae said to Grayson.

"Thanks, but I'll do just fine out here," Grayson replied. He opened the smokehouse door and handed a plate to Billy, who took it eagerly.

"Thank you, ma'am," Billy called out to the Osage woman, and aimed a gracious smile at her young daughter, who blushed in return. Grayson shook his head, amused by Billy's obvious attempt to present a picture of a mistreated prisoner. It seemed to have the proper effect upon Cassie, for she cast an accusing glance in his direction. Grayson closed the door and hooked the padlock over the hasp without locking it, then sat down on the ground to eat his supper.

He waited until Billy had finished before opening the door to take the empty plate. "You want some more coffee?" he asked. Billy said that he did not, all the while watching to see if Grayson was going to close the lock on the hasp, hoping he would just hook it on there as before. Reading his thoughts, Grayson slowly shook his head and locked him in. "I'll be back to check on you later," he said and started toward the store.

"Go to hell," Billy snapped and crawled over to a corner of the dark enclosure, bumping his head on one of Earl's hams before he found the wall. He could hear voices coming from the store, muffled by the log walls between, and he scowled as he imagined Grayson sitting by the stove drinking coffee.

It seemed like an eternity, but he had been sitting there for only about a quarter of an hour when he heard a scratching noise near the back wall of the smokehouse. Some sort of critter, he supposed, and the thought of it made him a little uncomfortable, for he had nothing to use as a weapon. Even if he had one, he wasn't sure it would do him much good since it was so dark in the tomblike structure. He found himself hoping it was a rat, and nothing bigger, or meaner. The scratching continued and he was on the verge of yelling for Grayson when a small crack suddenly appeared in the wall, as a small piece of chinking was removed from between the logs, letting a thin ray of light peek through. Thoroughly puzzled now, Billy could only sit and watch.

"Are you gonna be all right?" the young girl asked, just above a whisper.

Fairly astonished, Billy answered back immediately. "I reckon, miss, as all right as a man can be that's been shot and hauled across the country for somethin' he didn't do." He was smart enough to see that the girl felt sorry for him, sorry enough to sneak out back so her folks couldn't catch her.

"Do you want me to bring you some more coffee?"

"No, miss, but I'm mighty grateful to you for carin' about me. It seems like nobody else in the whole world don't care what they're doin' to me."

"Mr. Grayson says you killed a deputy marshal," Cassie said.

"It weren't me that killed that deputy," Billy said. "I just happened to be there at that saloon when he got shot. I was tryin' to get back home, and I just stopped there to get somethin' to eat. It was some feller that looks a lot like me, I reckon. And Grayson, he's a mean one. He don't care if I did it or not, as long as he has some poor soul to take back to Fort Smith to hang. He ain't even a lawman. He's a bounty hunter, and he don't care as long as he gets his blood money."

"Did you tell him it wasn't you that did it?" Cassie asked.

"Oh, yes ma'am, I surely did, but he don't care, long as he gets his money." He had no way of knowing if his ruse was working on the young girl or not, since he could not see her. She said nothing more, but he could tell that she was still there, so he continued to try to gain her sympathy. "I ain't worried so much about myself, but I know it's gonna break my pa's heart. He knows I wouldn't shoot nobody. I've always tried to do what's right. I just happened to be in the wrong place at the wrong time, and it was easier to arrest me than try to find the feller that really shot that deputy. It was just my bad luck that I looked like the killer." He waited for her response.

She didn't answer for a long moment, trying to decide what to say to the unfortunate young man. He seemed sincere, and far from the wanton killer Grayson had described to her father. If what he said was true, it would be a horrible injustice to an innocent victim, but could she believe what she had just heard? Finally, she responded. "I'm truly sorry for you. I wish I could believe you, and even if I did, I don't know what I could do to help you."

"Don't worry yourself on my account, miss." He paused, still playing the sham. "Can I ask you your name?"

"Cassie, my name's Cassie."

"That's a right pretty name," he said. "It's one of my favorites 'cause that was my mama's name. She passed away a few years ago and I sure miss her. But don't you fret no more about me, Cassie. They may be hangin' the wrong man, but maybe I'll see my ma again. I just hope it don't break my pa's heart."

Thinking this gentle boy could not be the hard-hearted killer they said, Cassie felt certain that he was speaking the truth. The helplessness he expressed, she felt as well. "I wish there was some way I could help you," she finally confessed, "but there's nothing I can do."

"Like I said, I don't look for you to do anythin' on my account. I just appreciate your kindness. I ain't seen much kindness in my life."

"Can I do anything?" she asked, feeling she should

do something to ease his discomfort. "Do you want something more to eat—or more coffee?"

"I don't think they'd let you bring me anythin' else," he replied. "I think Grayson didn't like it much when you brought me a plate the first time. I am still hungry, though, 'specially in the middle of the night. He didn't give me anythin' to eat before we got here."

"I can bring you some more of that ham," she quickly volunteered.

"No, Cassie," he immediately responded. "It wouldn't be good if he saw you bring me somethin' to eat. It'd make it harder on me after we leave here in the mornin'." He paused for effect, then continued. "I know what would work," he said, as if it just occurred to him. "If I had a knife, I could slice off some more from one of your daddy's hams here, and Grayson wouldn't even know about it. But I ain't got no knife." He paused again as if a thought just occurred to him. "Maybe that's somethin' you could do for me. If you could just slip a knife through that hole, then I could just slice me off some ham when I get hungry in the middle of the night."

"But that ham's not even cooked," she responded. "It would be awful."

"No, not so bad," he assured her. "I've et it uncooked before, and it'll fill my belly."

"Mama says you can get worms if you don't cook it," Cassie said.

"I ain't hardly worried about that," he countered, "since they're liable to be hangin' me in a week or so, anyway."

She was still not comfortable with such a decision. "I don't know—they'd be awful upset with me if I sneaked a knife in to you."

"They wouldn't never know," he was quick to assure her. "I surely wouldn't tell nobody. You could just poke that clay chinkin' back between them logs, and nobody will ever know that I had somethin' to eat. When he takes me outta here in the mornin', I'll leave the knife stickin' in one of the hams. Nah, better'n that, I'll drop it on the ground outside the door, and you can be close by and pick it up. That's the best way to do it."

Cassie was still torn between empathy for the young man's plight and her parents' instructions to stay away from the prisoner. "I'll tell Mama to give you some cooked ham, so you don't have to eat that raw meat."

"No, no," he was quick to respond. "Don't do that! That'll just make him mad, and I'll pay for it for the next week. If you won't bring me the knife, then don't say anythin' about it, and I'll still thank you for carin' enough to talk to me. I'm glad I got a chance to meet you, Cassie." He waited for the response he was hoping for. It came after a long pause.

"I'll bring you the knife."

"Bring a good sharp one," he said. "That salt-cured ham's hard to slice." A moment later she was gone. *There still ain't nobody better when it comes to working the ladies,* he told himself with a smug smile. *Somebody's going to be in for a big surprise come morning.*

He didn't have to wait long for his escape weapon, for within ten minutes' time, Cassie was back at the rear wall. "Hurry," she whispered as she pushed a butcher knife through the slit between the logs. "Grayson's coming!"

"Good girl," he whispered in response. "God bless you. Don't forget to be close to the door when he lets me out in the mornin'." Then she was gone. A moment later he heard Grayson's boots on the hard ground outside the smokehouse.

"Who are you talkin' to," Grayson said, thinking he had heard Billy's voice.

"Talkin' to myself," Billy replied sharply, "if it's any of your damn business."

When the first rays of morning light filtered through the trees bordering the river, Grayson rolled out of his blanket. His first thought was to check to make sure the lock was still in place on the smokehouse door. While he stood rolling up the blanket, Billy called out from inside. "You gonna let me outta here to pee, or you want me to do it in here?"

"I don't expect Earl would appreciate it if you used his smokehouse for that purpose," Grayson answered. "I'll take care of that little business for myself. Then I'll let you out so you can pee."

"Well, hurry up," Billy replied, "or I might decide to piss on one of these hams in here."

Grayson didn't bother to respond, but walked down behind the hog pen in preference to the outhouse behind the store. Finished with nature's call, he returned to unlock the smokehouse door. Before opening it, he cocked the rifle he was holding, so Billy could hear it in case he had any ideas about any sudden moves. He lifted the hasp and stepped back a few steps. "All right, Billy, come on out." Squinting against the morning light, Billy came out and paused to look around him before moving in the direction Grayson pointed. He seemed docile enough as he walked down behind the hog pen.

"Just so you know," Grayson said, "I'd like to get

off to a peaceful start this mornin', but this rifle is aimed right between your shoulder blades. So get your business done quick and we'll get some breakfast before we get back in the saddle." Billy seemed inclined to cooperate. Ordinarily, Grayson would have started out right away and stopped for breakfast only when it was time to rest the horses. Since they were at a place where someone could fix them a good breakfast, with eggs as well as bacon, he decided to take advantage of it. Already he could smell the aroma of frying bacon on the crisp morning air.

As he was walking Billy back up the slope from the hog pen, he noticed Earl's young daughter standing in the half-open back door, watching them. Billy hung his head and began to limp a little. *Trying to look as pitiful as he can*, Grayson thought. He didn't know why he bothered. He was quite surprised, however, that Billy remained docile and went back into his makeshift jail cell with no fuss. Before leaving him to go in the store, he took a good look at him to see if he looked all right. The complete lack of insults and threats set him to wondering if Billy had taken ill. "I'll bring you some breakfast in a little while after I saddle the horses," Grayson told him as the padlock clicked shut. "You can eat it in there, so both of us can have our hands free while we eat."

After breakfast was finished, Grayson settled up with Earl and they walked out in the yard to the smokehouse, where Grayson had tied the horses. Neither man noticed Cassie when she slipped out of the back door and walked casually over toward them. Grayson unlocked the padlock and handed the key to Earl. "Come on out Billy," he said and stepped back. When Billy came out, Grayson told him to turn around, face the door, and put his hands behind him. Billy did as he was instructed, but turned only partially around. Grayson started to step closer to tie his hands behind his back, but at that moment, Cassie, who had moved up to stand at her father's elbow, suddenly moved in closer to Billy. Quick as lightning, Billy spun back around with the butcher knife in his hand. Before she could react, he grabbed Cassie with his other hand and pulled her hard up in front of him, his forearm drawn tight across her neck and the butcher knife pressed against her throat.

Earl blurted, "Cassie!" and started to go to his daughter.

"Step back, old man," Billy crowed, "or I'll run this blade right through her pretty little neck." He pressed the point just hard enough to draw a little blood, causing Cassie to cry out and stopping Earl in his tracks. "Now, by God," Billy swore, "things are gonna change around here." Cassie's mother, alerted by the sounds, came running from the house, screaming her daughter's name. "Tell her to shut up," Billy said, "or I'll cut clean through to her gizzard."

Frantic, Earl yelled for Mae to stay where she was, then turned back to Billy, who was almost choking Cassie in a stranglehold. "Please let her go," he pleaded. "We'll do anythin' you say. Just don't hurt her. What do you want us to do?"

"First, I want that son of a bitchin' bounty hunter to bring that rifle over here and prop it against the wall, then step back, or I swear I'll kill her. Then I want you to untie my horse and drop his reins, and you and that Injun you're married to can see how you like it in the smokehouse till me and the little missy, here, are out of sight."

Terrified to near paralysis, Cassie began to cry and begged Billy to let her go. "I tried to help you," she pleaded. "Why are you doing this?"

"'Cause I ain't ready to hang, you dumb little bitch. Now shut up and don't cause me no trouble." For emphasis, he pressed a little harder with the knife blade, causing Earl to cry out again.

"You ain't said what you're fixin' to do with me after I prop my rifle against the smokehouse," Grayson said, his voice calm and emotionless. It was the first thing he had said during the frantic moments since Billy had grabbed Cassie. As casual as if passing the time of day with a neighbor, he gazed at Billy, the rifle still in one hand by his side. "You also ain't asked me what I want." He paused while his gaze remained locked on to Billy's eyes. "So I'll tell you." He pulled the Winchester up against his shoulder and aimed it at Billy's head. "Cassie," he went on, still deadly calm, "I want you to hold just as still as you can. At this close range, there's no way I'm liable to miss, so you hold real still. The noise will be a little sudden. Don't let that bother you, but I have to apologize for the blood. When the bullet hits Billy's head, there's liable to be a little splatter, and I hope it won't mess up your dress too bad. It'll be over before you know it."

Stunned momentarily when things didn't go as he had anticipated, Billy clutched Cassie even tighter, trying to shield himself as much as possible with the girl's body. When Grayson calmly stepped to one side to keep a clear target line to Billy's head, Billy tried again to threaten. "Drop that rifle, or I'll slit her throat!"

"You really think you can push that knife through her throat before I can squeeze the trigger?" Grayson asked. "I'm already thinkin' how much easier it will be to tote your carcass back to Fort Smith instead of puttin' up with your mouth all the way." He sighed patiently. "But I promised John Council I'd give you the choice, so I'll give you one more chance before I put a hole in your head where a brain was supposed to go." He steadied himself for the shot. "Hold still, Cassie, we're about done here."

"All right! All right!" Billy screamed and pulled the knife away from Cassie's throat. "You win, dammit!" He released the girl and dropped the knife on the ground at his feet, then obediently turned to face the smokehouse door with his hands behind him, waiting to be tied. Cassie ran to her mother's arms, sobbing as she sought her protection, shamed by her naïve willingness to believe the smooth-talking young outlaw.

Grayson glanced at Earl, whose face had drained of color and looked as if he was about to faint. "Why don't you take your women in the house, Earl? I'm finished up here, so we'll be on our way. Tell your missus I'm sorry about this little show Billy put on, and don't be too hard on the girl." He didn't say it, but he had a feeling he knew how Billy got his hands on the knife. Earl nodded and turned to join his family while Grayson tied Billy's wrists.

"Well, you've had yourself a nice little show this mornin'," he told him as he tightened up on the knot. "I reckon I can't really blame you for tryin'. I s'pose I would if I was in your shoes. But I reckon I'd best make sure you understand a little rule I've got. I don't see no sense in givin' a prisoner more'n two chances to do like I tell him to. When you took your first chance, I put a bullet hole in your leg." He took him by the arm, turned him around, and led him toward the horses, talking as he did. "Now this thing this mornin', well, that was your second chance, and I'd ordinarily put a hole in the other leg for that. But you already had the ladies upset, what with you stickin' a knife to that young girl's throat, so I didn't wanna give 'em anything else to upset 'em." He paused to steady Billy while he got him up in the saddle before continuing. "So now you're lookin' at your third chance, and like I said, I don't normally give a fellow but two. The third time usually gets a bullet hole between the eyes. I wanna be sure you understand that, 'cause to tell you the truth, I was kinda hopin' you'd go ahead and start to cut that girl, so I coulda blowed you to hell and made my job a helluva lot easier."

There was not much that Billy could say in defiance, but he was still obstinate enough to try. "They're payin' you to take me back alive. They ain't gonna give you nothin' if you kill me."

"That's where you're wrong, Billy. You're just as good to me dead as you are alive. All they want is your worthless body."

"You ain't got me all the way to Fort Smith yet. If you don't let me go, my pa and my brothers will hunt you down like the lowdown dog you are. Don't matter if I hang or not; you'll be just as dead as I am. I guarantee it."

"I reckon we'll just have to wait and see about that," Grayson said. "Every man will die when his time comes—and not a minute before." He nudged the gray with his heels and pointed the horses east,

Chapter 5

Jacob Blanchard was furious. When Stump returned to report Billy's capture by the bounty hunter, Jacob went into a rage like none his crew had ever seen before. He cursed Stump soundly for letting Grayson ride away with Billy in tow. Cowering in the storm of Jacob's wrath, his foreman, Yancey Brooks, and Yancey's right-hand man, Lonnie Jenkins slumped like scolded dogs before their master as he fumed. Jacob could interpret Stump's flight from the line camp only as pure cowardice, thinking he should have fought to protect his son. Unable to understand why they could be held responsible, Yancey and Lonnie nonetheless hung their heads and accepted the blame.

"Yancey!" Jacob roared, "send somebody to town and tell Slate and Troy I want them out here right now. Then you and Lonnie get saddled up, ready to ride. I want that son of a bitch that took my boy! I want you to take two extra horses, so you can swap off when they get tired." It added to his ire that time would be wasted going back to the line camp on Rabbit Creek to pick up Grayson's trail. The bounty hunter already had a couple of days' head start, but there was little chance of cutting him off in the vast prairie land when there was no way of knowing the route he might take. The general picture only increased Jacob's frustration and fanned the fire of his rage.

"And Yancey," he charged, "I want you in the saddle night and day. I don't care if you kill a couple of horses—catch up with that bastard before he gets to Fort Smith."

Yancey looked at Lonnie and nodded solemnly. Looking up at Jacob again, he said, "We'll do our best, Mr. Blanchard."

This was not enough for Jacob. He wasn't convinced that his foreman grasped the full responsibility he was charged with. "I want better than your best, dammit. I want Grayson stopped, no matter what you have to do to stop him. You bring my boy back, and Grayson's scalp, and I'll pay you three hundred dollars apiece." He was satisfied to see a look of deepened interest in the eyes of both men at the prospect of obtaining a sizable reward. Both men had killed for Blanchard before, nesters or sheepherders, but always for wages. It was just part of the job as they saw it, for they had been hired primarily for their guns.

"Yes, sir, Mr. Blanchard," Yancey responded. "We'll get him. We'll take Stump with us to make sure we start out on the right trail."

"Leave Stump here," Blanchard ordered. "He'll just slow you down, him and that damn mule he rides. Somebody needs to stay here and help Jimmy do the chores, anyway. Now, get movin'. Don't waste no more time."

"Yes, sir, you're right." He turned to Jenkins. "Come on, Lonnie, let's get ready to ride. Jimmy can go get Slate and Troy."

It was after midnight by the time Jimmy Hicks slid off his weary horse and stepped up on the stoop to knock on the door of the sheriff's office. Only after a continuous rapping on the door did he see a light appear in the window. Moments later, he heard the bolt drawn back and the door opened just enough for the barrel of a pistol to appear. In another moment, however, the door was opened wide to reveal Slate Blanchard standing in his long johns, holding a lamp.

"Jimmy, what the hell are you doin' here?"

"Your pa sent me to fetch you and your brother," Jimmy replied. "He said to tell you to come right now."

"Why? What's wrong?" Slate responded. "Is Pa all right?"

"Yes, sir, he's all right. It's Billy. That Grayson feller that came through here caught Billy up at the line camp, and he's haulin' him back to Fort Smith."

"Damn," Slate swore. "I knew we shoulda took care of that bastard as soon as he rode into town— shoulda known he was after Billy." He turned to yell over his shoulder. "Troy! Wake up!" He turned back to Jimmy again. "Come on inside." When there was no response from the cell room behind the office, he called Troy again, this time receiving a groggy grunt and a request to keep his shirt on. Slate continued his questioning of Jimmy. "Did Pa tell you anythin' else?

What does he want us to do?" He understood the importance of immediate response, but he didn't know in what direction.

"He just told me to fetch you right now," Jimmy replied.

"For what," Troy said as he stumbled into the room, still half asleep. Slate repeated the little bit of information Jimmy had given him. Troy thought it over for a moment, and like his brother, wasn't quite sure what to do about it. "What good is it gonna do us to ride fifteen miles back to the house, if we gotta try to catch up with the son of a bitch goin' the other way?" He looked at Slate for an answer, but received none. "How the hell do we know where to even start lookin' for him?"

"Mr. Blanchard sent Yancey and Lonnie up to Rabbit Creek to try to pick up his trail," Jimmy said. "They took off with extra horses. Mr. Blanchard told 'em to ride 'em into the ground if they have to."

Fully awake now, Troy couldn't help but comment. "Yeah, we need to rescue Pa's favorite son every time he gets his ass in trouble." Being the middle son, Troy had always felt he never got a fair share of his father's affection. He knew Slate didn't share his jealousy, but figured it was because Slate was the eldest and felt no competition for his status in the family. Billy, however, was the pet and could do no wrong in his father's eyes.

Fully aware of Troy's envy of his brother's place in his father's heart, Slate felt it necessary to remind him. "Billy's our brother, and nobody gets to harm any one of us without payin' for it. Now we need to get out to the ranch and find out what Pa wants us to do."

"What about sheriffin'?" Troy asked. "Are we just gonna close the sheriff's office and ride outta town?"

Slate shrugged and paused to think about the uselessness of his position in the town his father had created. There had been no one arrested in almost a year, primarily because of the shadow cast over the town by Jacob Blanchard and his hired guns, more so than the sheriff and his deputy. Everyone in town knew the Blanchard brothers were the law in name only and served mainly to harass drunks. "I reckon the town can do without us for a few days. We'll see what Pa wants us to do. Then maybe one of us can come back to keep an eye on things here in town."

While Slate and his brother rode back to their father's ranch, the object of their search was sleeping in a camp beside the Cimarron River. His prisoner, bound hand and foot, was trying to sleep as best he could, forced to abide an uncomfortable position on his side. From time to time, the constant singing of the frogs in the nearby river was accompanied by a gentle tinkle of bells whenever Billy tried to move in his limited state. of freedom. The tiny bells, which Grayson attached to the rope that bound Billy's wrists, were meant to alert him of any excessive movement on the prisoner's part during the night.

Grayson was satisfied with the time they had made since leaving Rabbit Creek, and was confident that he could maintain the lead he had on anyone trying to follow. Blanchard's boys would have no choice other than riding to Rabbit Creek to pick up his trail.

Upon leaving the Cimarron the next morning, he continued almost due east across Indian Territory, planning to maintain that course until reaching the Arkansas before following that river all the way into Fort Smith. By the time he reached the Arkansas River, he figured he might need some additional supplies, primarily coffee and bacon, so he planned to strike the river at a point where it took a double loop, forming a wide U. There was a trading post situated at the bottom of the U, run by John Polsgrove, a giant bear of a man, and a friend of Grayson's, which made him unique, because Grayson didn't have many friends. Polsgrove was well known in the Cherokee Nation and appreciated by the Indians because of his sense of fairness in trading and his general pleasant nature. His easy-going manner seemed in sharp contrast to his physical features, which more nearly resembled those of a polar bear. Grayson almost smiled when thinking about his friend. It would be good to see him again, and possibly enjoy some of his wife Belle's fried corn cakes. *That might even help Billy's disposition,* he thought with an amused grunt. After a week of constant riding, his prisoner had descended into a dismal silence, his string of threats and profanity apparently exhausted. Grayson figured the monotonous, sleep-deprived journey might make Billy look forward to a hanging, if only for the variation.

He saw the smoke long before he was in sight of the log buildings that sat close beside the river. A long thin column that etched an almost invisible brown ribbon against the clouds hanging low over the river drifted straight up until it was snatched and scattered by the wind. Immediately alert, Grayson guided his horses farther north, thinking it best to come in above the trading post, instead of riding straight in.

The fire could mean anything, good or bad, but it always paid to be careful, so he continued on the altered course until striking the river about what he estimated to be two hundred yards north of Polsgrove's Store. A thick belt of oak trees hovered close to the river at this point, and when he entered their cover, he pointed the gray gelding down river, picking his way carefully through the trees and underbrush.

"Hey, what's goin' on?" Billy blurted, aware of Grayson's sudden caution. Oblivious of the altered course up to that point, he now realized that his captor was taking precautions not to be seen by someone. Thinking that whatever it was might pose some danger to him, he came out of the monotony of the rocking motion of the saddle to become fully awake. "What's goin' on," he repeated. "Injuns?" The possibility of a renegade gang of Indians struck his mind. "Don't leave me back here with my hands tied and no gun!" When Grayson ignored his questions, he demanded, "Untie my hands, dammit!"

"Shut the hell up," Grayson finally responded. It was plain to him that he wasn't going to be able to keep Billy quiet. It posed a problem for him, for he sensed something wrong at John Polsgrove's store, and he wanted to get close enough to see for himself. It could be nothing, he told himself. Maybe the knowledge that Jacob Blanchard would go to any extreme to rescue his son influenced his extra caution. Then he told himself that it would be almost impossible for Blanchard to overtake him this soon. Still, he wanted to take a look at John's store before riding in with his prisoner. The problem, then, was what to do with Billy. He decided he would risk leaving him with the horses while he worked his way closer along the riverbank to a point where he could get a good look at the compound John had built by the water. "Come on, Billy," he said, pulling him from his horse. "I reckon you're tired of sittin' in the saddle all day, so I'll let you stand up for a while."

He took an extra coil of rope from his packhorse and tied Billy securely to a sizable cottonwood tree, standing with his back to the trunk. For good measure, he wound the extra rope around him enough times to almost make him look like a mummy. Totally alarmed, Billy complained, "What if somethin' happens to you, and you don't come back?"

"If that happens," Grayson told him, "just untie yourself and we'll call it even."

"You son of a bitch!" Billy cursed him.

"I won't be long," Grayson said, ignoring the outburst. "I just can't take a chance on puttin' you in any danger," he added sarcastically.

"Yeah, and you can go to hell," Billy fumed, "leavin' me here like this."

Satisfied that his prisoner was unlikely to escape, Grayson left him and disappeared into the trees along the river. He had not gone far when he began to smell the smoke he had been seeing for the last couple of miles. Working his way even closer along the bank, he reached a point where he had a clear view of the compound, so he paused there to see if anything looked amiss. Nothing did at first glance, but upon longer observation, several things caught his eye. The smoke that had prompted his caution was not coming from the yard as he had first thought. Instead, it came from the front part of John's store, and although merely smoldering now, it had burned out a large portion of the front wall. He shifted his gaze to the smokehouse and the barn, then back to the corral when it occurred to him that there were no horses there—and there should have been at least a half dozen. It was obvious that John had been hit by raiders. Without conscious thought, Grayson cocked his rifle. Whoever had caused the damage was gone now, for there was no sign of any other horses. Anxious to find out what had happened, he rose to his feet and hurried along the bank toward the house. Just as he emerged from the trees, a woman appeared in the burnt-out door frame, pointing a rifle in his direction.

"Belle!" Grayson called out. "It's me, Grayson!"

Still holding the rifle on him, she hesitated. "Grayson?" she finally responded. "Is that you?"

"It's me," he replied. She let the rifle fall to her side and walked out the door to meet him. "What happened? Where's John?"

"I was afraid it was them coming back again," Belle replied, her voice hoarse and weary. "John's hurt bad. They shot him in the back."

"Who shot him?" Grayson responded.

"They was Pawnee," Belle answered, "wild young men. They run off with the horses and tried to burn the house down."

She looked to be about to fall exhausted, but she turned to lead him back inside the burnt-out doorway to the house where he found the big man lying on the bed where she had been trying to administer to his wounds. "Damn, John," Grayson exclaimed softly when he saw his friend's face covered with fresh blood. He was unaccustomed to seeing the huge man in such a vulnerable state.

"Grayson?" Polsgrove replied with considerable effort.

"Yeah," Grayson answered. "What happened?"

From the wounded man and his wife, Grayson was able to piece together the details of the raid on the trading post. He was not totally surprised to hear them. From as early as 1873, the federal government had been moving the Pawnee from Nebraska to reservations there in the Cherokee Nation. There had been very little trouble between the tribes as a result of this, but there had been occasional incidents of friction. According to Belle, a group of five men, all young, rode into the compound purportedly to trade some hides. They said they wanted tobacco, but when John turned to fetch it, one of them shot him in the back. He did not go down, but turned instead to charge them, and was shot in the face by another member of the party. While he lay helpless on the floor, they stormed over the counter to help themselves to anything they fancied, including a shotgun and two pistols that were under the counter. "When I hear the guns," Belle said, "I run to bedroom to get the rifle. They try to get me, but they run when I start shooting. When I try to help John, they run off with the horses."

Grayson nodded, concerned. "How bad is he hurt?"

"Bad, but he not die I think." She tried to smile, and added, "Take more than two bullets to kill bull."

"I reckon," he responded as he took a close look at the wounded man. In his opinion, the facial wound looked worse than it probably was. The bullet had entered at the corner of his mouth, shattering teeth on one side and ripping a hole in his cheek where it

BLACK HORSE CREEK

went out. It left a ragged wound that bled profusely, but luckily missed the point where his jawbone hinged. The wound in his back was more serious, since the bullet entered low on his rib cage, perilously close to his lung. "He been spittin' up any blood?" he asked. She said no. "Well, that's a good sign." He tried to give her a reassuring smile. "Maybe the old bull *is* too tough to kill." There wasn't much he could do for him that Belle had not already done, so he said, "I reckon all you need to do now is rest." He stepped back and watched the Cherokee woman fashion a bandage around John's face. "Is there a doctor in the Cherokee village?"

"No doctor," Belle answered.

"Well, John, looks like you're just gonna have to heal on your own," Grayson told him.

"I'll heal," Polsgrove said, forcing the words through painful lips. "But they stole my horses and the cow, too, I reckon." He paused to grimace with the pain of talking. "I need them horses."

Grayson turned to Belle. "How long have they been gone?"

"About noon," she replied.

"Noon, huh?" Grayson said. "About three or four hours," he guessed. "Maybe I can catch up with 'em tonight." He saw the look of gratitude on both faces, and knew he could not have second thoughts about it, even with the complications it would cause. "I got a little problem, though. I left a fellow tied to a tree back down the river a ways. I'm gonna have to put him someplace while I go after them Pawnees. You got someplace where I can lock him up?"

Belle paused to think for a moment before replying, "Barn, smokehouse, maybe."

He considered the two choices and remembered that the barn had too many loose boards. "I'll put him in the smokehouse. Billy's used to stayin' in the smokehouse. It'll be like comin' home. I reckon I'd better get started." He certainly hadn't counted on any delays in getting Billy back to Fort Smith, and didn't care much for the thought of lingering here. But what choice did he have? He could not refuse to help his friends. *Oh, well*, he thought, *I'll trust to luck and hope it won't take me long to track those Indians.*

He returned to the riverbank to find Billy securely tied, just as he had left him, and the horses grazing peacefully near the water's edge. At first sight of the stoic bounty hunter, Billy railed against the treatment he had been subjected to. "Get me off this damn tree!" he demanded. "You ought not treat a dog this way."

"I reckon you're right, but you ain't hardly on the same level as a good dog," Grayson said, and meant it. "I'm fixin' to untie you right now. I've fixed you up with a nice room for the night, one you'll like, and nobody's gonna bother you—feed you, too, if you behave yourself."

Billy was so relieved to be set free from the cottonwood that he refrained from cursing or threatening Grayson while he was taken to the trading post. When he saw Belle standing at the smokehouse, holding the door open for him, however, he let loose another tirade, protesting a second confinement in the dark cell. The solemn Cherokee woman gazed at him without compassion as he stood just inside the smokehouse door, his back now toward her, waiting for Grayson to untie his wrists. A big, sturdy woman, she had no sympathy for Billy's plight. Her sole concern was for the giant of a man lying on her bed in the house. When Billy was relieved of his bonds, she slammed the door shut and Grayson tapped an iron spike into the hasp in lieu of a padlock. With Billy safely put away, he walked toward the corral where his horses waited. Belle walked with him, and he told her what to do about the prisoner.

"I don't hardly see how he can get outta that smokehouse," he told her, "but you be careful. He'll try anythin' to get away, and he ain't particular about who he kills if they get in his way. I don't like to leave you with John stove up like he is, but if I don't go after those raiders while their trail is still fresh, I won't likely catch 'em at all."

"No worry," Belle said, her voice confident. She picked up the rifle she had momentarily propped against the side of the barn and held it up before her. "He break outta there, I shoot him in the ass."

"You do that," Grayson said, pulling the saddle off of Billy's Appaloosa as he spoke. "I don't know how long I'll be gone, but I'll get back as soon as I can. If I'm lucky, I'll catch 'em when they're sleepin'." Working as quickly as he could, he took the pack saddle off his sorrel and turned all the horses except his gray out into the corral. Belle helped him replace the poles the Pawnee raiders had taken out to steal John's horses. Then with one last caution for Belle to be careful, he stepped up in the saddle and headed downriver in the direction the Pawnee had fled.

Far from oblivious to all the action taking place outside his darkened cell, Billy listened attentively to all the conversation he could hear between the Cherokee woman and Grayson. As soon as he heard Grayson's horse leaving the yard, he called out, hoping to catch Belle's ear before she went back in the house to care for her husband. "Ma'am," he called, doing his best to sound meek. "Ma'am, I don't wanna be no bother, but can I speak to you for just a minute?"

Hearing his plaintive request, Belle walked back to stand outside the smokehouse door. "What you want? Grayson say don't trust you."

"I don't know what I ever did to make that man come after me. He's haulin' me to Fort Smith for somethin' I didn't even do. I can prove I'm innocent, but he won't let me. I don't mean to bother you, but if you'd just give me some water I'd be mighty obliged. Grayson ain't give me nothin' to eat or drink since yesterday, and I'm awful parched."

Belle did not answer at once, but stood there for a few moments, thinking over his request. She was not without pity for any suffering animal, but neither was she witless. "I bring you some water, maybe some food."

"Oh, thank you, ma'am, and bless you. I surely do appreciate it. I could tell by your sweet voice that you were a kind Christian woman." Inside the dark enclosure a malicious smile spread across his face. He was confident in his charm with the ladies, whether they were gullible young girls or weathered older women, and this time Grayson would not be around to interfere.

Due to the Pawnee raid, there had been no food prepared for her husband's supper, but Belle got some deer jerky and filled a jug with water and returned to the smokehouse. Hearing her approach, Billy positioned himself at the door, ready to spring on the surprised woman as soon as the door was opened.

"You stand back from the door," she said, "and I put water and jerky inside."

"Yes, ma'am," Billy replied. "I'll stand way back against the back wall until you close the door again, and I sure thank you for your kindness. I'm backin' up now." In a crouch, he moved up silently before the door, his feet set solidly under him to launch his body like a battering ram as soon as he saw daylight in the opening.

Certain now that she was doing the right thing, she set the jug of water on the ground at her feet and carefully removed the spike that latched the door. Inside, Billy heard the grating of the iron spike as it slid up from the hasp. He readied himself to attack. As soon as she pulled the door open, she was affronted with a body hurling up in her face. Prepared for the possibility of such an occurrence, she took a step back and delivered a blow to his forehead with her husband's hand axe, which she had brought with her as a precaution. Knocked senseless, Billy landed in a heap across the sill of the smokehouse door, where he lay motionless. Still with no show of emotion, Belle took hold of Billy's belt and dragged him back inside the smokehouse. She then set the jug of water inside, along with the jerky, closed the door, inserted the spike, and returned to the house to check on her husband.

"Grayson said be careful, you might try something," she said as she was walking away, but the figure lying prone inside the smokehouse didn't hear her comment.

The trail was not hard to follow. The raiders had taken no pains to hide it, probably, Grayson thought, because they didn't think there was anyone that might follow them. Down along the riverbank they had fled, crossing over to the other side at a point where a sandbar extended halfway across. This is where he found John's cow. Evidently it had balked at going for a swim and the Indians decided it too much of a bother to try to drive it to the other side. Grayson was mildly surprised. He had figured to find the remains of the cow after the Indians had butchered it for supper. According to what Belle had told him, the raiders had gotten away with a generous supply of bacon, dried apples, and a case of canned peaches that John had ordered all the way from Omaha. Evidently they were satisfied to feast on this, he supposed, and let the cow go when it became a nuisance.

With a nudge of his heels, he guided the gray into the water, and picked up the Pawnees' trail where they came out of the river. It continued to follow the river. He was glad they had felt no need for caution, for it was already beginning to get dark. He estimated no more than another half hour at the most before the sun dropped below the distant horizon, and then light would disappear as if someone had blown out a lantern. He followed the tracks for as long as he could see them, and they never left the river. When darkness finally descended upon the prairie, he continued to ride down the river, for they were sure to make camp next to the water. As he watched for a fire, he hoped they had stopped to make camp early, since he had started several hours behind them.

After a couple of hours passed, a full moon climbed over the hills to the east, casting enough light on a sandy patch in the bluffs to clearly reveal the tracks of the horses he followed, telling him that he had not lost them to that point. He rode no more than a mile farther before he saw what he had been alert for, the flickering of a flame through the branches of the trees beside the river. He reined the gray back immediately and dismounted. He tied his horse to a tree with a split trunk, one he could recognize easily in the dark in the event things didn't go the way he planned and he had to run for it. After checking to make sure he had a full magazine in his Winchester, he started making his way closer to the campfire.

He had covered a distance of about fifty yards when he reached a point on the riverbank where he was forced to stop and look the situation over. To proceed, he would have to leave the cover of the trees and cross an open patch of grass, perhaps thirty yards across. The campfire was on the other side of the opening where the trees began again. The Indians had hobbled the horses in the open patch and left them to graze. The rising moon didn't help matters, for it would only make it easier for him to be seen when he crossed the opening. So he backed away and dropped down below the bank, thinking it safer to make his way along the slippery edge of the water.

Once he reached a point almost directly below the Indians' campfire, he raised up from his crouched position just high enough to see the camp. It was as he had hoped to find it. The raiders had evidently filled their bellies and retired to their blankets. Belle had said there were five raiders, and he counted five sleeping forms like spokes around the fire. He remained there for a few minutes, trying to decide how best to handle the situation. It would be risky to try to sneak off with the horses without waking the

Pawnees. There was also the matter of punishing them for raiding the store and shooting John Polsgrove. And that would require a gun battle between him and five Indians, all armed, probably, since they stole weapons from the trading post. If he walked in among them, shooting as fast as he could, he was sure he could kill at least three of them before they could all react. But that would leave two that had a chance to retaliate. He discarded the idea, thinking that just wasn't his style to fire away at sleeping figures. *First, I'll see about the horses,* he decided.

Drawing away from the edge of the bank, he backtracked to a point opposite the edge of the clearing. Then he climbed up the bluff and made his way as quietly as he could in among the group of horses now watching him as he approached. John's horses were easily distinguished from those belonging to the Pawnees, for the Indian ponies backed away as soon as he came near. One of John's horses wore a halter, so Grayson went to it first; then one by one he untied the hobbles on the others. After he finished removing the restricting ropes on John's horses, first one, then another of the Indian ponies allowed him to approach and remove their hobbles as well. The remaining three shied away; one of them, a shaggy looking paint, reared his head and snorted his defiance, causing Grayson to drop to one knee, rifle ready, in case the pony woke those sleeping by the fire. When there was no response from the camp, he decided to leave well enough alone and forget the three renegade ponies, although he would have liked to put the Pawnees on foot.

Not at all sure whether it would work or not, he took hold of the halter on John's horse and led it across the clearing toward the trees where the gray was tied, hoping the others would follow. At first, the others simply stood where they were and watched as he neared the tree line. Then one, and then a second, and then the others followed, including the two Indian ponies he had freed from their hobbles. Grayson was amazed. He made it back to the split tree and the gray, with the horses still following, although a couple began to lose interest and turned around. Still, he decided he was ahead in the game, so he climbed aboard the gray and rode back to herd the two stragglers before they reached the clearing again. The sudden crack of a rifle shot as it whistled over his head was the signal that caused the camp to erupt in an uproar of loud yelling and cries of alarm. It was followed by rifle and pistol shots thrown indiscriminately toward the trees around him. The sudden commotion caused the horses to bolt, and Grayson worked hard to keep his from rearing up. Out in the clearing now, he saw two figures running to try to catch their ponies. He settled his horse down enough to get off a couple of fast shots, hitting one of the Indians in full stride. There was immediate return fire from the edge of the clearing when the others spotted his muzzle flashes. Spending only enough time to throw three more shots at the flashes he saw from their weapons, he decided it best to retreat. He wheeled the gray and galloped after the gang of horses that had bolted away from the river, luckily in the direction he had first come.

Leaving the river behind, the small herd of horses galloped out onto the prairie, with Grayson content to follow, as long as they continued in that general direction. He would let them run until they tired themselves out, even with the risk of breaking a leg on the dark prairie; then he would attempt to herd them back toward the river and John's place. His thoughts were interrupted once again by the zip of a rifle slug over his head, followed by the report of the rifle behind him. *Damn,* he thought, sure it was the same Indian that sent the first shot over his head earlier. *If he ever figures out he's shooting high, I'm a goner.* Bending low over his horse's neck, he galloped on until coming to a line of low hills. Charging straight over the top of one of them, he pulled the gray to a hard stop as soon as he crossed over the crest, coming out of the saddle with his rifle in hand. As soon as his feet hit the ground, he scrambled back to the top of the hill and dived on his belly. He didn't have to wait long before he saw two Indian ponies charging after him at full speed, the dark forms of their riders leaning low over their horses' necks. He took his time to make sure the front sight was squarely in the center of the dark form on the lead horse. He squeezed the trigger and the rider disappeared from the horse's back. Grayson cocked the rifle and quickly shifted to aim it at the second Indian, but he veered away when the rifle spoke, causing Grayson to miss. He immediately cocked it again, but the Indian was galloping away at an angle by then and lying low on the side of his pony. Grayson watched to see if the warrior would attempt to come after him again, but after a few minutes, he decided that the Indian had had enough. With thoughts of his little herd of horses scattering in all directions, he sped off after them again, only to lose them in the darkness. "Dammit!" he cursed, afraid he had gone to all that trouble in vain.

* * *

He found them right after dawn the next morning. They had evidently run until forced to rest, then drifted back to the river. They were grazing near the bank, as if waiting for him to show up, and paid him no mind when he guided the gray among them. Knowing his horse was in need of rest, for he had continued to look for the horses most of the night, he pulled his saddle off and turned him loose to drink and graze. Apparently fully domesticated, John's horses were content to mill around close to him, so he figured it worth the gamble to remain there until the gray was fully rested. He felt sure the Pawnee raiders had suffered enough grief to be discouraged from continuing the chase. To be safe, however, he kept a sharp lookout from the top of a low swale during the entire morning. It was midmorning before he saddled his horse again and began the job of herding the horses back up the river to the trading post. He didn't expect it to be an easy job, for he never fancied himself to be much of a wrangler.

Chapter 6

"You busted my head," Billy wailed. "It's still bleedin'."

"You lucky I don't shoot you," Belle replied. "You want food, or not?" After the first time she brought him coffee and jerky the night before, she was wary of any more of his attempts to escape. "You want food, push the door open and get it." After placing a cup of coffee and a plate of bacon and biscuits on the ground beside the smokehouse door, where he could reach them from inside the open door, she had removed the spike from the hasp and stepped away.

He could see her through a crack in the weathered door, standing with the rifle against her shoulder, aimed at the door. There was little chance he was going to make any surprise move on the sturdy Indian woman. As she had instructed, he pushed the door open, slowly, until wide enough to see the cup and plate before it, and the stoic woman standing ready to shoot. Squinting against the sudden light, after being confined in his dark cell, he eagerly took her offering, and sat back on his heels to gulp it down. "You put a bad cut on my forehead," he complained after he had eaten one of the two biscuits she had brought and washed it down with half the cup of coffee, "and a pretty damn good-sized knot on my head."

"You don't behave, I don't give you no more food," she said, her face expressionless. "Grayson say it all right to shoot you if you cause trouble."

"What Grayson says ain't always gonna be the way things are gonna be done," Billy responded angrily, venting some of his frustration before checking his emotions. "But I ain't gonna cause you no trouble, ma'am," he hastened to say. "You can count on that. I'm real sorry I scared you before. I surely didn't go to." He could tell by her expression that she was not moved by his attempt to appear contrite. *Damn hardheaded Injun,* he thought. *If I get half a chance, I'll put a bullet between those dead eyes.* "I could sure use another cup of that coffee," he said, but she was distracted by something on the far side of the river. He followed her glance to see a string of horses loping toward the river. *Grayson,* he swore to himself.

"Close the door now," Belle ordered and gestured with her rifle. When Billy didn't respond at once, she lifted the rifle to her shoulder again. "Grayson say I can shoot . . ."

"I know, I know," he interrupted impatiently. "I'm closin' the damn door."

"Belle said you got all my horses back and two Injun ponies to boot," John forced out of one side of his mouth. It was obviously painful for him to talk at all.

"Yeah," Grayson replied. "You got a couple extra horses, but I don't reckon they were worth the price you paid for 'em."

"Reckon not," Polsgrove groaned. With great effort, he shifted his huge body around, trying to find a position that lessened his discomfort. His massive body looked too big for the small bed. Grayson couldn't help but wonder how they made out when Belle climbed in with him. "I guess I'da had to pull my wagon myself if you hadn't got 'em back."

It appeared that the bullet in his back was not enough to put the big man down for good, just as Belle had said. But it was going to be a while yet before he would be on his feet again, and this was the present cause for concern for Grayson. The need to transport Billy Blanchard to Fort Smith as quickly as possible was still his main focus. The Pawnee raid on the trading post had in no way altered that, but it had thrown a snag in his plans, and given him a difficult decision to make. John Polsgrove was in a vulnerable state with no one to help him but the one Indian woman. Grayson could not ride off and leave them in this fix. His big friend's next statement made it even worse.

"Grayson, I thank the Good Lord that you showed up when you did. I reckon I'd be under the sod now if you hadn't. I think the Lord sent you and I want you to know I'm beholden to you."

Grayson thought he detected the start of a tear in the huge man's eye. *Oh, Good Lord*, he thought, *don't do that*. John's expression of thanks was enough to make Grayson uncomfortable. He didn't need tears on top of it.

"Hell," he replied, in an effort to shift John's

thinking to something else, "it was Belle that run 'em off when she gave 'em a taste of that rifle. She's the one you should be beholden to."

"You ain't told me what happened when you caught up with them Pawnee," John said. "There was five of 'em. Did they join up with any more?" He was concerned with the possibility of even bigger trouble to come.

"No, they were by themselves," Grayson answered. "You saw 'em, just a few young bucks lookin' to steal some horses and whatever else they could find. I doubt you'll see that bunch again."

"I know they didn't just run off and let you have the horses back. Did you get any of them?"

Grayson nodded. "Two that I know of. I don't think I hit anythin' else." John nodded in return. Grayson moved on to a question of more importance to him at the moment. "What about you and Belle? Have you got anybody helpin' you at all?"

"Sometimes," John answered. "I ain't needed him lately, but Belle's sister's boy, Robert, comes to help me when I have to take the wagon to meet the boat to pick up supplies. He's a hard worker, and he knows how to handle a gun."

"I expect you could use him right now," Grayson suggested. "I'm gonna have to take Billy on in to Fort Smith before some of his crowd come lookin' for him. Where is this boy, Robert, now?"

"He lives in a village about a half day's ride east of here," Belle said, having heard the question as she entered the room. "You gonna send for Robert?"

"I think it'd be a good idea," Grayson said. "I have to get movin', and you need the help."

"I go," she said. "You stay with John till I get back?"

"Well, sure," Grayson replied, "but I figured I'd go get Robert."

"I go. Be quicker. Then you take that man outta my smokehouse. He pee in corner. I smell it at back of smokehouse. Ain't good for the meat."

Grayson almost laughed, but he was concerned about the wisdom of sending the woman off across the prairie by herself. His concern must have shown in his face, because John told him not to worry. "She always goes to fetch him when we need him. Besides, he's liable to run if he sees you come ridin' in. He's been in a little trouble from time to time, and he gets kinda spooked when he sees a deputy marshal show up in the village."

"I ain't a deputy," Grayson reminded him.

"Yeah, but you look like one," John said.

Early the next morning, Belle crossed the river and set out across the prairie to the east. After making sure John didn't need anything, Grayson took Billy his breakfast. He had given some thought to the pos- sibility of escape with Billy locked in the smokehouse for that length of time, but he now reasoned that if his prisoner hadn't found a way out by now, he was not likely to at all. For Billy's part, however, he was about to go crazy in the dark confined cell. Grayson was not without sympathy for the young outlaw's plight, but there were no other choices for Billy's incarceration unless he was tied hand and foot the entire time.

"You gotta let me out of this damn hole," he com- plained to Grayson as the bounty hunter watched him eat, much the same as Belle had. "I'd rather you just go ahead and shoot me instead of keepin' me locked up in this rat hole," he wailed, knowing that Grayson wouldn't.

"One more night's all you gotta do," Grayson said. "Then we'll be on our way and you can go back to cryin' about your hands bein' tied." He watched Billy eat for a while longer, before commenting, "You kinda found out the hard way not to try pullin' anythin' on Belle, didn't you?" Billy scowled, but didn't reply. "That's a right nasty cut you got there on your forehead. What the hell did she hit you with?"

"That bitch come at me by surprise," Billy said. "I didn't give her no reason to hit me with that axe. She said to come out to eat, and that's all I done—damn Injun bitch."

"Yeah," Grayson said. "Women are like that, always tryin' to trick a man." He knew the true version of how Billy got knocked in the head, and he knew that Billy knew he did. But he couldn't resist japing him about it. Still, never far from his thoughts was the threat of pursuit by Billy's father and brothers. They would come after him. That was something he knew for a fact from the start. The thing he didn't know was how close they were now with the delay caused by the Pawnee attack.

"Earl," Mae Johnson called to her husband as he came up from the hog pen, "there's a couple of riders coming down from the bluff, and they're leading a bunch of horses behind them."

Earl quickened his step in an effort to see for himself. It was a little late in the day for his usual customers to show up at only an hour or two before sundown. He already had an increased sense of caution ever since Grayson had stopped for the night with his prisoner. "You know 'em?" he asked as he joined his wife in the front yard.

"Nobody I ever saw before," Mae answered, still staring back at the bluffs along the river. Like Earl, she was feeling cautious about seeing any strangers since the incident with Grayson and Billy Blanchard. When Cassie walked out of the house to throw the dishwater out in the yard, Mae turned to her and said, "Go back in the house, and stay there till we find out who's coming down the path."

"Why, Mama?" Cassie asked, sensing her mother's caution. "Who is it?"

"I don't know, so you just stay out of sight till I do."

When Cassie hurried back to the house, Earl turned to his wife. "It don't look like none of them bucks from the village. I expect we'd best go on in the store, and just wait to see what they want. Might be somebody needin' some supplies." He paused for a moment before suggesting, "Might be a good idea if you went back in the house with Cassie." He was certain he would feel better behind the counter with his pistol on the shelf just under it. Without further comment, they turned and went back inside, he to the store, she to the house behind it. Both wondered if the strangers approaching were from Black Horse Creek.

"Look here, Yancey. Looks like he turned off the trail, and there's more'n a few tracks leadin' down to that place there—looks like a store or somethin'. They musta stopped off here for a spell. I wonder why." The simple fact that Grayson had stopped to go to a trading post made him uncertain. "I hope to hell we been followin' the right trail all along."

"It's the right trail," Yancey Brooks insisted. "Who

the hell knows why he stopped here? It's sure as hell the same trail we followed through that gap where Stump said he found his mule. Besides, look at them prints." He pointed to a distinct hoofprint in the sand. "Billy said he just had that Appaloosa shod before he came home. Looks to me like Grayson musta wanted to stop for somethin' to eat, or a drink of whiskey, or somethin'. It don't matter why he stopped, but them tracks are Billy's."

"I reckon," Lonnie Jenkins replied. "I expect it'd be a whole lot simpler to go down there and ask 'em if Grayson came this way, instead of arguin' about horse tracks."

"Reckon so," Yancey replied. Both men had been sufficiently impressed with the task Jacob Blanchard had charged them with—that they were to ride night and day, never stopping to rest until they had killed Grayson and brought Billy back home. The subject had never been discussed between them, but they were of like mind in thinking that the six hundred dollar reward would be well worth the strain. But in case of failure to catch Grayson, it would be healthier for both men to keep on riding, rather than face Jacob Blanchard's wrath. "Well, let's quit wastin' time." He started down the path, and Lonnie followed, their spare horses behind them.

Earl stood beside the door watching the two strangers as they rode down the path to his store until they pulled up at the hitching rail. Then he walked back to stand behind the counter to await them, his hand feeling under the counter to make sure his pistol was in easy reach. In a moment, they walked in the door—two rough-looking men with trail-weathered faces, heavily armed with both rifles and handguns.

"Howdy," Yancey said as he paused to look the room over. "Don't suppose you got any whiskey, do ya?"

"No, sir," Earl answered. "I don't carry any spirits of any kind. Seein' as this is Indian Territory, I ain't supposed to."

"But seein' as we ain't Injuns," Lonnie said, "you might could sell us a shot or two outta that whiskey you *ain't* got." He gave Earl a wink of his eye and turned to grin at Yancey. "We've been ridin' long and hard, and a little drink would sure help cut the dust in our throats."

"I'm sorry as I can be, fellers," Earl replied, "but I wasn't japin' you. I don't have no whiskey on hand, not even for my personal use. If I did, why, I'd be tickled to offer you a drink. Is there anythin' else I can help you with?"

Disappointed, Yancey looked at Lonnie and shook his head. "Well, maybe you can help us out a little," he said to Earl. "Me and my partner, here, are government agents, and we're on the trail of two outlaws. One of 'em's name is Grayson and he's got an innocent man as a prisoner who ain't done nothin' wrong. We think they mighta stopped here. Maybe you can tell us how long ago that was." He glanced at Lonnie again to receive his partner's look of appreciation for his original story.

Earl was at once undecided as to which way he should respond. One thing he was at least ninety-nine percent sure of was that the two men standing before his counter were not government agents. They could only be men who worked for Jacob Blanchard. It might be honorable on his part to say he had not seen Grayson, but he feared that there would be serious consequences if he tried to cover for him. Under the impatient glare from both men, he finally blurted the information they asked for. "Two days ago, they stopped for some supplies, then left right away."

"Headed which way?" Yancey demanded.

"I don't know," Earl replied.

"Followin' the river?"

"I don't know," Earl repeated. "I guess so. He didn't say where he was goin'."

Yancey studied the obviously nervous storekeeper for a long moment before remarking aside to his partner. "You know, Lonnie, I don't think this feller is bein' honest with us. I think he knows damn well which way Grayson took Billy when he left here."

"That's what it looks like to me," Lonnie replied, "lyin' to government agents."

Earl's hand stole over to rest on the handle of the .44 revolver under the counter, but he couldn't bring himself to grasp it and pull it out. The men were obviously hired guns, and he feared that if he drew the weapon, it might cost him his life. "I swear to you, he didn't tell me where he was headin' when he left here."

"Damn you . . ." Yancey cursed and reached across to grab Earl by the collar.

"East!" Earl fairly screamed in fright. "They rode east when they left here. They didn't follow the river!"

"That's better," Yancey said and released him, while Lonnie chuckled at the frightened man's response to Yancey's impatience. "You know why that's better?" Yancey went on. "'Cause when I got back on that trail and found them prints we've been followin' headin' east, instead of down the river, I'da come back here and put a bullet in your lyin' ass."

Earl quickly moved his hand away from the pistol, as if afraid it might discharge on its own. "No, sir," he said. "I wouldn't lie to you. I sure wouldn't lie to government agents."

"All right, then, we'll let it go this time," Yancey said. Thinking to take advantage of Earl's apparent acceptance of his concocted story, he said, "We'll be needin' some supplies. The government will be payin' for 'em. Lonnie, why don't you go ahead and get what we need off the shelves there." Turning back to Earl, he said, "You'd best get you a piece of paper and write down everythin', so you can charge the government for it. I'll just wait right here with our friend while you're at it, Lonnie."

Mortified by the criminal farce taking place, and his fearful reluctance to try to stop it, Earl could only stand and watch as Lonnie raked items off his shelves at random. "Ain't you gonna write that stuff down?" Yancey goaded. "You don't wanna miss nothin'." Earl watched helplessly as Lonnie emptied a gunnysack of corn on the floor, then stuffed the sack with tobacco, coffee, cartridges, and anything else he fancied. When Lonnie was finished, Yancey said, "Get your piece of paper, and I'll sign it for you. I reckon you don't need to have everythin' down, just tell 'em how much it costs."

It was plain to see that the outlaw was going to insist that he play the game they seemed to be enjoying, so Earl got a piece of paper and put it on the counter along with a pencil. With a wide grin of amusement, Yancey picked up the pencil and wet the lead with his tongue; then with a great show of importance, he fashioned a careful X on the paper. As a special effect, he drew a little cross on one leg of the X. "There, that's so they'll recognize my mark."

Humiliated, Earl continued to go along with the robbery of his store. "How do I get paid? Who do I send this to?"

The question stumped Yancey for a moment, so Lonnie gleefully answered for him. "Why, you just send it to Washington, in care of the government agents office, and they'll send you some money." He hefted the sack on his shoulder and started toward the door.

Ashamed to have been taken so brazenly, Earl was finally disgusted enough to comment, "I'd feel a helluva lot better if you would at least hold a gun on me."

"Glad to oblige," Yancey said, and leveled his rifle at him. "The only reason I don't blow you to hell is because you had enough sense not to pull that gun from under the counter." With the rifle trained on Earl, he backed out the door.

On the other side of the door, Mae stood with her ear pressed up against it. When all was silent in the store and she felt sure the men had gone, she eased the door ajar, enough to see her husband standing dejected in the open front door. She hurried to console him as he hung his head in shame, for they could hear the outlaws' laughter as they rode back up to the river trail. Earl turned to her and confessed. "They robbed me without ever holdin' a gun on me," he lamented. "I coulda pulled my gun from under the counter, but I was afraid I wouldn't be fast enough."

"Thank the Lord you didn't," she said. "What good would it have done to try to fight them. I'd rather

have you alive than a dead hero. Those men are nothing but hired gunmen for Jacob Blanchard. They
would have killed you, and then where would Cassie
and I be?"

At the head of the path, Yancey and Lonnie dismounted to inspect the commonly used trail that followed the river, trying to distinguish which tracks
might be those they had followed to this point. There
were too many to be sure, some fresh, some old. They
had no choice but to follow the trail, hoping to find
tracks that split off and verify the direction the storekeeper reported. They were just about ready to return
to confront Earl again when Lonnie sang out. "Here
he is!" He stood over the tracks and waited for Yancey
to confirm it. "There it is—that sharp edge on those
new shoes." Yancey agreed, and they followed the
tracks down through a narrow draw until sure it was
the same number of horses they had been following.

"That ol' bastard back there wasn't lyin'," Yancey
remarked. "Grayson didn't keep followin' the river,
he headed east, all right." He looked toward the horizon in the direction indicated by the hoof prints.
"He's cuttin' across, headin' for the Cimarron. If what
that feller said was a fact, and he was here a couple of
days ago, we still got some catchin' up to do."

"I wish we'da had more time to take that place
apart," Lonnie said. "I wonder if that ol' boy had a
woman back of that store." Earl would never know
that he had one thing to thank Jacob Blanchard for.
Had he not instructed Yancey and Lonnie to stop for
nothing—and had not the two gunmen feared their
employer too much to disobey—he well might have
lost something more valuable than merchandise.

Thanks to their raid on Earl Johnson's store, the two outlaws had plenty to eat while they raced across the prairie, riding late into the night every night, able to make good time because of the straight line their prey had ridden. With a good head start, Grayson had not wasted time changing directions in an effort to hide his trail. He had not thought it necessary. Now the two killers were making up the distance between them and Grayson. When they found Grayson's campsite by a creek two days' ride from Earl's trading post, almost a half a day beyond the Cimarron, they were sure they were catching up to him. Still, the trail never varied as it held to an easterly course. "When is the son of a bitch gonna head for Fort Smith?" Lonnie wondered aloud.

"He's headin' straight across to the Cherokee Nation," Yancey said. "But it ain't gonna do him no good. We keep this up, and we'll catch him a long time before he cuts back south to Fort Smith." They switched horses and continued on into the night, leaving the two worn-out horses behind and leading the final two.

While the two assassins raced across Oklahoma Territory, Jacob Blanchard waited impatiently for word of their success in overtaking Grayson and rescuing Billy. It had been four days since Yancey and Lonnie left to pick up the ex-lawman's trail, and Jacob had reached the limits of his mental endurance. He called for Jimmy Hicks to saddle his horse, and he rode into Black Horse Creek late one morning, the horse near exhaustion from the pace he had set. Plodding slowly down the street on his way to the sheriff's office, he met his two sons as they were coming out of the hotel dining room. They stopped abruptly upon confronting the old man.

"Kinda late to be eatin' breakfast, ain't it?" Jacob asked when he pulled the tired horse to a halt and dismounted.

Almost too surprised to respond, both men sputtered for a few moments before Slate blurted, "Pa, what are you doin' in town?" His father never came to the town he created except on grave emergencies, or to personally make his anger felt if one of his merchants was causing trouble.

"I came in to see what you boys are doin' about findin' your brother," Jacob replied. "I told Yancey to let me know somethin' as soon as he could, and I ain't heard nothin' since they've been gone."

"Maybe it's just too soon to know if they've caught up with 'em," Slate said. "They might have, already, but I don't know of any place they could find a telegraph office before they get halfway across The Nations. Most likely Yancey and Lonnie ain't come across any place to send a telegram, so we'll have to wait till they get back."

This was not good enough for Jacob. He was not by nature a patient man, especially in his concern for Billy's safety. "Yancey's a good man—damn good with a gun; Lonnie's a fair hand, too—but I don't know if the two of 'em are smart enough to take Grayson down. I mighta been wrong to send them." He cast a serious gaze upon his sons. "If that son of a bitch makes it to Fort Smith with Billy, they won't waste much time before they hang him." As a matter of habit, he handed his reins to Troy, and they started walking toward the sheriff's office. "Billy's got a wild streak, but he don't deserve no hangin'. If they kill that boy, there's gonna be a helluva lot of blood spilled, startin' with that son of a bitch, Grayson. And it ain't gonna stop there. We'll get that do-gooder judge in Fort Smith and the hangman, too. Everybody who had a hand in it is gonna pay if they kill my boy."

"What do you want us to do, Pa?" Troy asked.

"What I shoulda had you do in the first place," Jacob answered. "I want you boys to get over to Fort Smith as fast as you can. And get me some information, dammit!"

"Pa, there ain't no way me and Troy can get to Fort Smith before Grayson gets there, unless he takes his own sweet time," Slate said. "And I doubt he'll do that. He's bound to know he's got somebody on his tail."

"I know that, dammit," Jacob responded. "But you can find out if Grayson made it or not. If Billy ain't there in that damn jail, then chances are Yancey and Lonnie took care of business and Billy's on his way back home."

"What if Billy's in the jail when we get there?" Troy asked.

"Then the first thing you do is to find that damn bounty hunter and kill him," his father told him. "Then you send me a telegram and let me know. We'll figure a way to get Billy outta that jail somehow." He paused to think about the likelihood of accomplishing such a thing, a feat that most would consider impossible. "Maybe when they're takin' him back and forth for the trial," he speculated. "We'll find a way."

"You figurin' on goin' over there?" Slate asked. "Maybe you'd best leave this up to me and Troy."

"Don't go thinkin' I've lost my fire just because I'm old," Jacob replied. "If somethin' happens to that boy, I want vengeance by my own hand." His piercing gaze was evidence enough of the smoldering fire within. "You two get yourselves ready to ride, and go help your brother."

"What about the town?" Slate asked. "We can't just ride off and leave the town with no sheriff or deputy, not for as long as we're liable to be gone."

"Hell, nothin's gonna happen here," Jacob replied. "Go pin a star on that young feller that works at the stable. He oughta be able to handle a drunk or two."

"Burt?" Slate asked. "Yeah, I reckon he'd be about the best choice. He'd probably be tickled to be in charge for a while."

It was settled then. A typical lazy morning for the two brothers in the peaceful town of Black Horse Creek had turned into a breakneck ride to get to Fort Smith in time for a rescue or a killing, or both. One thing the two brothers knew for certain was that there would be no acceptance of failure on their part to avenge their brother. And both boys were smart enough to know that their mission was leaning more toward the impossible side, because there was no way of guessing Grayson's trail back to Fort Smith.

Chapter 7

"Whaddaya think, Lonnie?" Yancey Brooks reined back to let Lonnie pull up beside him.

"I don't know. Looks like a tradin' post or somethin'," Lonnie said. "Sizable outfit, ain't it?" Both men were traveling in country they were not familiar with. Judging from the size of the waterway, however, they felt certain that they were looking at the Arkansas River several hundred yards ahead of them. From the ridge they were on, they could see that the river made a double turn, forming a U-shaped bend with a cluster of small buildings nestled in the bottom of the U.

"He knows this damn country," Yancey said, "so I'm bettin' he was headin' for that place on the river. That's gotta be the reason he's been holdin' to a straight line across the territory." Although it had been apparent that Grayson had not taken pains to hide his trail, it had become harder and harder to follow. A day and a half of rain had done its part to erase some of the tracks, forcing the two assassins to gamble on long stretches where there were none.

"He must know the folks that run that place. I reckon there's one way to find out," Lonnie said, and gave his horse a nudge with his heels. "Maybe if we're lucky, this is where we'll catch up with him. We'd best look that place over pretty good before we go ridin' in, though—look them horses over in that corral to see if Billy's Appaloosa's in with 'em. We don't wanna spook Grayson if he sees us comin' and runs."

"Hell, we'll just ride right on in," Yancey disagreed. "I ain't ever seen Grayson. Have you?" When Lonnie said that he had not, Yancey exclaimed, "Then, hell, he ain't ever seen us neither. He don't know we're comin' after him."

Lonnie considered it for a moment. "I hadn't thought about that," he finally confessed.

Robert Walking Stick paused on his way from the barn to look at the two riders approaching from the west. Each man was leading one horse with no saddle and no packs. His first thought was that they were probably coming to see John Polsgrove with selling the horses in mind. He knew that Polsgrove bought horses from time to time, but he expected the two riders to be disappointed, because John had just acquired some extra horses as a result of the Pawnee raid two days before. Robert went on into the store to tell his aunt Belle that someone was coming. "Got some customers, Aunt Belle," he sang out when he didn't find her in the store.

Belle came in from the living quarters behind the

store after having just given her husband his dinner. She wiped her hands on her apron and walked to the door to look at the riders. "Ain't nobody I ever see before," she said. She turned to address her nephew. "Your dinner's on the table in the kitchen. If you don't eat it pretty soon, it's gonna be too cold."

"Yes, ma'am," Robert replied. "I'm goin' after it right now."

She watched him till he went through the door, thinking how fortunate she and John were to have his help. Robert was a hard-working boy—never had to be told what to do. He saw things that needed doing and he jumped right on them. He had a few run-ins with the Indian Police, but nothing really bad, just things that young boys get into. He had access to some illegal alcohol from time to time and had raised a little hell in the village on a couple of occasions. But Belle figured that was nothing more than the natural warrior blood of his ancestors. Although it caused concern for his mother, her sister, it merely made Belle smile. She walked over and closed the door to the house, then went back to the end of the counter to await the riders.

Right from the start, she had cautious feelings about the two strangers. There was something about the way they paused at the door to look the room over before entering. And when she asked what she could do for them, she didn't get a reply right away. Instead, they continued to scan the room as if there might be someone hiding behind the counter, or behind the stack of flour sacks in the corner. "We're government agents," Lonnie finally said, thinking to use the same farce that seemed to work for them before.

Belle Prairie Flower Polsgrove was not the simple Indian woman they took her for, however. "Government agents?" she asked. "What kind of government agents?" Her reply left Lonnie speechless. He looked to Yancey for help.

"The kind that puts people in jail," Yancey said.

"Nobody here need to go to jail," Belle replied. "You wanna buy something?" At that moment, the door to the house opened, causing both men to jump, their hands on their pistols, to startle a curious Robert, who simply wanted to see what they wanted. Belle was immediately alerted to a possible robbery attempt. "Don't shoot Robert," she said, almost without emotion, and she took a couple of steps to the side to stand next to her rifle propped at the corner of the counter. "He don't do nothing wrong."

Yancey relaxed and forced a smile. "Nah, we ain't lookin' for Robert. We're chasin' a killer name of Grayson, and we think he was here."

Belle frowned. "Grayson ain't no killer. You after the wrong man. Maybe you need some supplies— coffee beans, flour, dried beans—we got all that."

"No, dammit, we don't need no supplies," Yancey responded. "Now, was Grayson here or not?"

Belle wasn't about to give men as phony as these two any information about Grayson. Whatever they were up to, it wasn't good. She edged a little closer to her rifle. "People all the time come in here—we don't ask no name. I don't ask your name."

"A minute ago you said Grayson wasn't no killer," Yancey said. "Now you say you don't even know his name." He waited for her explanation, but she only shrugged. It was plain to see that he wasn't going to get anywhere with the impassive Indian woman, so Yancey shifted his attention to the boy standing in the doorway. "How 'bout you, boy? You see a couple of fellers—one of 'em ridin' an Appaloosa, and most likely had his hands in irons?" Robert hesitated to answer. Having witnessed the reactions of the two men when he opened the door, he wasn't sure how to answer. After another moment with no response, Yancey threatened. "Boy, I asked you a question, and if I don't get an answer right now, I'm liable to start shootin' this place to pieces."

That was enough for Belle. Before Robert could answer, she picked up her rifle and rested it on the counter before her. "You start shooting and I shoot you," she warned. "Now maybe you get on your horse and ride away."

"Why, you ornery ol' bitch," Yancey responded, "put that rifle down, or I'll blow your head off." When she made no move to follow his orders, he said, "There's two of us, so even if you got one of us, you ain't quick enough to cock that thing before the other'n gets you. So put it down," he demanded.

"Maybe she don't have to get but one of you." The words came from Big John Polsgrove, standing behind Robert in the doorway, his shotgun resting on the boy's shoulder. Awakened by the sound of angry voices, he had struggled out of his bed and made his way to the door to lean against the jamb. "Which one you gonna shoot if they go for them pistols, Belle?"

"I shoot the big one, doing all the talking," Belle said with a slight smirk. "He's a big target, no chance to miss."

"Good enough," John said, "I'll take the other'n.

All right, boys, either go for them guns, or get the hell outta my store."

Time stood still for a frozen moment with both Yancey and Lonnie weighing their odds in the stand-off. It didn't take a great deal of thought for both men to realize they had no chance to draw their weapons before being cut down. Finally Yancey admitted defeat. "All right," he said. "You got the upper hand this time. Me and my partner will walk out the door. Ain't no need for anybody to get shot." He looked at Lonnie, who still appeared to be caught in indecision. "Come on, Lonnie, let's leave these folks be." He held his hands out before him to show his intentions were peaceful, and turned toward the front door. Lonnie followed.

As soon as the two gunmen went out the door, John started to sag against the door jamb, having held on for as long as he could. Robert was able to get a shoulder under him before he went to the floor. Belle ran from behind the counter to help. "Watch 'em, Belle," John gasped, a growing stain of crimson spreading on his shirt. "Watch 'em," he warned.

"I watch 'em," she said. "Robert, get him back to bed." She took but a second to make sure Robert was enough support to get her giant-sized husband back to his bed. Like John, she had a feeling they weren't through with the two strangers claiming to be government agents. So her rifle still in hand, she hurried over to take a position behind the stack of flour sacks piled up in the corner opposite the counter where she could watch the door.

Outside, the tempers were hot, fueled by the humiliating defeat at the hands of the Indian woman and her husband. Had they known that her husband was on the verge of collapse, they might not have backed down. As they stood ready to climb on their horses, Yancey glanced back to notice that no one was even standing in the door to make sure they left. "That Injun bitch," he muttered. "She's stuck in my craw, and that's a fact."

"Mine, too," Lonnie said. "I'm thinkin' about throwin' a few shots through that door before I ride off."

"There ain't nobody watchin' the door," Yancey pointed out. "We could shoot the place up before they knew what hit 'em." It was all the encouragement Lonnie needed. He nodded and drew his .44 from his holster, and they both suddenly charged through the door with guns blazing.

With both men concentrating their fire on the counter, after first discovering there was no longer anyone standing in the doorway to the house, their barrage succeeded in shooting holes in the front of the counter and the shelves behind. So intent upon their surprise attack, neither man noticed the Winchester rifle resting on the top sack of flour on the pile in the opposite corner of the room—or the Indian woman carefully taking aim on the one man who had stepped all the way inside the room. The unlucky man was Lonnie, and he let out a grunt and staggered backward into Yancey when the slug from Belle's rifle slammed into his chest. Yancey escaped injury when Lonnie unintentionally shielded him from the second shot that struck not six inches from the first. Not wishing the same as his partner, Yancey ran for the horses. Lonnie, still on his feet, staggered drunkenly after him, and managed to grab the saddle horn when his horse started to follow Yancey's.

The two extra horses were left behind in the panic to escape out of rifle range.

Yancey did not look back until reaching cover in the trees along the river. Only then did he realize that Lonnie was still alive. The wounded man, unable to lift himself into the saddle, was holding on desperately to his saddle horn while his horse dragged him along, his feet plowing the dust as he went. After taking a look behind them to make sure there was no pursuit, Yancey pulled to a stop and dismounted to help Lonnie up in the saddle. "Damn, partner, I thought you was in the saddle," he lied. "I didn't know you was hit that bad." Once Lonnie was settled, Yancey put the reins in his hand and asked, "Can you ride?"

"I damn-sure will," Lonnie gasped. "I ain't stayin' here." He fell over on his horse's neck.

Yancey hesitated a moment to make sure Lonnie was going to stay on, and when it appeared that he was, he hurried back to his horse and mounted. "Let's get the hell outta here," he said, and started off at a gallop. He didn't ride more than half a mile before reining the horse back to a fast walk and waiting for Lonnie to catch up. "You ain't lookin' too good," he told him when his horse pulled up beside his. Lonnie could only shake his head slowly as he suffered through his pain. Yancey took a longer look at him, trying to decide what to do. "Well," he said, "we might as well find us a place to camp, since we ain't got but one horse apiece now. We'll let 'em rest tonight and see how you're feelin' in the mornin'." This was welcome news to Lonnie, because he knew he couldn't stay on his horse much longer.

Yancey picked a place to camp close to the water's edge, and helped Lonnie settle himself next to a cottonwood trunk for support. "I'll take care of the horses. Then I'll take a look at them wounds," he said. With the horses watered and hobbled, he returned to build a fire before tending to Lonnie's needs. "Two of 'em," he muttered, looking at the twin holes in Lonnie's chest. "Both of 'em bleedin' like hell. There ain't nothin' I can do for you. Looks like they both went deep inside." He was fairly satisfied that his partner was a goner, but he didn't want to tell him that. Lonnie had a coughing fit that lasted for a couple of minutes before he was again able to control it. However, the coughing brought up a small quantity of blood that ran down the corner of Lonnie's mouth and into his chin whiskers. That was enough to confirm Yancey's suspicions. "We'll see how you feel in the mornin' after you've had a little rest." He made him as comfortable as he could, even tried to feed him something, but Lonnie couldn't eat without a choking sensation, so Yancey let him rest.

In an effort to take his mind off his pain, for Lonnie was groaning with every breath, Yancey rambled on about his plans for them to continue the search for Grayson. "We ain't got no tracks to follow, but I figure he was plannin' to follow the river right on into Fort Smith. He's been trying to swing wide, so nobody would look for him this far north, but he'd be a damn fool to keep goin' east now, past the river. He's got to cut back sometime, and this is where he's doin' it. I'd bet my share of that reward on it." He paused to see how Lonnie was doing, and the suffering man could only groan. Yancey decided he wasn't hearing a thing he said.

Somewhat to Yancey's disappointment, his partner was still alive the next morning, and determined to gut it out in the saddle, although he still could not eat. "You just help me up in the saddle," Lonnie said, "and I'll make it all right."

"Damn, partner," Yancey told him, "I wasn't sure you'd make it through the night, but you must be tougher'n a bull elk. We'll get saddled up and get on down this river. We'll catch that son of a bitch before long." He decided to make an effort to remain positive in hopes of encouraging Lonnie to gut it out. He was sure they had been rapidly closing the gap between themselves and Grayson, and he was reluctant to lose what they might have already gained.

The ride was hard on the wounded man that day, but he stubbornly held on, determined to make it until dusk. Before, they had ridden on into the night, but they had to be more concerned with their horses now. So when they came upon a bend in the river that looked like it was made for camping, Yancey suggested they stop there for the night. There was ample evidence that testified to the fact that the spot they picked was a popular one. After he got Lonnie reclined against a tree, he looked around the area to see what he could find. There were six or eight spots where campfires had been, their ashes dead and gray now, but some were more recent. Farther down the riverbank, he found a recent camp, indeed, for there were horse droppings that still looked moist, almost fresh. *Somebody was here not long ago*, he thought. Then a hoofprint in the sand by the water caught his attention, and his heart skipped a beat, for the edges were sharp, like the ones he and Lonnie had been following. *Billy's Appaloosa*, he thought, *I'm sure of it!* He couldn't believe his luck. It was unusual to find the edges on those shoes still fairly sharp after traveling so many miles. More likely they had stumbled upon somebody else's trail who had recently had his horse shod. "No, hell, no!" he said defiantly. "That was Billy's horse that left these tracks!" They were back on Grayson's trail, and from the looks of the droppings he had found, they weren't far behind. He hurried back to tell Lonnie about the tracks.

"We'll get on his trail in the morning," Lonnie forced through pale lips when Yancey reported his find. His face looked even more haggard than before, but his will was there and he was determined to heal from his wounds. He tried to sip a little bit of coffee, and he went into another of his coughing fits. Yancey studied him carefully, and began to think the situation through. It didn't take much thought before he came to the conclusion that there were decisions to be made.

In spite of Lonnie's determination, Yancey wasn't convinced that his partner was going to make it. The wounds he suffered were deep and involved his inside organs. He wasn't even confident that a doctor could save him. *Hard to say, though,* he told himself, *I've seen some fellows shot to pieces and live to talk about it.* He looked again at the suffering man lying next to the tree, trying to find some position that would lessen the pain. And he had to think that it was a hell of a time for Lonnie to get shot, for he was certain now that they had almost overtaken Grayson and Billy. Then he began to feel a little perturbed by the constant moaning that seemed never to cease. He couldn't help thinking that if Lonnie would go on and die, he could get hot on Grayson's trail, and he would once again have a spare horse to alternate with his. Mr. Blanchard had offered six hundred dollars to the two of them to get the job done. It seemed to Yancey that the money should be the same, even if just one of them came to collect it. *I'll see how Lonnie passes the night,* he thought. *We've been riding together, on one job or another, for a good many years now.*

His thoughts of compassion were interrupted by a loud groan from the wounded man, and he told himself, *Ain't neither one of us gonna get any sleep with that going on. Hell, he'll likely be dead by morning. There ain't no sense in letting him keep me awake all night.* Thoughts of that six hundred dollars riding farther away from him were enough to make up his mind.

Lonnie rolled his eyes up to gaze mournfully at his partner when Yancey walked over to stand before him. "I'm beholden to you for standin' by me," he said, and tried to smile.

"Well, hell, I wouldn't leave you out here on the prairie to die," Yancey replied. "How you feelin'? Is it gettin' any better?"

"I'm gonna make it," Lonnie answered. "I think I'm a little bit better, but I'm still hurtin' right smart."

"I think I can fix that," Yancey said, and whipped out his .44 Colt and shot the surprised man in the head. He intended to put the bullet right between his eyes, but Lonnie had tried to turn away in that last fatal instant causing the bullet to hit him in the side of the head, right at the temple. The recoil banged his head against the tree trunk, and he slumped in death. "No hard feelin's," Yancey said, "but you was slowin' me down." He went about stripping the body of anything useful to him, then looked around to determine where best to drag it out of the way. Making a quick decision, he grabbed Lonnie's feet and dragged him over to the embankment of the river, and rolled him over the edge to drop about four feet to rest on the sand at the water's edge. With that chore done, he went back to the fire he had built and began to cut some bacon to put in his frying pan.

He lay down to sleep that night feeling satisfied to roll up in his blanket without the constant groaning of his late partner to keep him awake. Sleep did not come easily, however, and when it did, it was not for long, for he was wide awake long before sunup. He told himself that he was just too anxious to get started on Grayson's trail in the morning, and that was the reason he found it difficult to wait out the morning light. In truth, however, he found it hard to forget about Lonnie's body lying below the riverbank. Did he check real closely to make sure Lonnie was dead? How could he be alive with a bullet in his brain? *He couldn't*, his common sense told him, and yet he finally got out of his blanket, and with the light of a full moon, walked back to the riverbank to make sure the body hadn't moved.

Lying face up, the body appeared to meet his gaze, causing him to leap back from the edge of the bank, startled, almost falling down. Regaining some measure of control over his emotions, he moved cautiously up to the edge of the bank and looked again at the cold dead eyes of his late partner staring up in the moonlight to meet his. "Lonnie?" he couldn't help asking, not sure what he would do if there was a response. When there was none, he breathed a sigh of relief. Then his heart skipped a beat when Lonnie seemed to stir slightly. Yancey's frightened reaction was to jerk the trigger and shoot the corpse of his friend once more, realizing immediately after that he had just let himself get spooked. "Damn you, Lonnie, you're dead as you can get. Whaddaya wanna devil me for? You was gonna die anyway." The corpse shifted slightly again, but this time Yancey realized that the river had risen just enough during the night for water to inch up on the sand and gently rock Lonnie's body.

There would be no more sleep that night, his nerves having been thoroughly frazzled, but he thought it necessary to wait until sunup to give him a better chance to follow Grayson's tracks away from the camp. He was still convinced that the bounty hunter was riding the river down to Fort Smith, and he was bound to overtake him before another day, two at the most. But he wanted to see the tracks of his horses leaving the camp to verify it. So he went back to his blanket, built up his fire, and waited for the sun to appear.

"You a religious man, Grayson?" Billy asked, not expecting an answer. Grayson seldom bothered to answer his prisoner's cocky rambling, but that never seemed to discourage Billy. He did it just to annoy the somber bounty hunter. "Whaddaya reckon it's gonna be like when one of my brothers puts a bullet in your brain? You reckon there's gonna be a big ol' angel waitin' to take you by the hand—maybe lead you up them golden stairs to a mansion in the sky?" Seated at the base of a cottonwood, his hands tied around the trunk, he watched Grayson preparing their supper. "Maybe it'll be one of the devil's boys that comes to meet you instead," he started again. "That'd be more like it, 'cause there ain't nothin' lower than a bounty hunter when it comes to pure scum." There was still not even a glance in his direction from the object of his taunting. "You'd better hope it's Slate that gets you. He'll most likely put a bullet right through your head, make it quick-like, and you'll be right on your way to hell. Now, if it's Troy, well, that'll be a different story. Troy's got a real nasty streak. He's gonna wanna kill you slow-like, so he can enjoy it longer."

Grayson pulled his coffeepot to the edge of the fire when it started to boil. After it simmered down a bit, he poured himself a cup of coffee and sipped it cautiously to keep from burning his lips. Then he stirred the bacon around in the pan, and turned it over to fry the other side, all the while ignoring the constant rambling of Billy's mouth. Although he never showed any indication that Billy's attempts to annoy him had any effect upon him, he secretly wondered if he was going to make it to Fort Smith without cutting the brazen killer's tongue out.

The wound in Billy's thigh, although swollen and a little red around the bullet hole, was healing to the point where it was not so painful. Grayson suspected this to be the reason that his prisoner was feeling sassy enough to try constantly to annoy him. *I should have shot him in the head instead of the leg,* he thought as he pulled the pan from the hot flames. When he lifted some of the meat out of the pan and placed it on a tin plate, Billy stopped talking, in anticipation of eating his supper. Just as he had ignored the senseless banter, however, Grayson ignored his silence. He picked up his coffee, took his plate, and walked several yards away to sit down against a tree to eat.

At once alarmed, Billy sang out, "Hey, wait a

minute! Where's mine? I'm hungry, too. You gotta feed me, dammit, it's the law."

Grayson took a deliberate look at him and had a couple more sips of his coffee before speaking. "There ain't no law that says I gotta feed you. Even if there was, I ain't a lawman." He tore off a bite of bacon with his teeth and chewed the tough meat for a few seconds. "Besides, it seemed to me that you were more in the mood to use your mouth for talkin' instead of eatin', so I figured you could decide when the talkin' was done, and maybe you'd let me know."

"Ah, come on, Grayson," Billy pleaded, his cockiness gone now. "I been ridin' as hard as you have. You gotta feed me." Grayson was not moved by the contrite tone he had adopted, so Billy promised, "All right, I'll shut up if you let me eat."

"You sure now?" Grayson paused, then took another bite of bacon. "'Cause if you don't, I'm gonna have to bend my rifle barrel over your head to shut you up."

"I'm sure," Billy replied meekly. "I'll shut up. Just untie me from this tree." *You hard-ass son of a bitch*, he thought to himself, *you just get careless one time, and I'll cut your gizzard out.* He had no sooner thought it when he noticed something that might offer his opportunity. During all the long days since leaving Rabbit Creek, Grayson had never been careless once. When Billy was not tied hand and foot, he was under Grayson's constant vigilance. He never made a mistake— except for this one time—when he left the knife he had used to slice off the bacon sticking in the butt end of a large limb by the fire. The sight of the long, razor-sharp skinning knife caused the wheels in Billy's mind to churn anxiously, and he tried not to stare at it while Grayson was untying the rope that held him to the tree trunk.

Billy was past the point where he might consider desperation attempts as too risky. Too many days had already passed with no sign that he was going to get help from his father, and the harsh reality that he was on his way to be hanged made any attempt worth the gamble. He shifted his gaze to directly lock on the stoic bounty hunter as he pulled the knot loose. *Is he going to remember that knife he left by the fire? Or did he leave it there as bait, hoping I would make a move for it?* There was no way to tell by studying the impassive face of his captor.

As soon as Billy's hands were free, Grayson backed away and leveled his rifle, ready to fire. "You can take a minute to take a leak," he said, and kept the rifle on him while he emptied his bladder.

When he had finished, Billy made a show of stretching his arms and neck. "A man gets awful stiff and stove-up settin' there huggin' a tree all night," he said. "Wouldn't be no harm in lettin' me set by the fire to warm up a little, would it?"

"It ain't that cold this mornin'," Grayson said. "I think it best if you sit on that log where you sat last night." He nodded toward a fallen tree a few yards from the fire. The warmth of the fire reached that far, and he felt no need to risk having Billy grab a flaming limb and flinging it in his direction.

"Whatever you say," Billy replied. The fire was between him and the log Grayson insisted upon, so he thought he could pass close by it without arousing Grayson's suspicions.

Billy's cooperation without his usual vocal rebellion should have alerted Grayson that something was wrong, but he didn't give the matter much thought. He stood back to let Billy go before him, his rifle held waist-high before him, but not really expecting any trouble, for Billy typically was prone to cause trouble after his belly was full. As they approached the fire, Billy held his hands out, palms down, as if to warm them as he passed by. Grayson was not ready for the move that followed. Beside the fire now, Billy apparently began to stumble, and before Grayson knew what was happening, Billy suddenly reached down and drew the knife from the limb. Thinking his prisoner had put his hand down to keep from falling, Grayson was unaware of the coming attack until Billy turned back toward him with the knife in hand. Grayson's reflexive action in that initial instant was to slap his hand against his empty knife scabbard, shocked to find he had been so careless. It was no more than an instant, however, as he braced himself to meet Billy's charge, prepared to use his rifle in defense, and shoot only if he had to.

Billy was quick, but no quicker than the older and larger man, who stood his ground when Billy lunged, striking out with the knife. Grayson blocked Billy's attempt to bury the blade in his chest by catching it on the barrel of his rifle, then hit him hard on the side of his neck, causing him to stagger backward in order to stay on his feet. The intense fire in the young killer's eyes burned hotter still. Grayson tried to talk him down. "Let it go, Billy. You made your play, but now it's over. Don't make me have to shoot you."

It was too late to try to talk sense to Billy. Although the advantage was Grayson's, Billy was reluctant to surrender now that he had a weapon in hand. "You're gonna have to shoot me, you son of a bitch," Billy snarled, "but I'm takin' you with me." He flung himself recklessly at his jailor. Grayson heard the solid thud of the bullet against Billy's back, followed a split instant after by the sound of the shot fired. There was no time for thought. The next few seconds were dependent upon instinct and reflexes. Grayson dived for the ground, rolling several times until he reached the cover of the log that Billy had been directed to. With the log to shield him, he took time to figure out what had just happened. The shot had to have come from the trees behind him. From whom and for what, he could only speculate, but he assumed the shot had been meant for him. From the end of the log, he could see Billy's body, and from all indications, it appeared that his prisoner was dead. If he was right in his assumption, and he was the intended target, then he had better decide what he was going to do, and quickly. The shot had come from the same side of the river he was on, from a distance of at least seventy-five yards, maybe a hundred. How many was he facing? There was only one shot fired. As if his thought was intercepted, a second shot came, imbedding itself in the log. "Time to move," he muttered and pushed his body back away from the log.

Doing his best to keep the log between himself and the spot he thought the shots probably came from, he kept as flat as he could while pulling his body back into the brush before the trees. When he reached a point where the bushes between the trees were thick enough to conceal him, he got to his feet and quickly moved deeper into the brush, hoping to gain a position to see who was shooting at him. He was safe for the moment, the fact confirmed by several more shots aimed at the log he had vacated. The possibility that it was an Indian with stealing the horses in mind had to be considered, but he still had a strong feeling that it was just one man. He would have wanted to try to work around his assailant by crossing over to the other side—especially if it was only one man—but the river was wide at this point, although not deep, and with a fairly lazy current. If the bushwhacker caught on to his intention to circle behind him, he would naturally move to cut him off. And Grayson didn't like the prospect of being caught in the middle of the river while his assailant took pot-shots at him.

He finally decided the first thing to do was to get Billy and the horses and pull back away from the clearing at the river's edge. The trouble with that was the fact that Billy was still lying in the open where he had been shot, and it was too dangerous to try to remove the body since it would expose himself as an open target. There was no problem with the horses. He could easily get to them back in the trees without exposing himself. And he would not have bothered to risk saving Billy's body, but it was worth one thousand dollars. Council had insisted that he had to produce the body to collect the reward. "Damn," he cursed, frustrated. He had plenty of evidence to support Billy's death, his horse, his weapons, his personal items, but John Council was adamant—no body, no money.

"Damn the luck," Yancey cursed under his breath. His front sight had been set squarely on Grayson's chest, and if Billy had kept walking beside the fire, his reward money would have been as good as in his pocket. But Billy had lunged right at the point when

Yancey squeezed the trigger. The bullet was already on its way when Billy's back suddenly appeared in his sights. Yancey felt no real loss in the death of Billy Blanchard. Very few people had any use at all for the loudmouth braggart, but he was Jacob Blanchard's favorite son, so it was going to be a difficult task to explain Billy's death as an accident, and caused by Billy, himself. "Damn," he swore again when picturing the old man's reaction. *He's liable to shoot me*, he thought, *even if I kill Grayson*. There was no decision to be made; he would tell Blanchard that Grayson shot Billy. When he returned to Black Horse Creek with Billy's horse and possessions, as well as those of the feared bounty hunter, Blanchard might even reward him with a bonus. Without witnesses, there was no way Jacob could ever know that it was him who shot Billy. The thought brought a wicked smile to Yancey's face, for he couldn't help appreciating the irony of getting rid of a hated bounty hunter, along with Blanchard's pain-in-the-ass son, and collecting double the reward for doing it. His thoughts were interrupted by the sound of horses crashing through the brush on the other side of the clearing. *He's running!* he told himself, and immediately left the cover of the trees, hoping to get a shot off before Grayson was able to get away. When he reached the edge of the clearing, however, there was no sign of the fleeing man, only the sound of horses pushing through the brush-covered riverbank, growing more and more faint by the second. With his horses tied some seventy-five or eighty yards behind him, there wasn't much chance of overtaking the bounty hunter in a flat-out race. *But the day ain't over yet*, he told himself.

Unwilling to charge into the clearing, being

naturally wary of an ambush, in spite of the fact that he was pretty sure he was now alone, he dropped to one knee and looked the campsite over before exposing his body. There was Billy, lying facedown next to the fire, still clutching Grayson's skinning knife. It was a good shot, he thought, even if it was not the right target. He remained there on one knee for a few seconds, listening until he could no longer hear the sound of the horses farther down the river. He's long gone, he decided, disappointed that he had not gotten an opportunity for one more shot. *You're running*, he thought, *but you're leaving a trail easy to follow from the sound of it.* He resigned himself to more time in the saddle, tracking. He had never bumped into the man known simply as Grayson, but based upon the way he had hightailed it after a couple of gunshots, he suspected his reputation was more words than deeds.

Yancey rose to his feet again and walked over to the fire to examine Billy. He turned the body over to find Billy looking up at him with the same vacant gaze he had gotten from Lonnie Jenkins. It was not as unsettling in the light of day as it had been in the middle of night. "Don't look at me like that, boy," he joked and reached down to close Billy's eyelids. Since it was still too early for rigor mortis to set in, Billy's eyes remained closed. "That's the first time you ever done what I told you," Yancey couldn't resist taunting the dead man.

Still clutching his rifle before him, ready to fire quickly, he scanned the tree line and shrubs by the river bank. Satisfied that he was indeed alone, he relaxed his vigilance and glanced around him at the abandoned camp. "Left his coffeepot," he said with a chuckle. There was a cup lying on the ground where Grayson had dropped it, so Yancey picked it up, wiped off the dirt, and poured himself a cup of coffee. After a couple of sips, he glanced again toward the shrubs by the river. The cup dropped from his hand when he discovered the grim man standing there, where there had been no one only seconds before, a Winchester rifle pointing at his midsection.

"Who the hell are you?" Grayson asked. He had half expected to see Slate or Troy Blanchard, but he had never seen this man before. There was no answer to his question. In a panic, Yancey tried to yank his rifle up, but was immediately cut down by a slug from Grayson's Winchester, followed in less than an instant by a second shot that slammed into his breast bone. Grayson walked up to stand over the body, stuck the toe of his boot in the chest and rolled it over. A big man, rough and dirty-looking, he was no doubt one of Blanchard's hired guns. Grayson wondered how many more had been sent to stop him, and how far behind they were. He shook his head slowly when he thought about the time spent at Big John Polsgrove's trading post. It had cost him his lead, but he had been given no other choice. He wondered if this man lying here had stopped at John's store. He hoped not, since John was in no condition to deal with a hired gun, and he had no help but a young boy and his wife. "Well, there's work to do," he announced to the two corpses in the clearing.

The first order of business was to recover all the horses, so he started down along the river at a trot. As he expected, his gray gelding was not far away, grazing peacefully on a patch of grass near the water. "Come'ere, boy," he called calmly, and the horse looked up, thought it over for a second or two, then walked slowly over to his master. Grayson climbed in the saddle and followed the obvious trail left by the other horses when he had chased them through the trees. Like his gray, they had not run far before settling down to graze on the water lilies at the river's edge.

Once his horses were secured, he scouted the perimeter of the clearing until he came across Yancey's footprints. He followed them back through the trees until he found the outlaw's two horses tied to some tree branches. He became a little wary when he discovered that both horses carried saddles. It caused him to scout all around the area where they were tied, but he could not find any footprints other than the set he had followed. He couldn't help wondering if maybe there had been two, and if a visit to John Polsgrove might have had something to do with the empty saddle. Whatever the reason for both horses being saddled, he felt quite certain that his assailant had acted alone on this morning. He had quite a string of horses now, more than he cared to fool with, but too valuable to cut loose. The next thing to attend to was Billy.

Returning to stand over him, he took a few minutes to think about what he should do about the corpse. He wondered how firm the governor and John Council were in their insistence that he had to bring Billy's body to Fort Smith. It would take him at least three more days to reach Fort Smith, maybe a half a day more, and from prior experience, he knew that a man's body would start to smell pretty high in that amount of time. He decided he'd better not waste any more time and get in the saddle right away. But first, he had to wrap Billy up the best he could, so he scratched his head for a while over that one. The solution came to him in the form of a wide piece of canvas he found rolled up and tied behind the saddle of one of the two horses acquired that morning. It appeared to have been used to make a shelter of sorts. He found it was big enough to wrap Billy's body up fairly securely. So he rolled the corpse in the canvas and tied it together with rope. "There you go, governor," he said when he was finished, "all wrapped up like a Christmas package." Billy had not started to stiffen up yet when Grayson hefted him up across the saddle of the Appaloosa and tied the ends of his package under the horse's belly. *I guess you'll ride there all right*, he thought, although the Appaloosa seemed a bit skittish with the rope tied under its belly. It settled down and accepted the awkward bundle after a few minutes, however, and Grayson was able to break camp and start out for Fort Smith.

Things went well enough for the rest of the morning as he followed the river southeast, veering from the trail along the shallow banks only when approaching Fort Gibson near the confluence of the Arkansas with the Neosho River. He had no reason to stop at the fort, and he preferred to avoid the town that had grown up near it. There was no need to leave witnesses to his passing that way, in case there were still others on his trail. To make sure there was no contact with anyone, he led his horses through a range of low hills that stood between the river and the prairie to the southwest. Descending a narrow ravine to the prairie again, he felt his horse jerked up short by the string of horses behind. He looked back to find that

Billy's Appaloosa was suddenly pulling against the lead line, and trying to sidestep the awkward burden wrapped in canvas. The reason was apparent. The rough terrain of the hills had caused the package to slip upside down, with Billy's body now hanging under the Appaloosa's belly, the sensation of which caused the horse to try to step around it.

Grayson stopped to haul the corpse back up across the saddle where it had started out. Billy's body had gotten quite stiff by then as rigor mortis had set in. He took an extra length of rope to loop around the saddle horn to secure the package, thinking he would improve on it when he stopped to rest the horses. It wouldn't be long, because it was already getting along in the afternoon, but he determined to be far removed from Fort Gibson when he did stop. Another hour in the saddle and he approached the bank of the Arkansas once again, and looked for a good place to stop to let the horses drink and rest. There were any number of sites to choose from, since the river was lined with a heavy band of trees at this point, and he finally decided upon one where the river split to flow around a sandbar that formed a small island of willows with one solitary oak tree right in the middle. He led his horses across the shallow channel onto the island.

Billy's corpse was totally stiff, and in the shape of a U. When Grayson untied it, it sat on the saddle like a great horseshoe, so he had to roll it to one side, then pull it straight off the horse from the side. He checked it to make sure the ropes he had bound it with were still tightly tied. Satisfied that Billy was wrapped as snugly as could be expected, considering the wrap available to him, Grayson dragged the body over and leaned it against the trunk of the large oak. After pulling the saddles off the horses, he left them to graze on the thin grass growing on the sandbar while he gathered some dead limbs to start a fire for coffee.

Chapter 8

"What the hell has he got leanin' up agin that tree?" Stover asked. He crawled up closer to Rampley, who was lying on his belly, peering through an old army telescope at the camp on the willow island. "Lemme take a look."

"Just hold your horses," Rampley said. "I ain't got a good look yet." After a minute more, he commented, "Damned if I know what that thing is, but he's sure as hell got it all tied up like it's somethin' he don't want nothin' to get to."

"I don't give a damn what it is," Iron Foot snarled impatiently. "What do them damn horses look like? They any good?" Being a half-breed Pawnee, he was naturally more interested in the horses the man had hobbled. To his naked eye, they looked like they might bring a lot of money in Muskogee, especially the Appaloosa. "Let's go down there and get them horses."

"Just keep your shirt on, you crazy Injun," Rampley said. "That feller's got a Winchester rifle settin' close by him, and I ain't in no big hurry to find out if he knows how to use it." He could see the rifle through the branches, although it was more difficult to see the man.

"You talk like a woman," Iron Foot spat. "Ain't but one man down there. I'll go down there and kill him, and you two stay up here and peek through your damn long-see'um."

"What's your hurry, Iron Foot?" Stover asked. "You afraid they'll run outta whiskey at Tarver's before you can get some more money?" He was answered with a sneer from Iron Foot. "Ol' Bob Tarver ends up with every penny you come by. That watered-down rotgut he sells you ain't fit for nobody but a damn half-breed."

"Maybe one of these days I'll take my knife and open a new airhole in your throat, Stover. Maybe I'll take your scalp, too, and tie it on my rifle barrel."

"It'd look a helluva sight better'n that stringy old gray thing you've got on it now. That thing looks like it came offa muskrat," Stover replied and winked at Rampley. It wasn't the first time he had been threatened by the shiftless half-breed, so he wasn't really worried that Iron Foot might one day follow up on one of his threats. Without him and Rampley to tell him what to do, Iron Foot would probably starve to death. The scalp tied to Iron Foot's rifle barrel was not a trophy from a life or death combat with a fierce enemy. Actually Rampley was the one who killed the original owner, a gray-haired old trapper whose misfortune it had been to share his camp with the three cutthroats. Iron Foot was the only one who wanted to take the scalp, and he made such a mess of it that Stover teased him for displaying the ragged piece of hair on his rifle.

Iron Foot fixed a doleful stare upon Stover as he drew his long skinning knife from his belt and made a show of testing the keenness of the blade with his thumb. Then he favored him with a wicked smile as he fondled the weapon playfully. "I bet your skin would split just like a fat pig," he taunted.

"Why don't you two shut up? You're makin' me tired," Rampley said. "We need to decide how we're gonna go after that son of a bitch down there on the river. He's gonna be hard to sneak up on, settin' on that island like he is." While the bantering was going on between his two partners, Rampley had been considering the best way to jump the rider without one or more of them getting picked off with his rifle. As always, his first consideration was whether or not it would be possible to shoot him at long range, but due to the willow thicket, it might be difficult to get a clear shot. He extended the telescope again to its full thirty-inch length and took another look at the man tending his fire. Because of the willow branches, he could see only parts of him whenever he moved. *If I was a hundred yards closer, I might could see enough of him to get a kill shot in,* he thought. *But if I missed, then he'd dig in and we'd play hell trying to root him out.* His thoughts were interrupted by Stover asking again to use the glass.

"Hell," Stover exclaimed, while trying to locate the target through the glass. "Where'd he go? Oh, there he is," he said when the breeze ruffled the limbs, giving him a glimpse of the man kneeling by the fire. After a few moments, he suggested, "Why don't we just shoot that thicket to pieces? He's bound to catch a slug if we throw enough at him."

"I'll tell you what," Rampley retorted. "Why don't you do that? Me and the chief will set back here and see how you do. Right, Iron Foot?" His proposal was met by two blank stares, so he went on to point out the problems with that approach. "We could waste a whole lot of ammunition tryin' to smoke him out. And the first shot fired is liable to send him to diggin' a hole in the sand where we couldn't hit him. He could set there a helluva long time while we shot up all our cartridges. I expect he'd be hopin' we'd try to rush him, knowin' we'd have to come across that wide open stretch of sand. I expect he'd enjoy it."

"Talk like women," Iron Foot muttered under his breath. "I go root him outta there by myself." His partners ignored him, accustomed to his boastful claims.

"So what are we gonna do?" Stover asked Rampley, who usually had the final say on most decisions involving their unlawful activities.

"I reckon we'll go in peaceful-like," Rampley said, "just stoppin' to pass the time of day, and maybe share some coffee if he's got any. Then first time he turns his back, shoot him. That's a helluva lot better'n startin' a shootin' war that's liable to get one of us killed."

"Well, let's get goin', then," Stover said. "I wanna see what that thing is leanin' agin the tree. We mighta hit us a big payday."

"Take that damn thing offa your rifle," he told Iron Foot. "We don't want him to think we've got a wild Injun with us."

"I am an Injun," Iron Foot replied, insulted. "Pawnee, and proud of it." Nevertheless, he removed the scalp, folded it carefully, and put it in his pocket.

Grayson paused to listen when he heard a couple of his horses whinny, which usually told him someone or something was coming. As a precaution, he walked over to the oak tree, and with a little effort, climbed up on a lower limb. From this perch, he could look through the willow branches and see a couple of hundred yards in any direction. His first concern was his back trail, in case someone else had managed to catch up with him, but he could see no one traveling the river trail. Turning to search in the opposite direction, he found the same, no one in sight. Then he saw them, three riders coming from a line of hills west of the river, and apparently headed straight toward him. He remained on his perch for a while longer, trying to get as good a look at the riders as possible, hoping they would turn to follow the trail when they reached it. It was hard to tell much at that extended distance, but he assumed they were outlaws as a matter of precaution. So he dropped back down to the ground and prepared to meet them. Maybe they knew he was there, maybe they didn't. But they sure seemed to be heading directly toward his island, and if that was the case, they should arrive within fifteen minutes.

As a matter of habit, he had scouted his temporary camp when first arriving, a practice he had found necessary over the years, so he picked up his rifle and a cartridge belt and positioned himself between the fire and the oak tree where he could see them if they proceeded to ford the narrow channel. His horses were behind him near the back edge of the island and the wider, deeper channel—not impossible to reach from the other side of the river, but much more difficult. There was nothing to do now but wait and see if he was going to be lucky and they would pass on by without knowing he was there. In a few minutes' time, he got his answer.

"Hello the camp!" Rampley called out as the three of them pulled up before the tracks leading into the water. "Mind if we come across?"

"What's your business?" Grayson called back.

"We're just passin' through," Rampley replied. "On our way to Muskogee to build a new church. We've camped here before. Didn't know you was here. We're needin' to rest our horses for a spell." When there was no response, he continued. "We wouldn't wanna crowd you. We'll ride on if you'd ruther, but if you've got a fire goin', it'd be mighty neighborly of you to share a cup or two of coffee— and we'll supply the coffee beans."

They were common road agents, Grayson was sure of it. The horses were most likely the main reason for their interest. He had dealt with many of their type over the years when serving as a deputy marshal. The claim that they were on their way to build a church was a nice touch, he thought, one he hadn't heard before. He figured that he was going to have to deal with them, either now, or later, after darkness. Since it appeared he was to have the choice, he decided he preferred to handle the situation now when he could see them plainly. "Well, if you've got peaceful intentions," he called out, "come on across."

Rampley looked at Stover and grinned. Then he called out again, "We're peaceful enough, and we thank you kindly. We're comin' across." He reached

down and made sure his rifle was riding easy in its
scabbard, then did the same with the .44 handgun on
his belt. "Let's go, boys," he said softly and started
across. Stover and Iron Foot fell in behind him and
they entered the water in single file.

They could not clearly see the man kneeling on one
knee beside the oak, a Winchester '73 resting across his
thigh, until they pushed through the outer branches of
the willows. At first sight, Rampley almost jerked his
horse to a stop. *Grayson!* He recognized the ex-lawman
immediately from the time the deputy had brought
Fletcher Tyler in to hang at Fort Smith. Rampley had
been in the crowd at the gallows. His initial reaction
now was to run, but it was too late to turn around. He
told himself to be calm. There was no reason to believe
that Grayson knew him—Stover or Iron Foot either.
Just remain cool, he told himself, *and maybe we'll get out
of this without setting off the chain lightning he's supposed
to be.* He glanced over at Stover, to see if he had discovered the same thing, without knowing if he had ever
seen the notorious lawman before. If Stover recognized Grayson, he gave no sign of it, still wearing the
same smug grin he had left the river trail with. Rampley could see that his simpleminded partner's con-
centration was on the odd horseshoe-shaped bundle
leaning against the oak tree, opposite Grayson. Though
odd in shape, he could guess what might be wrapped
in the laced-up canvas, once he knew the identity of
the man they had encountered. It was about the right
size.

"How do?" Grayson offered without emotion
while watching his visitors closely. Of the three, only
the one in the lead seemed intent upon focusing on
him. The other white man was more curious about

Billy's body, it appeared, while the third—an Indian, or breed, Grayson knew he was one or the other—was more interested in the horses. One thing he was certain of, not one of the three was a carpenter. He was already certain that he had sized up the three accurately, but he played along for a few minutes longer. "So you're goin' to Muskogee to build a church, are you?"

"Uh, th-that's right," Rampley stammered, wishing now he hadn't said it.

"Yes, sir, that's a fact," Stover volunteered cheerfully, having failed to be aware of Rampley's sudden caution. "Gonna build a big ol' church, so all the sinners can be saved."

Grayson nodded thoughtfully. "That's right interestin'. What denomination?"

His question left Stover unable to answer, since he didn't know the meaning of the word. "What, what?" he finally responded.

"We're just gonna build it," Rampley came to his rescue. "We ain't got nothin' to do with who goes to it." He wished again that he had come up with a different story. He was afraid there were going to be more questions asked that neither he nor Stover could answer.

"Let me save us all some time," Grayson said. "I'd be willin' to bet ain't one of the three of you ever seen the inside of a church. Now you wanted to come in here to look me over and see what I might have of value. Well, you've seen it, so I expect you'd best turn those horses around and look for someone else to take advantage of. Because I warn you, you're gonna pay a price for my horses, and the price might be higher than you wanna pay. The way I see it, we got us a standoff. Now, I'm gonna guarantee you, I'm gonna get two of you, 'cause when the shootin' starts, I've already got my rifle cocked and ready to fire, so I'm gonna get one of you before any of you can draw your weapons. And by the time you do, I will have cocked my rifle again and got another one of you. So it all boils down to which one of you is left standin' when it comes to who wins, me or him. I feel pretty good about my odds."

His discourse resulted in a pregnant silence, leaving all three outlaws stunned by his accurate appraisal of the situation. Both Stover and Iron Foot looked to Rampley to respond. What the man said made good sense unfortunately, and the scene he described was not in the style in which they usually operated. Back shooting was more to their way of operating, and certainly more to their liking. The silence extended as Rampley tried to decide the best way to retreat without one or more of them taking a shot in the back, for he could not be sure Grayson would actually permit them to withdraw peacefully. But to make a play for their weapons would ensure casualties among him and his partners, and that was a certainty. It was not worth the gamble. Then he reminded himself that Grayson had no reason to arrest them. They hadn't committed any crime as far as he knew, so finally he answered. "I think there's been a little misunderstandin' here, and it don't sound like you're lookin' for company, so we'll just move on up the river to rest our horses. We'll just say good day to ya since you don't appear to want no company." He wheeled his horse. "Come on, boys. We'll leave this man alone."

Stover and Iron Foot, still somewhat dumbfounded

by the unexpected turn of events, and still wondering how they could be retreating when they outnumbered the victim three to one, wheeled their horses and obediently followed Rampley back into the water. Upon reaching the riverbank, Rampley didn't stop, turned his horse up the river, and broke into a lope. When out of sight of the island, he reined his horse back to a stop and waited for his partners to pull up beside him.

"Well, that didn't come off worth a shit, did it?" Stover was the first to comment, after silently following Rampley's lead. "He sure as hell buffaloed us."

"You know who that was?" Rampley asked. When Iron Foot and Stover both shook their heads, he told them. "That was Grayson. I saw him once at Fort Smith."

The man was still a mystery to Iron Foot, but Stover was familiar with the name. "Well, I'll be damned," he muttered. "You sure of that?"

"I saw him at Fort Smith," Rampley repeated. "It's him, all right."

"Well, I'll be . . ." Stover started again, then paused to think about it. "If he's as much hell as ever'body says, then I reckon he wasn't just braggin' when he said he'd get two of us."

"I wasn't gonna give him a chance to show us," Rampley said.

"Reckon why he didn't try to arrest us?" Stover wondered.

"Hell, he don't know what we've been up to. Besides, he ain't a marshal no more," Rampley answered. "He quit a few years back."

"He had thick hair." That was Iron Foot's first comment on the matter. "Look good on my rifle barrel."

Stover looked at him and scoffed. "It might be a little bit harder to take that scalp than that scraggly old man's you've been totin' on your rifle."

"Maybe," Iron Foot replied, his thoughts still on the horses he had seen back on the little sand island. "He might be big medicine, but he's got to sleep sometime. I think maybe I might sneak in his camp tonight and kill him, and take his horses."

"I don't know," Rampley hedged. "I've heard talk that some folks think he don't ever go to sleep."

"I am Pawnee," Iron Foot declared grandly. "Nobody can sneak into camp better than Pawnee. He'll never hear nothin' till he hears the sound of the wind comin' out of his windpipe."

"You ain't but half Pawnee," Stover ridiculed. "Maybe you didn't get the half that sneaks good. You just got the half that talks big."

"Maybe you and Rampley too scared to steal them horses, but after I kill Mr. Big Medicine Grayson, then I bet you help me steal 'em."

Stover started to respond with sarcasm again, but Rampley cut him off. "You might have a good idea there, Iron Foot, you havin' all that Injun blood in you. You think you could sneak into his camp at night and kill him?" Stover was about to scoff at the idea again, but Rampley motioned for him to keep silent. He had been thinking about the opportunity they had just missed—not just the horses, which were reason enough—but he had seen other spoils in addition. There were at least four saddles that he had seen, plus weapons, cartridges, supplies. And Stover could be right: there might be something valuable in the odd-shaped bundle of canvas. It was a lot to pass up. He had nothing to lose if that crazy breed got himself killed, and all that to gain if Iron Foot succeeded in killing Grayson. "Yes, sir," Rampley said, "there'd be a helluva lot of respect for the man that killed Grayson." He could tell by the gleam in Iron Foot's eyes that the half-breed was thinking about it.

"I'm gonna kill that son of a bitch," Iron Foot announced confidently. "There ain't no doubt about it."

"It's a while yet before dark," Rampley said. "So we'd best get to a place where we can watch that camp." He guided his horse off the river trail and headed back toward the hills where they had first discovered Grayson's camp.

When they returned to the original spot, they dismounted and prepared to wait out the daylight. Stover sat down on a rock next to Rampley while Iron Foot was pulling the saddle off his horse. "What the hell was all that talk about ol' Iron Foot and all his Pawnee blood? That damn fool's gonna get himself killed. He couldn't sneak up on a deaf and dumb rock."

Rampley smiled. "But what if he does? We stand to gain. Right? And if he don't, then we ain't lost a helluva lot, have we?"

"Hell, I reckon not," Stover replied, matching Rampley's smile with a wide grin when he saw the reasoning behind Rampley's actions. "I reckon we got nothin' to do but set back on this hill and wait till dark, then watch ol' Iron Foot take to the warpath."

Rampley got his army telescope out of his saddlebag and laid it on the rock, then made himself comfortable. "I believe we could make us a little fire if we keep it down behind those rocks." He pointed to a notch at the top of a gully.

"Don't want no smoke," Iron Foot said as he walked up to take a position to watch the island.

"Hell, he can't see smoke from a little fire," Stover said. He had a hankering for some hot coffee, and it would be a few hours before sunset.

It was going to have to wait, however, for before they could argue the point Rampley exclaimed, "He's on the move! He's leavin'!" He came sliding off the rock and ran to grab his saddle. "Saddle up," he directed.

If his three visitors had been more observant, and noticed something other than what he might have of value, they might have noticed that he had made no efforts to set up camp. He supposed the fire he had built may have caused them to think he was there for the night. He had never intended to stay longer than necessary to give the horses a little rest, for he figured there were at least three more hours before dark. As soon as his guests had left, he started saddling horses, and when Billy was secured back across the saddle on the Appaloosa, he kicked dirt on his fire and climbed aboard his horse. It had not been much of a rest stop for the horses, but he figured it might be best to move on before the three outlaws thought it over and decided to have another try—this time without announcing themselves. It didn't figure that they would give up that easily, but if he was lucky, they might not see him pull out right away. The horses would have to wait until dark to rest.

Leaving the little island behind, he continued following the river as it made its way toward the southeast. From time to time, he looked back over the way he had come, but he saw no sign of anyone on his trail. Maybe they really had ridden on up the river, deciding it not worth the risk of losing one or more of their number. He could hope that was the case, but he would assume that they were tracking him and be ready, just as a precaution.

As darkness approached, he swung over closer to the river, searching for a suitable place to camp. Although he had seen no sign of anyone on his trail, he was intent upon finding a campsite that afforded him some protection, for he still had a feeling he had not seen the last of the "carpenters." And with four extra horses to protect, his choices were limited. Finally, when the light of day began to fade, he found what he was looking for, and he guided the gray down into a gully created by a wide creek that flowed into the river. It was wide enough for the horses to stand hobbled for the night with some protection from a five-foot bank. As was usually the case on a long journey, the horses never got enough time to graze. When he had come looking for Billy, he had brought a small supply of grain to make sure his horses were fed. But he didn't plan on a return trip with extra horses. He knew they needed a long grazing period, but they weren't going to get it until he reached Fort Smith.

Still acting with caution in mind, he pulled the horseshoe that was Billy's body off the Appaloosa, and dumped it on the edge of the gully, above the spot where he intended to build his fire. *You might as well be useful*, he thought. *You can act as a redoubt against anybody coming up behind me.* The macabre breastworks might have been more useful had he been able to straighten it, but in its U-shaped form, it wouldn't provide much cover. He grunted in appreciation for his attempt to make a joke.

"I reckon I'd better get somethin' to eat before it gets any later," he muttered, with an attack on his camp still in mind. So he settled for some buffalo jerky he had bought at John Polsgrove's store, and the always necessary coffee. While he waited for the coffee to boil and the jerky to roast, he climbed out of the gully and walked a few yards away into the deepening darkness to listen to the prairie around him. All was quiet, broken only by the howl of a coyote off in the distance. He squatted down on his heels for a few minutes longer, listening. But even the coyote went silent, and the dark prairie became so quiet that he became aware of the sound of the water in the creek. *They'll be coming pretty soon*, he thought, almost certain he would have visitors on this night. He rose to his feet and returned to the gully to prepare for the attack.

He decided to move the horses farther up the creek to get them out of the way of any stray bullets. Even though he knew they would not be intentionally targeted, for dead horses would be of no value to the thieves, he deemed it best not to take a chance. After that, he proceeded to gather blankets from all the extra saddles he had acquired, and used them to fashion what he hoped would appear to be sleeping forms lying randomly around the fire. When he was finished, he had four dummy blanket rolls positioned in a circle around the fire, which he hoped would cause confusion for anyone attacking the camp, as well as give him a chance to see their muzzle flashes and locate the shooters. When all was to his satisfaction, he hung a cartridge belt over his shoulder, picked up his rifle, and moved a couple dozen yards away from the fire. Wrapping his blanket around his shoulders, he backed into a trench in the side of the gully and waited.

He was almost ready to say his gut feelings had misled him, for he must have waited in his cramped ambush for almost two hours, long enough to become sleepy, because he caught himself nodding several times. *Go to sleep and you'll never wake up*, he told himself, but still he fought the desire to close his eyes. In the next instant he was wide awake, alert to the shadow moving up to the edge of the gully close to the canvas-wrapped body.

His confidence high now that he had made his way right up to Grayson's camp with no sign of alarm, Iron Foot peered over the side of the gully into the sleeping camp. *What the hell?* he thought when he saw the four sleeping forms like spokes around the dying fire. *Where did they come from?* He started to back away, reluctant to set off a gun battle when outnumbered four to one, while Stover and Rampley waited a short way back upstream, and in no position to help him. Then it struck him: the "sleeping bodies" were set up to confuse him so he wouldn't know which one was Grayson. A slow smile spread across his simple face. *I ain't that easy to fool. I'll just shoot all of them*, he thought, but then he remembered how quickly Grayson had assured them that he would get two of them before they got him. That thought made him hesitate again, and he looked hard at the blanket rolls, trying to decide which one had a real man sleeping inside it. In the dim light, he couldn't tell, so he asked himself which one was closest to the fire, thinking that would be the place he would pick—and

Grayson probably would do the same. He aimed his rifle at that one and pulled the trigger. The result was like a lit fuse, for he saw the sudden flash of a muzzle blast at the same time. A fraction of a second later he was slammed in the chest and knocked over on his side.

Moving immediately, lest his muzzle flash had provided a target for the wounded man's two partners, Grayson scrambled to a new position up closer to the edge of the bank. Much to his surprise, all was silent again except for the horses stirring around behind him, reacting to the two sudden gunshots. He had expected an all-out attack upon his camp, but there was no sign of the other two outlaws. It was enough to cause him to turn quickly and splash through the creek to the other side, thinking that the others must have somehow circled around behind him. He strained to see in the darkness on the south side of the creek, but he could see no sign of anyone. Looking back at the opposite side of the creek, at the position he had just left, he saw no signs of an attack, only the wounded man lying near Billy's corpse. From all signs, the man had acted alone, so where were the other two?

"You think that fool got him?" Stover wondered aloud. He got to his feet and walked to the top of the mound they had taken refuge behind, peering into the darkness between him and the river.

"I don't know," Rampley replied. "I doubt it, else he'd be whoopin' and hollerin' and doin' some kinda crazy war dance." They had heard two shots. The first was definitely Iron Foot's Spencer, but the second one was a Winchester. That was not a good sign, especially since there were no shots after that.

"Whaddaya reckon we oughta do?" Stover asked, now that Iron Foot's boastful plan seemed to have failed. "I knew that damn-fool Injun couldn't sneak up on nobody." He stared off into the darkness for a few moments more. "You reckon they shot each other?"

"I don't know," Rampley said. "Maybe . . ." His voice trailed off as he considered that possibility. He didn't think much of the idea of walking up to the creek to see. "I'd feel a little bit better about it if we'd heard Iron Foot's Spencer last, instead of the other way around."

"Yeah, me too," Stover remarked. "I reckon it'da been smarter if we had moved up a little closer. Then maybe we'da seen what happened."

"That son of a bitch is settin' up there waitin' for us to show up," Rampley said.

"You reckon they shot each other?" Stover repeated the question. "As quiet as it's got—wouldn't it be somethin' if they're both layin' up there dead, and we could walk right in without no worry?"

They were both envisioning the amount of plunder in the form of horses and saddles, plus guns and ammunition, that waited to be taken. Unfortunately, there was also the image of the ominous bounty hunter, lying in wait as well. "We could just wait him out till mornin'," Rampley suggested. "Somethin's bound to happen by then, one way or the other. And we could see then." They thought about it for a while longer until a three-quarter moon climbed up over the hills far to the east. "Won't have to wait much longer before we'll be able to see a little better."

This gave Stover something more to think about.

"You know, that son of a bitch coulda come outta that creek and he could be sneakin' around behind us while we're settin' here decidin' what to do." He glanced around, thinking about how exposed they would be with a moon overhead. He voiced as much to Rampley.

"Well, we need to do somethin', instead of waitin' for him to come after us," Rampley decided. "Looks to me like ol' Iron Foot's dead, so we're either gonna sneak up closer to that creek and see if Grayson's dead, too, or get on our horses and get the hell outta here."

There was a short silence, with both men considering their choices. Neither man was enthusiastic about moving on the camp, but the possibility of gaining all the plunder gathered there was too much to abandon. Stover was the one who broke the silence. "It's still two to one, us against him. I don't care how big a stud he is, the odds are in our favor. I think we oughta move in a little closer to see what's goin' on, and if it turns into a shoot-out, we got him outnumbered. I can't stand the thought of ridin' off and leavin' all them horses and stuff for some Injun to find, and all the time Grayson bein' dead."

"That suits me," Rampley said. "Let's get goin'."

Leaving their horses tied to some berry bushes close to the riverbank, they made their way cautiously along the bank until seeing the dark outline of trees that bordered the creek and the gully it formed. It was only a short distance of perhaps forty yards or so to the gully's edge, but there was very little cover in the open ground between it and the point where they now stood. There they remained, reluctant to cross the open area and chance the possibility that he was watching and waiting for that to happen. After a short while, they realized they were no better off than they had been back on the mound. They had come this far, however, so they were not ready to give up and run. Neither did they want to risk crossing the open ground.

"Why don't we work on down the river to the mouth of that creek, and come up on him that way?" Rampley suggested. "Chances are pretty good that, if he ain't dead, he's probably watching for us to come across that open piece, same as Iron Foot."

"That might work," Stover agreed, and they climbed back down the riverbank and started making their way through the thick brush that lined the water. It was not easy in the dark, but by the time they reached the mouth of the creek, the moon had risen high enough to enable them to see to push through the brush more quietly. They then split up, one on each side of the creek, and began their cautious advance toward Grayson's camp.

They had not gone twenty yards when they first heard Iron Foot's weak call for help. "Rampley," the pitiful wail called out. "I'm dyin'. Help me. Stover." Over and over it went as the dying half-breed moaned, his breaths coming in shorter gasps. It was an unnerving plea, stopping both men in their tracks.

At first, Stover was confused, thinking that Iron Foot was somehow aware that they were working their way up the creek. If Iron Foot knew they were in the creek, then Grayson might, too. But then he reasoned that the half-breed didn't know where they were. He had probably been babbling out of his head ever since he was shot. Still, Stover was getting a worried feeling about the wisdom of their approach. "Whaddaya think we oughta do?" he whispered across the creek to Rampley.

"Nothin'," Rampley replied, also in a whisper. "It was his damn-fool idea, so I reckon he oughta knowed he could get shot." He paused to consider what effect, if any, this development had on their plan to stalk the camp. The thought occurred that maybe Iron Foot had succeeded in killing the ex-lawman. Otherwise, Grayson would most likely have shot Iron Foot again to shut up his moaning. "Come on," he whispered. "Keep goin' and we'll see about helping Iron Foot after we take care of Grayson."

"You sure we wanna get any closer?" Stover asked, starting to get cold feet. The mournful wailing of their wounded partner served to put a lethal pall over the dark gully.

"Keep goin'," Rampley replied, feeling more confident now. Moving in a crouch, carefully placing one foot in front of the other so as not to misstep and make a sound, he continued until reaching a slight bend in the gully. He hesitated, for he could now see the embers of the fire a dozen yards up ahead and the pale image of the canvas-wrapped bundle lying on top of the gully just above it. He also saw Iron Foot's body beside the bundle. He held his rifle ready to fire, but there was no sign of Grayson. Hearing a sound like the splashing of a fish, he looked across the creek for Stover, but Stover was gone. And he realized that the sound he had heard was made by Stover running down the creek. Instantly furious to discover Stover had run out on him, he started to back up when his foot slipped on a sizable rock at the edge of the water. Stumbling awkwardly to keep from falling in the water, he glanced up to see the dark outline of the man he sought to kill standing above him at the rim of the gully. The two rifles fired barely an instant apart, and Rampley staggered backward before falling in the water, while the bullet from his rifle plugged harmlessly into the side of the gully.

Grayson ejected the cartridge and walked along the gully's edge, watching Rampley's body bobbing gently in the creek. By all appearances, Rampley was dead. Grayson pumped one more shot into him to make sure. His partner had run when he glanced up and saw Grayson standing, waiting, at the edge of the gully, so he felt pretty sure it was the last he would see of him. Still, it was his careful nature to make sure, so he set out after Stover. It was too dark to pick out tracks, but there was no doubt the two men had come down the river, so he cut directly across to the riverbank, instead of going down to the mouth of the creek and then turning upriver. He had run almost thirty yards along the bank when he heard the sound of horses' hooves beating a hasty exit on the prairie floor on the other side of a low mound. He was satisfied then that he was finished with the "carpenters" as the sound of the hooves faded away. He turned to walk slowly back to his camp.

It had been a long night and he was tired, so he took only a few moments to look at the body beside Billy. The half-breed had suffered a painful death, and Grayson felt that he had most likely deserved it. But he would have put the man out of his misery if he had been certain his partners were not set up close by to ambush him. He couldn't help wondering why the breed came in alone, but he didn't give it more than a moment's thought. "I reckon the folks in Muskogee will have to find somebody else to build their church for 'em," he said with a grunt of amusement, as he looked down at the pained expression on Iron Foot's face. He reached down and picked up the Spencer carbine lying beside the body and checked the action of the lever. He would pack it with all the other weapons he had collected, more weapons than he knew what to do with, he thought. But the weapon seemed to be in good working order, so he pulled out his knife and cut the twine that tied a poorly looking scrap of gray hair to the barrel. He left the half-breed's body where it was, thinking it could feed the buzzards and coyotes, and probably serve its only useful purpose.

It might have been a wise decision to pack up and move his camp someplace else for the rest of the night, but he felt certain enough that when Stover lit out, he had no plans to come back. So he built the fire up a little and turned in for the night.

Chapter 9

He was slowed considerably by the string of horses he had acquired, so he pushed on as far as he could before daylight faded away, but he figured he was still a good two and a half days from Fort Smith. And this was depending upon whether or not he encountered any more trouble along the way. He constantly checked his back trail, watching for any sign of someone else trying to overtake him, because he felt certain that Jacob Blanchard was not the kind of man to accept defeat in his efforts to save his son. As he sat watching his herd of horses grazing peacefully near the river, he almost forgot the danger stalking him. He had to admit they were a fine-looking lot of animals, especially the Appaloosa, the blue roan Tom Malone had ridden, and his gray. His pack horse, a sorrel, was a pretty stout horse as well. And the two he had acquired from the two would-be assassins were strong, broad-breasted horses, built for endurance, but he wouldn't rank them above his packhorse. The herd was a sizable bonus to the thousand dollars he was to receive when he reached Fort Smith. However, he would certainly turn Malone's blue roan over to the marshal, but the others he would keep. So this could be considered a profitable endeavor for him—*if* he made it to Fort Smith without further trouble.

This thought brought his attention back to the inflexible canvas horseshoe now lying several yards away, far enough from the fire to hopefully keep it as cool as possible. To this point, Billy's body was still stiff, and had given off no unpleasant odors. He didn't know how much the tightly wrapped canvas had to do with this, but he knew it would be only a matter of time before he was going to have to make sure Billy was downwind. This reality was incentive enough to get an early start the next morning.

Another day of hard riding found him still a full day's ride from Fort Smith. At least there had been no trouble from any of Blanchard's people. All was not rosy, however, for he was struck by a putrid odor from his canvas bundle when he started to remove it from the horse's back. "Damn!" he gasped and took a backward step to recover. Knowing that he couldn't leave it on the horse overnight, he summoned his resolve and stepped up to the body again. Thinking to roll the corpse off the horse as before, he was surprised to find that it was no longer stiff, and sagged when he took hold of one end and attempted to heave it over on the ground. He didn't know much about dead bodies, but he had seen bodies that had begun putrefying, so he knew that they had no longer been stiff at that stage, and had given off the foulest odor he had ever smelled. "Damned if you ain't makin' me earn my money," he charged as he grabbed the canvas sack and dragged it off the horse to land on the hard ground with a muffled thump. There was no trouble in deciding which way the wind was blowing that night, and no doubt about the time it shifted in the predawn hours. As a result, Grayson was awake and saddling the horses long before the sun made an appearance.

Near the end of the day, there was no improvement in Billy's bouquet. Grayson was sorely tempted to rid himself of the foul-smelling burden, and to hell with the thousand dollars. But he was within five miles of Fort Smith, he had endured for this long, and he couldn't help feeling resentment over the governor's insistence that the body be produced. "By God, they think they want this stinkin' piece of shit. Well, I'll sure as hell deliver it, and we'll see what they think then." With only five miles to go, he would have pushed on into town, but it was too late to catch John Council in his office that night, and he wanted to make sure there would be someone there to receive the trophy. After one final night, worrying about possible shifts in the wind, he loaded his putrid cargo and rode into Fort Smith.

Knowing he would be turning the late Deputy Tom Malone's horse over to the marshal, he had put Billy's saddle on Malone's horse and loaded Billy's corpse across it. He intended to keep Billy's Appaloosa, and he figured Billy was in no position to object. Besides, he felt he had earned it. His first stop was at Bob Graham's stable at the edge of town where he normally kept his horses when in Fort Smith. "Mornin', Bob," Grayson said as he rode up.

"Howdy, Grayson," Bob returned. "Looks like you've been doing some horse trading."

"You could say that," Grayson replied. "I wanna drop off all but mine and the black. I'll be back in a little bit, soon as I deliver him to the marshal's office."

"All right," Bob said, his interest now attracted to the blue roan and the bundle lying across the saddle. "I'll take care of 'em for you." As he moved to take possession of the horses, he suddenly wrinkled his nose and remarked, "Whatever you got in that bundle is startin' to spoil."

"Yeah, I reckon," Grayson replied. "It was rotten from the start."

The streets of the town outlaws called Hell on the Border were already busy when Grayson led the deputy's horse down the center. People walking or riding close to him paid little more than casual curiosity to the canvas bundle lying across the saddle, but parted to form a wide wake as soon as it passed them. He proceeded to the courthouse, which housed the offices of the court and John Council, as well as the jail on the lower floor, and tied the horses out front.

"What the hell?" Sid Sowers murmured when he spotted Grayson as he descended the porch steps. Sowers was a clerk in Judge Isaac Parker's court and he was more than familiar with the somber ex-deputy. It was certainly not the first time he had seen Grayson bringing a prisoner in, but they were usually sitting up in the saddle. "Is that a body on that horse?" he asked while still halfway down the steps. When Grayson answered that it was, Sid asked, "What are you gonna do with it? Why don't you take it to the undertaker?" Then the wind shifted slightly. "Damn! That thing's ripe."

"I didn't take him to the undertaker's because John Council told me to bring him here," Grayson answered. "My instructions were to bring him in, alive if possible, dead if not. And I'd just as soon get him offa my hands."

"I can sure see why," Sid replied. "I'll fetch John for you." He turned to go back up the steps, only to meet John Council coming down.

"I saw you from the window," John said as he passed Sid on the steps. The look of astonishment on his face was noted by the clerk, and prompted him to follow John down to hear the story. "Grayson," Council exclaimed. "Is that a body on that horse?"

"Yes, sir," Grayson replied. "That's Billy Blanchard. I brought him in, just like you said, and I'd like to see about gettin' my money for him."

"Jesus!" Council snorted like a dog that had gotten too close to a skunk. "How long has he been dead?" Not waiting for an answer, he charged, "You were told to bring him in alive. You weren't supposed to shoot him."

"I didn't," Grayson answered, without emotion as usual, "at least not the shot that killed him. I did put a bullet in his leg, but it was one of Jacob Blanchard's own men that killed him. So I brought him in, anyway, 'cause that was the deal I struck with you." He waited for a few moments for Council's response, but the usually calm U.S. marshal was obviously flabbergasted. In was not the scenario he and the governor had envisioned when they sent the notorious bounty hunter after Billy Blanchard.

"Damn," Council swore softly. "We can't put him on display if his body is deteriorated as bad as he smells through that canvas you've got him wrapped in. For Pete's sake, how long's he been dead?"

"Four days or so," Grayson answered, then paused while Council grimaced. "I woulda preferred that he'd shot him closer to Fort Smith, but he didn't seem inclined to cooperate." He waited again while Council stewed over the situation some more. "I haven't looked inside that canvas since I first wrapped him in it, but I suppose you can still tell that it's Billy. But like I told you when we made the deal, I brought his guns, and saddle, and horse, if you have to have proof that it's him."

"Oh, hell, Grayson." He was thinking now what he could tell the governor. "Take him on over to Wainwright's. I don't want to open that damn package up here. The whole courthouse will smell to high heaven."

"You sure you don't wanna check to make sure that's Billy Blanchard in there?"

Council looked exasperated. "Hell, I take your word for it. Take him to Wainwright's and tell him to see if he can fix him up somehow."

"All right," Grayson said with a shrug. "I reckon I can do that, but I'd like to collect my money as soon as possible. I had a lot of expenses goin' all the way to Kansas to get him."

"I'll have to talk to the governor about that," Council said. "It may take a little time. I don't keep that kind of money in my office. I guess you've got Billy's horse, haven't you? You can keep it to make up for some of your expenses."

"Much obliged," Grayson said, having already

decided that he would claim the horse, and in the event he was told it belonged to the court, he planned to tell them the horse had been shot. He also did not see fit to volunteer the information concerning the other horses he had acquired along the way back from Kansas. "I hope I don't have to wait too long for my money," he reminded Council one more time before taking the body to the undertaker. "I took care of my end of the deal."

"I know, I know," Council replied impatiently. "I'll see what I can do." He knew, however, that it was going to be a difficult task to convince the governor to authorize one thousand dollars for a putrefied corpse.

Grayson delivered Billy's body to the undertaker, and Wainwright was as equally enthusiastic about receiving it as Council had been. "I don't know what they expect from me," he complained. He took a knife and cut a big enough hole in the canvas to give him an idea of the state of the corpse, although he could guess fairly accurately by the foul odor escaping. As he suspected, the body had advanced well into putrefaction, with eyes and tongue bulging, the skin having already gone from green to purple to black. "Why in the world don't they just let me put him in a box and bury him. I can't get him looking anywhere close to an open casket, if that's what they're thinking."

"I don't know," Grayson said as he prepared to leave. "That ain't my department." He stepped up in the saddle and turned his horses back toward the stable, relieved to be rid of the remains of Billy Blanchard. His thoughts now were of a good hot bath to soak all traces of Billy out of his skin, then to see if his usual room was available at Wanda Meadows's boarding-house.

* * *

The room that he usually rented whenever he was in Fort Smith was not available. So the large room on the second floor, with the windows that allowed him to look out on Garrison Street, had to be given up for a small room on the first floor near the kitchen. "You're lucky I've got that room in the back, Mr. Grayson," Wanda Meadows told him. "I'm getting more long-term renters lately, and they're all wanting the larger rooms on the front. If you had left me a deposit, I could have saved it for you, but I didn't have any idea when you'd be back. I never do."

"It ain't no problem, ma'am," Grayson said. "I reckon I'll do just fine in the other room." Over the years, he had had a couple of different arrangements with Wanda when it came to his room. When he was enjoying periods of prosperity, he often paid for his room two months in advance. Other times, as in this latest case, he had been hard-pressed to save enough money for cartridges before heading out after Billy Blanchard. He could always ride a little way out of town, make camp by a stream, and roll up in his blankets for the night. He even had a favorite spot to do this, where a stream flowed into the Poteau River. After just getting back from a long trip, and sleeping on the ground every night, however, he had a hankering for a bed with clean sheets, and the opportunity to sit down at Wanda's table for a good home-cooked meal. Wanda had a reputation as the best cook in Sebastian County, and she was a handsome woman to boot, and a church-going woman. He knew that she was a widow, and he sometimes wondered what was wrong with the bachelors living in Fort Smith.

There should be a line of them starting at her front steps.

His first night back in town went a long way toward making up for the many restless nights spent on the trail from Black Horse Creek, so much so that he might have slept right through breakfast if his room had not been next to the kitchen. Feeling refreshed, he went to the outhouse, then washed up at the well instead of using the dry sink in his room. After a hearty breakfast of fresh eggs and ham, weighed down with a couple of Wanda's biscuits and honey, he went to the stable to see if Bob Graham was interested in buying some good horses. The two men came to no agreement, but Bob said he'd think about it. Grayson had traded with Bob before, so he knew the stable operator was just playing a bluffing game and they would come to some agreement before it was over. The bargaining for that morning over with, Grayson said, "Well, you know the price I've gotta have for 'em, especially that Appaloosa. You can think on it." Then he left to check with John Council again.

"I'm sorry, Grayson," Council told him. "I can't give you any final word yet. I'm gonna be honest with you, the telegram I got this mornin' said he wasn't pleased with the condition of Blanchard's body. And he let me know that under no circumstances was I to put a rotting, worm-eaten corpse on public display. In my wire to him, I asked him about your money, and he said he was gonna hold off on that until we see if the mortician can fix the body up so it doesn't look so bad."

"Sounds to me like the governor ain't fixin' to pay

me like he promised," Grayson said, "unless the undertaker can get Billy where he won't shock the good people of Fort Smith." Council didn't respond, but his expression told Grayson that what he'd said was true. "I thought the idea behind this thing was to give outlaws a picture of how they're liable to end up if they're robbin' and killin' in this territory."

"It was," Council agreed, "but like you just said, not at the risk of having the good folks of Fort Smith up in arms. We might have the women marching on city hall."

Grayson nodded thoughtfully as he considered Council's comments. He realized that he was in danger of losing the thousand dollars he was promised, and he needed that money. He had been damn-near broke when John Council approached him on the deal, and it had cost him even further to equip himself for the task. He could recoup all of his expenses with the sale of the horses and saddles. That much he was certain of, but that thousand dollars would have carried him a lot farther. He decided to go back to see Otis Wainwright.

"You're talking about making a silk purse out of a sow's ear," the undertaker said when Grayson asked about his progress to make Billy's body presentable for public viewing. "How long did you say you hauled him around after he'd been shot?" he asked, but did not pause to let Grayson answer. "His skin is already black, and his innards are coming out of every orifice. Any day now his skin will start sliding off every time he's moved. They don't need to be showing this body off. They need to get it in the ground right now to get rid of the smell. The only thing that ain't turned to complete mush is his head, and that's got his eyes and tongue bulging out like he's seen the devil, which I wouldn't be surprised if he had."

The last comment gave Grayson a glimmer of hope. "Can you fix his head up so it looks like Billy?"

Wainwright shrugged. "I can fix it up some, but you can't stick his head out in front of the gallows on a pole. The town won't stand for it."

"Yeah, but you could get his head lookin' pretty good from a distance, anyway?" Grayson asked. Wainwright shrugged again, so Grayson continued. "Who's that over there?" He nodded toward a body laid out on a table on the far side of the room.

"Him?" Wainwright answered. "Nobody. Some drifter that got himself shot in an argument at the poker table. Sheriff Thompson had him brought to me to get him ready for burial. He's going in the ground tomorrow."

Grayson stroked his chin thoughtfully, then commented, "Seems to me you could put Billy's head on that fellow's body."

Wainwright paused for a long moment before answering, not sure Grayson was serious. "Well, yeah, I reckon I could, but why in the world would I wanna do something like that?"

"I can think of one good reason," Grayson replied. "The state of Arkansas has authorized John Council to pay me six hundred dollars if I brought Billy Blanchard back in good enough condition to put on public display. With his body all rotted out like it is, they won't display it, so they won't pay me the money. Now I'm thinkin' if you can fix Billy's head up a little, and put it on that other body, I'd be willin' to split that six hundred dollars with you fifty-fifty." It was apparent that he now had Wainwright's full attention. He lied about the amount of the reward, but felt that three hundred dollars was a decent payoff for the deceit.

"I can't do something as unethical as that," was Wainwright's initial response, but Grayson could see that the undertaker was thinking about that three-hundred-dollar bonus. "What would people think if they found out I did something like that? Why, they'd run me outta town."

"I ain't gonna tell 'em," Grayson commented calmly.

Wainwright was still thinking it over. "I wasn't even gonna embalm that body. He was going in the ground right away, 'cause there's not going to be a funeral. There's nobody to come to a funeral."

"I expect you'd need to embalm him if he was gonna be on display for a few days or more," Grayson said.

"You surely would," Wainwright said, counting that three hundred dollars in his mind. "But, hell, that fellow over there is a good bit bigger than the corpse you brought in."

"Nobody around here knows how big Billy Blanchard was," Grayson said. "You're the only one here who knows how big a man you cut outta that piece of canvas. And from what you tell me, the only people who saw that drifter are the men around that poker game in the saloon. And they ain't gonna know the difference if he's got another head on him."

Wainwright's eyes were shifting back and forth as he considered the possibilities, but still he hesitated. "Oh, I ain't saying I couldn't pull something like that off. I could do a little surgery on Billy and sew his

head on that other body so you couldn't see the
stitches—close his eyes and mouth, so he'd look like
he was asleep."

"Anythin' you can do about the color of his skin?"
Grayson asked. "It's kinda black-lookin'."

"Oh, hell, I can paint him up a little. You'd have to
look real close to tell." He paused again while he
rehearsed it in his mind. "By the time I got him fitted
out in an open coffin, I could make him look like
President Rutherford B. Hayes if I wanted to."

"When can you have him ready for John Council
to see him?" Grayson asked.

Once again, there followed a lengthy pause while
Wainwright stopped to think about what he might be
risking. "Damn, Grayson, I don't know. . . ." He grimaced with indecision. "How do I know you won't
tell somebody?"

"Why would I?" Grayson answered. "It would cost
me the money I'm supposed to get for bringin' that
bastard in. To tell you the truth, there ain't no harm
done to anybody. Both of them are dead and gone,
and beyond carin' what we do with their carcasses.
So whaddaya say?" He stuck out his hand.

Wainwright shook it. "Three hundred dollars,
right?"

"Just as soon as Council pays me the money,"
Grayson replied, satisfied that Billy Blanchard was
going to be on display as a warning to those who
sought to ply their evil skills in Oklahoma Territory.

"Where you been, Ike?" Red Mullins, owner of Red's
Hotel, greeted a customer in the dining room of the
shabby inn in Okmulgee. "I ain't seen you in here in
over a week."

"I was over to Fort Smith," Ike replied, "went to see my brother and his wife. They got a little farm outside of town." He pulled out a chair and sat down at the end of the long table, nodding politely to several other men who took their meals routinely at Red's. Most of them he had seen at one time or another, except for the two strangers seated at the other end.

"What's the news from Fort Smith," Red asked.

"Nothin' much," Ike answered. "Damn place is gettin' too damn crowded to suit me. I never saw so many folks in one place." He took a sip from the cup of coffee Red set before him. "Tell you what I did see, though. You remember that feller that robbed the bank down in McAlester, and shot a teller? I saw him. They got him in an open coffin, propped up on the gallows with a sign on him that warns outlaws that think they can hide out in The Nations."

"He killed a deputy marshal that tried to arrest him, too," Red said. "I reckon they musta sent a posse of deputies out to run him down that quick."

"From what I heard, it wasn't a marshal that got him. A bounty hunter brought him in, feller name of Grayson."

"Did you see the hangin'?" Red asked.

"There weren't no hangin'," Ike replied. "He was dead when Grayson brought him in."

The conversation continued with none of the other patrons noticing the sudden tensing of the two strangers at the end of the table until one of them spoke. "Did I hear you right?" Slate Blanchard asked. "He was dead when Grayson brought him in?"

"Yes, sir, that's right," Ike said, "shot twice in the back is what they said, but you couldn't see no bullet holes in the corpse on account he was lyin' on his back in the coffin. Besides, they put a new shirt on him."

"The goddamned coward!" Troy swore in anger. "Murdered him!"

"Shut up, Troy," Slate warned when his brother's outburst caused the room to fall silent and everyone to stare at the two strangers. "We need to get movin'. We've got at least two days ride ahead of us. Come on." He pushed back from the table and got to his feet, a look of grim defiance on his face. None of the regular customers at the table said a word until the two strangers had left the room.

Chapter 10

"Well, I can certainly use the money," Wanda Meadows commented when Grayson handed her a six-month rent payment in advance. The money was to reserve his usual room upstairs when the present renter left. "You must have won big at the poker table or robbed a bank," she joked.

"I got paid for the last job I did for the marshal's office," Grayson said. "Figured it'd be a good idea to make sure I had the room I wanted, while I had some money in my pocket."

"I expect the least I could do is offer you a cup of coffee and a slice of that pie I made for supper," she offered, ". . . anybody that pays that much in advance." She had just finished baking two large apple pies to serve with supper that night, and she was sure there would be a serving for everyone, with a little left over. She had only three boarders in addition to Grayson at present, anyway. "Whaddaya say,

Grayson," she asked with a warm smile, "can I interest you in a piece of apple pie not an hour out of the oven?"

He smiled in return. "I reckon it'd be impolite to say no." It wasn't often he had the opportunity to enjoy fresh baked pie, and he couldn't recall if she had ever offered him anything between regular meals. "I swear, though, Mrs. Meadows, I'm already gettin' so fat from eatin' your cookin' for the last few days that I might need to buy some new britches."

"You could use a little fattening," she said with a laugh. It was not the first time she had entertained thoughts along those lines. "Sit down at the table and I'll get you some coffee. I might join you in a piece of that pie. I'm kinda interested in seeing how that crust turned out. When I rolled it out, I tried not to work it too much. The last one I made, I think I overdid it a bit and it made the crust a little tough. Or maybe it was that lard I was using. Anyway, I want to see how it turned out."

He smiled again. "I'll bet you ain't ever made a pie that wasn't good in your life."

"You wouldn't say that if you had tasted a piece of the first one I made after I got married," she replied. "And my poor husband, bless his heart, sat there and ate every bite of it." She had to laugh at the memory. There was a time when memories of her late husband would bring moments of melancholy, but enough years had passed to heal the pain of losing him so young in her life.

She cut two slices from one of the pies, placed them on the table, and poured two cups of coffee. Seating herself across from him, she smiled as she watched him staring at his pie for a moment before looking up to meet her eyes. His gaze was questioning and she was confused by it until he spoke. "I know there's some talk about what an uncivilized man I am, but I do know how to use a fork."

"Oh," she burst into laughter again, "I'm sorry. I guess we could use some forks." She jumped up and got a couple from the drawer. They said nothing for a few moments while they sampled the pie, but her thoughts were concentrated on the usually somber man sitting at her kitchen table. He had rented a room in her home, off and on, for quite a few years, and this was the first time she had had a conversation with him that consisted of more than a half a dozen words. His reputation was one of a cold, emotionless hunter of men, some said a cruel administrator of justice. For evidence of this, she could easily consider the wanted outlaw he had just brought in, dead from gunshot wounds. But he had never shown anything but polite respect for her and her boarders. Which was the real man she wondered? In fact, who was Grayson? No one really knew much about him, except that he had once been a deputy marshal. Where had he come from? She wondered if maybe she might be better off not knowing. Still, she could not deny a certain fascination for the man. She almost surprised herself when she suddenly asked, "Grayson, have you got a first name?"

He looked up, astonished. "Joel," he answered, surprised that she didn't know.

"Joel," she echoed. "Why, that's a nice name. I shall call you that from now on. Grayson sounds so stern." She looked up to see him pausing to gape at her, a large bite of apple pie in his mouth waiting to be masticated. She couldn't help but laugh at him. "You don't spend much time in the company of women, do you, Joel?"

"Reckon not," he said, then resumed his chewing.

"Well, we've known each other too long for you to keep calling me Mrs. Meadows. You must call me Wanda. All right?"

"Yes, ma'am," he replied.

"Not ma'am, either," she corrected. "Wanda."

He grinned. "All right, Wanda." He pushed his empty plate aside and reached for his coffee cup again. "You make mighty good pie, *Wanda*."

"Thank you, kind sir," she replied sweetly, and refilled his cup.

He was confused. It was almost as though the lady was flirting with him, but surely not, he thought. No woman ever had before, and he found himself wondering how old she was. *What the hell do I care?* he asked himself. She was a fine-looking woman, though. Odd he had never noticed before, but he had just never paid attention, his mind having always been focused on things of a more grim nature. He might have been astonished had he known that the lady was wondering about many of the same things he was.

She had never really given any man the slightest encouragement since her husband had almost chopped his foot off when a large tree he was cutting down bucked on the stump as it started to fall. It resulted in knocking him down and pinning his leg under the tree when it fell in the wrong direction. There was no one around to help him, and the only thing he could think to try was to attempt to chop the trunk in two and free his crushed leg. Able to reach his axe, he did the best he could to swing it from the awkward position on his back. But he soon found out how ineffective his attempts were. In frustration, he swung the axe as hard as he could muster. The axe glanced off the tree trunk and sank deep into his ankle, all the way to the bone. When her father-in-law found him, he had bled so much he was almost unconscious. The doctor told them that the leg might have been saved had not an infection set in. The infection spread so rapidly that his leg had to be amputated above the knee. He never really learned to use crutches, because less than a month after the surgery, he pressed his revolver to his temple and pulled the trigger, leaving a young wife widowed at the age of eighteen.

If I was interested in another man, she thought, *it surely wouldn't be someone who lived by the gun, even if it was on the side of law and order.* It was difficult not to compare the two—they were so different. She was certain that she would never love another man like she loved her late husband, even though she found a certain fascination for the somber man at her kitchen table—now that she had discovered there was a living soul inside the emotionless body. "Well, I've not got time to sit here and visit," she suddenly announced. "I've got to get supper started, or you all will be complaining and wanting your money back."

"Yes, ma'am," he replied at once. "I'm sorry I've took up so much of your time." He got up to leave. "I thank you very much for the coffee and pie. It was the best apple pie I've ever had."

She smiled. "Thank you. I'm glad you enjoyed it, but I've had better."

"You're sellin' yourself short," he said and started out the door where he paused, looked back at her, and added, "Wanda."

She gave him another smile and thought to herself,

I don't know, Wanda, girl. You might be thinking about taming a leopard.

By coincidence, the two brothers rode up before the gallows just as Otis Wainwright and his assistant were in the process of removing the casket from the platform where it had been on display. "Hold on, there," Slate called out as he dismounted.

"If you're thinking about taking a look at the body, you're a little too late," Wainwright said. "We've already put the lid back on." In fact, there were only a couple of nails tacked in to hold the cover in place until they carried it down the steps where it would be easier to finish nailing it shut. "Let's take it down, Johnny," he told his assistant, and picked up one end of the coffin. Johnny hefted the other end and they started down the steps with their awkward burden.

Slate motioned for Troy to remain calm when his brother started to react to the undertaker's refusal to let them see the body. "Let 'em tote it down," he said quietly. They watched silently while their brother's coffin was carefully carried down the steps of the gallows. It was not an easy task for two men, especially since neither was of a particularly brawny build. When they reached the ground without dropping the wooden box, and started toward their wagon to load it, Slate stepped in front of them. "Set it down right there," he said, "and take the lid off."

Wainwright hesitated for a moment while he and Johnny stood holding the coffin. "I'm sorry, mister, but the viewing period is over. If you wanted to see the body, you should have come before this. It's been on display for almost a week, and we have to get it in the ground right away."

Slate's heavy brows narrowed in an angry frown as he looked Wainwright straight in the eye. "Put the damn thing down and take the lid off," he commanded, "before I rip it off, myself." Troy stepped up beside him, his hand resting on the handle of the .44 in his holster.

"Whoa!" Wainwright exclaimed. "Hold on there, mister!" He turned at once to his assistant on the other end of the coffin. "Set it down, Johnny." When it was down, he stepped away from it as if it might explode, while he unconsciously looked around to see if anyone was witness to the confrontation and might come to his aid. "There's no need to get upset here. If you want to see the body that bad, we'll open it up for you." He had not paid that much attention to the two men when they first rode up. He decided now that it was best to do what they wanted, and without delay. "Johnny, hand me that hammer."

He backed the few nails out of the top and he and Johnny lifted it off. Then they both stepped back while the two strangers moved up to take a close look. The reaction shown in each man's face told him that they were not pleased with what they saw. "Damn," Troy muttered, drawing the word out in disbelief. "What the hell did you do to him?" Although the repair job Wainwright had performed on the deceased had suffered serious deterioration, he could still recognize the face as Billy's.

"You ought not'a had him stood up here that long," Slate said, giving Wainwright an accusing glance. "It's Billy all right, but his body don't look right. It don't look like Billy."

"It looks bigger'n Billy," Troy said.

At once distressed, Wainwright was quick to offer

an explanation. "After this amount of time, there's usually a certain amount of swelling in the body. Sometimes—as in this case—it can change the look of the body, so that it's difficult to recognize it." Slate and Troy exchanged uncertain glances. "You gentlemen understand that I have no connection with the law, I hope," Wainwright added. "I'm just the undertaker."

"Put the lid back on," Slate ordered, and there was no hesitation on the part of the undertaker to comply. "Grayson brought him in, already dead, right?" Wainwright said that was correct. "The bullet holes was in his back is what I heard."

"Well, he was killed by gunshots," Wainwright admitted, "but I have no way of knowing the circumstances of the shooting." He was reluctant to speculate on how Billy was killed, for he truly did not believe that Grayson murdered the outlaw, especially since his reward was originally based upon a living prisoner.

"He was shot in the back, though. Right?" Troy demanded.

"Well, yes, he was," Wainwright replied, afraid the menacing man might take the lid off to see for himself and discover no wounds in the back.

"That spells murder to me," Slate said. "That lowdown son of a bitch murdered him." He grabbed Wainwright's shirt and pulled him up to him, face-to-face. "Is Grayson still in town? Where does he stay?"

"I don't know," a severely frightened Wainwright blurted. "I don't have any idea, I swear."

"How 'bout you, Johnny?" Troy asked sarcastically. "Do you know where Grayson is?"

"N-no, sir, I don't have any idea," Johnny stuttered, shaken from a near-paralysis of fear.

"All right," Slate said upon deciding they would get no further information from the two frightened undertakers. "Give him a decent burial and do it quick."

"Yeah," Troy added, "you might be gettin' some more business soon."

Wainwright and Johnny busied themselves loading Billy's remains on the back of the wagon until the two strangers had ridden off toward Garrison Street. They paused to watch them until they rode out of sight. "Right in the middle of town!" Wainwright exclaimed, astonished, unable to believe what had just transpired. "I thought this was a civilized town."

"They must have thought they were still in Indian Territory," Johnny said. "I expect we'd better alert the sheriff about those two, and tell him to warn Grayson if he's still in town."

Grayson was still in town, and planned to be for some time yet, for there was nothing on his mind that needed tending to anywhere else. During the past couple of days, he had given a great deal of thought toward the rest of his life and what he might make of it. He really didn't know much about making a living beyond chasing after outlaws. There were very few pay days like the one-thousand-dollar reward he had just cashed in on. He thought of the extra horses he had acquired when he went after Billy Blanchard. Maybe he could take what he had left of the reward after the payoff to Wainwright and use it to set himself up to raise horses. At least that would be something he had an interest in, unlike farming. He supposed he could possibly go back to work in the U.S. marshal service as long as it was not in the Omaha office where his employment was ended over an incident with another deputy.

He hadn't thought about that in a long time—the events that caused him to leave the marshal service—for he felt no guilt or regret for doing what he did. It was the only time he had worked with a partner, and he was just unlucky enough to have drawn the wrong one. Now he recalled the attempt to capture Ned Dawson, vague images that flashed across his mind like sparks from a fire, bits and pieces—his partner, Red Sawyer, kicking a door open to find Ned's wife and two small children hovering frightened in a corner—the woman slumping against her children when Red's bullet hit her in the chest—Red's gun turned on the children—Red collapsing in the doorway, shot in the head. He had warned Red, yelled for him to stop. He remembered doing that, but Red had just laughed and turned his pistol on the smaller of the two children, a girl. *I had no choice,* Grayson thought. *If I had it to do over, I would do the same.* An ugly trial had followed, but the jury could not convict him, primarily because he had saved the lives of the two children. But it wouldn't do to retain a deputy in the service who had shot a fellow deputy. They graciously permitted him to resign. He was bitter at the time, but looked upon it now as the hand he had been dealt in a game that has no winners.

He was still young enough to start out on a new trail—one outside the violent world he had known in his earlier years. It was ironic that the town of Black Horse Creek came to mind when he thought about

the opportunities for settlements in the territories beyond The Nations. Black Horse Creek had the poten-
tial to become a growing center for farming as well as
cattle. But it was doomed for ultimate failure as long
as an outlaw like Jacob Blanchard owned it. Maybe
things didn't have to be that way. Maybe if the folks
who had invested their future in the town got together to set their own controls, they might successfully go up against Blanchard. *Just your mind wandering
off on a useless ramble,* he told himself. *Now it's time
for supper.*

He pulled the gray up in front of the stable door
and dismounted. Bob Graham walked out to meet
him, and stood talking to him while he pulled the
saddle off. "You come down on the price you're askin'
for them horses?" Bob asked.

"Hell, no," Grayson replied, "thinkin' about goin'
up on it. I might decide to keep all of 'em, myself,
anyway—might get into the business of raisin'
horses."

"You?" Bob asked. "That'll be the day."

"You never can tell," Grayson said as he turned the
gray out in the corral. "Make sure he gets a ration of
oats—my other horses, too." He spent a few more
minutes passing the time of day with Bob before
pulling his rifle from his saddle sling and leaving to
take the short walk to Wanda's boardinghouse. He
didn't notice the two men sitting on their horses in
the shadow of the dry goods store. It was a peaceful
evening. He felt a sense of contentment. He had a little bit of money on hand, and the satisfaction of having completed a difficult job. It crossed his mind, but
he wouldn't permit the prospect of a friendship with
Wanda Meadows to have anything to do with his

peaceful walk. There was nothing to alert him that it might become a walk into eternity.

"That's him, all right," Troy Blanchard decided. "That's Grayson. Look at him, strollin' down the street like he was on his way to church."

"Yeah, that's him," Slate agreed. There was no doubt the man they now saw walking away from the stables was the same stranger who had come through Black Horse Creek.

"Well, what are we waitin' for?" Troy demanded.

"Just hold it a minute," Slate said. "We're gonna get the son of a bitch, but we've got to make sure we get the hell out of this town and across the river to Injun country before the law gets after us."

"Hell," Troy persisted, "he's on foot and has no place to hide if we hit him before he gets to them other stores up there. Now's the time to get him while there ain't many people on the street. Pa will shoot both of us if we don't get the bastard."

"We're gonna get him," Slate said. "But we're gonna ride straight outta here before they can even think about a posse." He paused to look around for the best escape routes. "The river's yonder way," he said, and pointed to the west. "So we'd best head right between the blacksmith and the stable as soon as the job's done. All right?" Troy nodded impatiently. Slate went on. "I want him to see who's killin' him, so he'll damn-sure know why he's gettin' shot." Troy grinned to show his agreement. "Here's what we'll do," Slate said. "You take off around the back of this store and get up ahead of him. Then you cut back to meet him. I'll get in behind him and walk real slow to give you time. That way, we'll have him between us.

He won't have no place to run." Troy nodded thoughtfully. He liked the idea of letting Grayson know who shot him.

Grayson was aware of someone riding a horse at full gallop up the alley behind the dry goods store, but he had no reason to believe it was of any concern to him until the rider appeared from between two of the buildings ahead and turned back toward him. It didn't appear that the rider was going to give him any space on the street, for he walked his horse in the middle of the street, and gave no sign of yielding. *Maybe he can't see me,* Grayson thought, and prepared to step up on the boardwalk to let him pass. Suddenly it struck him that the rider was intentionally steering toward him and was now drawing a rifle from the saddle scabbard. In that instant, he recognized the smirking face of one of the Blanchard brothers. He pulled his rifle from his shoulder, where he had propped it, and quickly cocked it just as he felt the bullet slam into his back. The force of it caused him to stagger and try to keep from falling, only to be hit in the chest by the bullet from the rider in front of him. Down he dropped to his knees, firing one wild shot before a second bullet in the back knocked him face forward on the ground. Caught between a deadly crossfire, he was helpless to defend himself as another shot found his shoulder.

Alerted by the shots, people began to appear in the windows and doors of the shops along the street, and shouts to call the sheriff rang out. "Let's get outta here!" Slate shouted as he and Troy rode a circle around the body lying in a pool of blood in the middle of the dusty street. "He's dead! We got him!" Slate exclaimed as he fought to control his excited horse while trying to see if there was any sign of life in the motionless body. "Let's ride!" he shouted to Troy, and galloped toward the blacksmith shop. Troy threw one last shot into Grayson's back before chasing after his brother.

The two assassins did not spare their horses as they cut through the narrow alley between the blacksmith's forge and the stable, out onto the street behind that led to the ferry slips by the river. Down the hard-packed road they galloped, their horses' hooves thundering on the dusty surface, across the rail yards to the banks of the river, where they followed the river north. "We're gonna have to swim 'em across!" Slate yelled to his brother. "Maybe there's a better place up ahead." Indian Territory was on the other side of the river, so that was their first objective. Once they were in The Nations there would be a sense of safety even though they would still have to avoid the tribal police. There was considerable concern about the possibility of pursuit by a U.S. deputy marshal, but they figured to be long gone before that could be initiated.

After riding a quarter of a mile along the bank, Slate reined his horse to a stop and waited for Troy to pull up beside him. "We might as well put 'em in the water. One place don't look any better'n another, and if we keep goin', they're gonna be too wore out to swim against the current." They paused to listen for a few minutes, satisfied that there were no sounds of pursuit. "There ain't been no time for anybody to come after us," Slate said.

"Somebody woulda had to seen us get away," Troy

said. "We don't have to kill these damn horses; ain't nobody comin' after us."

Slate agreed with his brother's thinking, so instead of committing their horses to the river at that point, they continued on along the bank, letting the horses walk. After a couple of miles, they came to a section of the river where a sandbar extended out, almost to the main channel, reducing the distance the horses would have to swim. This is where they crossed. Once on the other side, they stayed close to the river as they continued north, looking for a place to camp, build a fire, and dry out. It was fully dark by the time they found the spot they were looking for.

With the horses taken care of and a blazing fire to warm them, it was time to have some bacon and coffee, and enjoy the success of their mission. They shared in the satisfaction of carrying out the family's demand for vengeance, and to make it even more satisfying, the only person who could have pointed them out as the killers was dead. "Let 'em send out the marshals," Slate gloated. "They ain't got no idea who they're lookin' for."

"You think there's any chance he ain't dead?" Troy wondered aloud.

"Shit no," Slate replied immediately. "I think that first shot in his back most likely killed him. And after we pumped him so full of holes, he was dead all right." He paused, thinking back. "How many did we put in him?" They both paused to recall and came up with a total of five shots. "If that didn't kill him, he ain't human," Slate said. "He had so much lead in him he'd be too heavy to pick up."

Troy laughed. "I expect so. I ain't seen nobody that

looked any deader'n him. He wasn't wrigglin' a finger."

"He didn't look so damn tough to me with his face in the dirt," Slate crowed. He was thinking that their successful revenge would go a long way in easing their father's pain over losing his youngest son. "I wish Pa coulda seen it," he said.

Troy nodded. "We'll get started early in the mornin' and get on back to Kansas," he said and poured himself another cup of coffee. "I wish we'da brought somethin' stronger than coffee to celebrate with."

"We'll save that till we celebrate with Pa," Slate said. They slept that night satisfied with themselves, Troy more so than Slate, for now he was Jacob Blanchard's youngest son, and perhaps his father would dote on him as he had with Billy.

Chapter II

How long he had lain in the middle of the street, he could not say for certain, for he remembered nothing after cocking his rifle and firing. He had floated somewhere on a plane between consciousness and deep sleep ever since. But now he became aware of his existence. He was—but in what state of life or death he could not determine, for he felt helpless to move his hands or feet. Gradually he became aware of someone else bending over him from time to time, staring into his eyes, which were barely open enough to permit light to enter. He might have attempted to speak, to ask where he was, for he knew he was no longer lying in the street, but he didn't care enough to try. And then a day came when he seemed to float gently back, and his eyes suddenly opened to see the ceiling above him. There were people in the room. He heard them talking. He tried to figure out where he was, and who were the people talking.

"I wouldn't get my hopes up, Wanda," he heard a male voice say. "I don't give him much chance of making it. I've done about as much for him as I can do. I was able to take out three of the bullets, but he's lost so much blood I don't think he can pull through it. It's mighty charitable of you to take care of him."

"He's paid for the room six months in advance," Wanda said. That may have been true, but it was not the sole reason she had accepted the responsibility of caring for him until he died. She felt that she had gotten to know the man who was Grayson in only the last week or so. He deserved to die in peaceful surroundings with someone to take care of him, and not in the hospital where no one cared. "Besides, he's really not that much to look after." She was about to say more, but she was suddenly distracted when she glanced down to see Grayson's eyes wide open. "Look!"

Dr. Shaw looked down at the patient, and studied the pale face and open eyes. He was about to explain to Wanda that it was not unusual for a patient's muscles to suddenly tense and eyelids to open wide moments before they slid under the veil of death, when Grayson spoke. "Where am I?" he forced between dry, crusty lips. The words were so weak they were barely audible.

Wanda was quick to respond to his call. She hurried to his side and placed her hand on his forehead. "You're here in your room," she told him, "and you're safe." Looking up at Dr. Shaw she said, "His fever's down. He's not burning up anymore." Standing at the head of the bed where Grayson could not see him, Dr. Shaw acknowledged her hopeful comment with a doleful shake of his head. He had seen too many patients appear to rally just before death, and there was no reason he could find to expect different in this case. Disappointed by the doctor's discouraging signals, Wanda turned her attention back to the wounded man. "Can you drink some water?" she asked. When he whispered yes, she looked up at the doctor again, a question in her eyes.

He understood her concern. "It's all right to give him some water, if he can drink it. Not too much, though. You'll find out straight away if he can drink it or not. Use that cloth there, you don't wanna choke him."

She soaked the cloth in the pitcher of water on the table and held it over his lips, squeezing gently until a steady flow of drops fell on his lips and in his mouth. He drank it eagerly, never stopping until she had repeated the process three times.

"Dr. Shaw says you've lost too much blood, and you need to build it back up. Can you eat something?" Her question went unanswered, for he had closed his eyes and drifted away again. At once alarmed, she looked to the doctor for an answer. He nodded solemnly and checked the patient for a pulse, but was once again surprised when he found a weak heartbeat.

"He's still with us," Dr. Shaw said, and again advised Wanda not to get her hopes up. "He's one stubborn son of a gun—I'll give him that—but he's fighting an uphill battle. The wounds are just too severe for any man to overcome." He closed his instrument case and prepared to leave. "Not much I can do for him that I haven't already done," he said. "You sure you don't want me to send Otis Wainwright to pick him up?"

"No," Wanda stated emphatically. "If this is going to be his last night on earth, I don't want him to spend it by himself in Otis Wainwright's back room. I'll send someone to fetch Otis in the morning—if it's his time." She looked back at the sleeping man, so vulnerable now, with all the traces of his usual rock-hard persona gone.

"Suit yourself," Dr. Shaw replied. "You're a kind-hearted woman, Wanda. A man like Grayson is destined to die alone in a back alley or a lonely prairie, and a violent death at that." It had been two days since Grayson was carried to Wanda Meadows's house—at the lady's insistence—and he should have been dead when they first reached him in the middle of the street. There was no medical reason for him to still be alive. The man simply refused to go when his number was called. "Well, good night, then," he said. "I'll see myself out."

"Thank you for your help, Dr. Shaw," Wanda replied. "I'll send word tomorrow." She remained by the bedside for a few minutes longer before leaving to clean up her kitchen. The dirty dishes were still on the table from supper.

She had not intended to fall asleep in the chair, so she was startled when she awoke to find the first rays of morning light filtering through the curtains on the lone window in the little room next to the kitchen. "Damn!" she muttered and jumped to her feet. Looking at the still figure lying in the bed, she was sure that he was dead. To be certain, she pulled his arm from under the blanket and felt his wrist for a heartbeat. Much to her surprise, she found one. *Good for you*, she thought. *I knew you wouldn't give up. Now I've got to go help Violet fix breakfast before I lose all my boarders.*

Breakfast over, she left Violet to clean up, and went to check on her patient. There were a few unpleasant chores that came with taking care of a bedridden man, and this was where Violet drew the line. Wanda wasn't thrilled to do it, herself, but she saw no way around it, and told herself that it was just like taking care of an oversized baby.

When she walked into his room, she was shocked to find Grayson struggling in an attempt to get out of bed, aware, obviously, that he had soiled it as well as himself. "Grayson!" she gasped. "What are you trying to do, kill yourself?" She hurried to the bed, grasped his shoulders and pressed him back down. He didn't possess the strength to resist.

"Where am I?" he asked.

"In your room. Now lay back and let me take care of you," she commanded, still astonished by the transformation from imminent death to a violent defiant struggle for life. He had no choice but to comply with her wishes, however.

"You have to leave me alone," he pleaded weakly. "You don't understand."

"I understand," she replied. "You've soiled your bedclothes again and you're ashamed for me to know it."

"Again?"

"Yes, again," she replied patiently. "And I cleaned you up every time."

Stunned, he asked, "How long have I been in this bed?"

"This will be the third day," she said. "And I expect

you should be about to starve to death. Do you want something to eat?"

"I don't feel like eatin'," he said, "but I'd surely appreciate a cup of coffee."

"All right. First I'll clean you up and then I'll get you some coffee." *We'll see what Dr. Shaw has to say about you coming back from the dead,* she thought. She had to admit that she hadn't doubted the doctor's prognosis.

Dr. Shaw was as astounded to find his patient alive as Wanda had expected him to be. He called it a miracle. "He must have the constitution of a grizzly bear," he told her after he had examined Grayson the next day. "And you say he finally started to eat something?" She said that he did. "Well, keep him at it. He needs to build his blood back up." He took another look back through the doorway of the tiny room off the kitchen and shook his head in amazement. "That's the closest to death of anyone I've ever treated—to come back like that." He looked at Wanda and said, "There's no need to let him drink up all the coffee, though. His physician could use a cup of it, too."

Wanda smiled. "Well, you just come on in the kitchen and set yourself down at the table. Maybe I still have a piece of cake to go with it."

Over the next week, the doctor had occasion to enjoy more of Wanda Meadows's coffee and sometimes a slice of cake or pie. He found the patient's will to survive and his determination to regain his strength truly astonishing. "Mister," he told Grayson, "you're a mighty lucky man. You were as close to dead as I've ever seen."

"If I was lucky," Grayson countered, "I wouldn't have got shot."

Wanda jokingly attributed Grayson's remarkable recovery to his embarrassment over having to be cleaned up by her. If truth be told, it was an important contributing factor to his rapid improvement. And after a few days of Wanda's cooking and care, he insisted that he was able to use the chamber pot she left in the room for him, although it was extremely painful to get in and out of the bed without help. Then it was only a matter of a couple days more before he was able to walk on unsteady legs outside to the outhouse. The real driving force behind his determination to recover, however, was the fiery hot hunger for revenge that burned deep inside him and would not be denied. Nothing else seemed to matter, and his biggest concern was his impatience to regain his strength and agility. He never spoke of this to Wanda, but she knew it was eating away at him until one day she broached the subject.

"You're doing a marvelous job of getting your health back," she said. "Dr. Shaw never seems to get over it, and you're so lucky to have survived such a terrible assault. I think you might do even better if you would forget about going after the men who attacked you. You might not be so lucky next time." When he responded with nothing but an emotionless gaze, she continued. "You don't know who they were, or where to find them, according to what you told the sheriff. So why not let the bitterness go, and put your whole mind on getting well?"

"I know who they were," he replied quietly.

"But you told Sheriff Thompson—" she started, but paused when it struck her. He told the sheriff he didn't know who shot him, because he had to have the satisfaction of vengeance for himself. Disappointed, she sat back in her chair to give him a look of disapproval. "So you're building your strength back up so you can go out looking for those murderers and kill them?"

He shrugged, then said, "That's about the size of it."

"But why not let the law help?" she asked, losing her patience. "Why risk your life again? It's their job to do, not yours. You're not a deputy anymore. You could do something else with your life."

He was not inclined to discuss his reasons for doing anything, but he figured he owed her an explanation after all she had done for him. "It's what I do, Wanda," he told her. "If the law wanted these two men, they'da probably come to somebody like me to go after 'em. The only difference is I'm the one who wants 'em, and I'll have to go clear over to Kansas to find 'em. The marshal don't wanna send anybody that far out of his jurisdiction, and the sheriff ain't concerned with 'em as long as they got outta town. That kinda leaves nobody but me to see that they didn't get away with shootin' me full of holes."

His calm demeanor told her that to argue with him was useless, so she decided not to pursue it. "All right, then," she surrendered with a long sigh. "I guess you'll do what you have to do. I certainly have no right to say, one way or the other." She gave him a patient smile and confessed, "I was getting kind of used to having you around. I'd hate to see something happen to you after we patched up all the holes in you."

"I 'preciate everythin' you did for me," he said.

"I'm thinkin' I might be outta your hair in a few more days."

"You paid for it," she told him.

"I think I got a lot more than I paid for, and I ain't likely to forget it."

Another week passed with Grayson getting stronger each day. Feeling close to ready now, he remained patient, content not to rush it lest he find himself not fully fit when it might count. He spent his days doing some carpentry work for Wanda, visiting Bob Graham at the stable, exercising his horses, and during the latter days, taking some target practice in the woods beside the Poteau River. The day finally came when he gave Wanda the news.

"I reckon I'll be headin' outta town for a spell tomorrow mornin'," he told her one night after supper.

Had he been looking directly into her face, he might have noticed the slight flinching of her eyes. Several of her other guests were still lingering over supper, so she made an effort to remain casual when she responded. "A spell? How long do you think you'll be gone?"

"I don't know for sure. As long as it takes to get the job done," he replied.

"I just wondered, because Mr. Bishop is leaving to return to Little Rock, so I can have your old room upstairs ready when you get back. I'm assuming you're planning to come back. You're certainly paid up for several months ahead."

"I'm aimin' to come back, all right," he said, and got up to leave the table.

"Well, I hope you have a safe trip, and I'll have

your room ready when you return." She wanted to say more, but she didn't feel comfortable talking in front of her other guests. So she smiled cheerfully and asked, "Will you be leaving before breakfast?"

"Yes, ma'am. I expect to get an early start."

Later that night there was a tap on his door, and he opened it to find Wanda standing there with several cold biscuits and some ham wrapped in a cloth. "I thought you might want a little something to take with you, since you're going to miss breakfast," she said. She could not help but feel that their relationship had changed dramatically in the last few days. For the best part of a month, she had come in and out of his room, oftentimes without knocking, to tend to his wounds and check on his progress. She had seen every part of the man as he worked to regain his health. But now, she felt awkward to be tapping at his door.

"Well, now, that's mighty nice of you, ma'am," he said, standing there with his hand on the doorknob. She noticed that he had reverted back to calling her "ma'am." Feeling equally awkward as she, he took the food from her. "This'll go mighty good in the mornin'. I 'preciate it." When she stood there, he finally asked, "Did you wanna come in?"

"Oh, no," she quickly replied. "I just wanted to make sure you had something to eat in the morning. Gotta look after my patient, you know." They both laughed, somewhat ill at ease. Suddenly she frowned. "Joel, please be careful. I know what you are going to do. Just promise me you'll be real careful." She turned at once and walked back down the hallway toward the parlor, leaving him to make of her visit what she would.

"I promise," he called after her, not knowing what else he could say.

The sheriff of Black Horse Creek walked into Reiner's Dry Goods late Saturday afternoon to find the proprietor and his wife cleaning the shelves and sweeping the floor, their usual weekly routine. "Can I help you, Sheriff?" Louis Reiner asked, with as much enthusiasm as he could manage. He was accustomed to the sheriff's, as well as his deputy's, visits to his store whenever they needed any merchandise he carried. They ran an account in his store, one that was never paid off, a problem that he was hesitant to complain about. Henry Farmer decided a while back that he was tired of the Blanchards' freeloading practices, and refused to give the sheriff any more hardware on credit. Shortly after, Henry's hardware store caught fire one night and burned to the ground. No one could say for sure how the fire was started, but one couldn't help but wonder at the coincidence. Henry went back to Arkansas, and Louis was visited by the old man, himself, when Blanchard told him he needed to expand his store to handle hardware in addition to his usual merchandise.

"I just stopped by to make sure you knew about the burial service we're holdin' next week for my brother Billy," Slate said. "The stone oughta be ready by then. We'll hold the service right after church lets out, and Pa figured everybody would wanna come and pay their respects."

"Yeah," Louis said, "we heard about it, and of course we plan to attend." He cast a sideways glance at his wife, who had stopped her dusting to listen.

"Good," Slate remarked. "I know Pa will be

pleased—me and Troy, too." He turned abruptly and left the store.

"Yeah," Louis said to his wife, "we'll be there, all right, since we don't want our store burnt down."

"The nerve of that old man," Eunice Reiner said. "What are they going to bury—an empty box? Billy's already in the ground. That drummer that came through here last week said that Billy Blanchard was buried in Fort Smith." She walked to the front window to make sure Slate was gone. "Marjorie Joyner said they've ordered a big ol' tombstone to put in the middle of the graveyard, like a monument to that murdering piece of trash. And now we're supposed to go to church and worship the Lord, then come out and pay tribute to the biggest sinner in the country. I think we oughta just get in our buckboard after church and go right home."

"Maybe," Louis said, "but I suspect we'll be there with the other spineless members of this town." Like a few of the other merchants in Black Horse Creek, he would like to pack up and move on to a legitimate town, but he was afraid to risk retaliation from the Blanchard clan. He thought again of Henry Farmer. He was allowed to leave, but without a penny's worth of all he had built up over the past two years. "Poor ol' Henry," he commented.

"What?" Eunice asked.

"Oh," her husband responded, "I was just thinking about Henry Farmer." That thought summoned another. "You know who I haven't seen in town in quite a while? That pair of scoundrels that work for Blanchard—Yancey Brooks and Lonnie Jenkins. They used to spend half their time next door at the saloon. Roy said they haven't been in for a long time."

"Blanchard probably sent them somewhere to rustle some more cattle for him," Eunice replied. She glanced out the window again as if afraid she might be overheard. "I'll be just as happy if we don't ever see the likes of those two again."

"Did you tell Roy?" Slate asked when Troy came in the office.

"Yeah, I told him. He said he never went to church. I told him I didn't care if he did or not, but he'd damn-sure better show up at the funeral." Troy was not any more enthusiastic about having a memorial service for his late brother than the citizens of the town were. He had always been envious of Billy's prominent place in his father's heart, and the sooner Billy was forgotten, the better. He was still smarting from the reception he and Slate received from their father when they returned from killing Grayson—a reception he had anticipated to be triumphant. Instead, they were treated as if they were to blame for Billy's death. He remembered the scene vividly.

The old man had seen them ride into the corral and had immediately walked out to meet them. "We got him, Pa!" Troy called out when he saw his father striding out across the yard. "We got Grayson!"

"Filled him so full of lead, it took four men just to pick him up," Slate said.

"Where's Billy?" Jacob demanded. "Where's my boy? I told you to bring Billy home."

"Billy's dead, Pa," Slate told him.

"Dead?" Jacob exploded. "Whaddaya mean, dead? Who killed him?" His craggy face became twisted with his sudden fury, and he glared at his sons as if accusing them. "I told you to bring Billy home," he repeated. He had always felt that Billy would survive. He could never accept the possibility that Billy would not come out on top. He was the most like him of any of his sons.

"There wasn't nothin' we could do to save him," Troy said. "He was dead before we got to Fort Smith. Grayson shot him in the back before he even brought him in."

"But we got Grayson," Slate quickly interjected. "We left him lyin' in the dust with five bullet holes in him." He barely got the words out before his father erupted.

Jacob released an angry howl, like that of a wolf, causing Slate and Troy to step back, lest he suddenly strike out at anything in range. They had never seen him that angry before. When he finally seemed to have his fury under control, he lit into them again, repeating his orders to them. "I told you to bring him home. Where's his body? Why didn't you bring his body with you?"

"We didn't think it'd be a good idea," Slate said. "We saw his body when they was fixin' it up to bury, and it was in bad shape. We decided you shouldn't oughta see Billy lookin' like that."

"You decided?" The old man exploded again. "You don't decide anythin'," he roared. "I decide." He calmed down after a few moments, then said, "Leave me alone for a bit. Go take care of your horses." He turned and started back toward the house, but before going more than a few steps, turned about again. "You sure you killed Grayson?"

"Yes, sir," Slate replied. "There ain't no doubt about that. He's dead."

Jacob said not another word, but continued on
toward the house. His anger and frustration were
about to overcome him and he regretted his decision
to send his two sons to Fort Smith. He should have
gone himself, for he deeply needed vengeance by his
own hand. He had counted upon Billy to help him
carve out his dynasty in Black Horse Creek. Billy was
vicious enough to handle the job. It was just a matter
of waiting for him to sew all the wild oats of his boy-
hood. Neither Slate nor Troy was qualified to be any
more than a gun hand, but Billy had swagger and
vision of greater power. Jacob would have gladly
given up both of his other sons if he could bring Billy
back.

Chapter 12

Although he had pronounced himself physically fit to make the long ride to Black Horse Creek, he was not really sure how well he would hold up under the long days in the saddle. He did know, however, that the only way to find out was to saddle up and start out through Indian Territory. He decided to take the same route back that he had taken with Billy, so he crossed over the river on the ferry and followed the Arkansas north. Before he left, Bob Graham bought Billy's Appaloosa from him, and agreed to board his other horses while he was gone. So he was able to use that money to take care of his needs for a good while and leave the balance of his reward money—close to seven hundred dollars—in his room at Wanda's boardinghouse. He rode his gray gelding and took the sorrel packhorse with supplies to last long enough to get him to John Polsgrove's trading post.

The gray had gotten a bit rank, having not had the

burden of a saddle for close to a month, but he soon settled down to his master's familiar weight on his back. The horses were not the only travelers out of shape on this journey, for Grayson found out in a short time that he was not one hundred percent recovered. During the first couple of days, he found himself grunting involuntarily upon encountering rough stretches in the trail. He called it a day sooner than he would ordinarily have, because of the stiffness and soreness he experienced. Consequently, the trip he had calculated to take five and a half days turned out to be a full day longer. By the time he approached the wide U-shaped curve in the river where Polsgrove's trading post stood, he was ready to rest awhile before continuing. He could not help feeling impatient with himself, thinking that he should be much closer to being fit again. Regardless, he planned to push on, even if he wasn't.

It was well past noon when he reached the path that led from the river to John's little group of buildings. It was evident that someone had been at work since he was last here. There were new logs partially completing the front of the store where the fire from the Pawnee raid had done most of its damage. As he turned the gray's head down the path, he saw Robert Walking Stick rounding the corner of the store carrying a load of shingles. When he spotted Grayson, he dropped the shingles and went inside the store. A few seconds later, he reappeared with John's wife, Belle, right behind him. Grayson held up his arm and waved.

"Hey, Grayson," Belle sang out and returned the rifle she had been holding to her side with the butt resting on the ground. "We heard you were laid up, shot full of holes," she said when he came close enough to hear her. She continued to visually inspect him while he dismounted stiffly. "You're lookin' a little peaked," she commented. "Need food—come in, I'll fix you a nice dinner."

"That sounds mighty appealin' to me," Grayson told her. "I could sure use some dinner right about now." He looked beyond her toward the door. "Where's that big grizzly you're married to?"

"Over here behind you," a booming voice announced as John walked out of the barn, holding a rifle. "How you doin', Grayson?" Polsgrove asked. "Like Belle said, we heard you was shot up pretty bad. Figured it was them two sidewinders that came through here, claimin' they was federal agents. Belle put a bullet in one of 'em."

"No," Grayson replied, "it wasn't those two. I reckon Belle did a better job than you knew, 'cause there wasn't but one man that tried to jump me. I figured he'd had a partner, since he had an extra horse with a saddle on it." He went on to tell them about being ambushed by the two surviving Blanchard brothers.

"Just you goin' after 'em by yourself?" Polsgrove asked. "Looks like the U.S. marshal coulda give you some help." Grayson responded with nothing more than a shrug, and Polsgrove realized after a moment's thought that Grayson probably wanted to do the job himself. Understanding, he nodded slowly, and offered any help he could give.

"I'm gonna need some supplies," Grayson told him. "When I left Fort Smith, I figured I'd buy what I need from you."

"Well, I appreciate that," Big John said, still studying

his friend closely. "I swear, partner, you don't look like you're ready to lock horns with anybody right now. Why don't you stay with us for a day or two and let Belle cook you up some grub to get your strength back. You hit here at a good time. Ol' Robert, there, killed a fat doe yesterday evenin', not more'n forty yards on the other side of that rise." He pointed toward the bank of the river.

"Yeah," Belle said, "you stay, I make you strong pretty damn quick."

It was hard to refuse the offer. He was reluctant to admit it, but in truth, the ride up the river from Fort Smith had taken a toll, and he was beginning to question the wisdom in pressing the issue too soon. A day or two more shouldn't really make much difference in the job he was bound to do, and he surely wanted to be physically able to get it done. "Maybe I'll take you up on that," he decided. "I guess I'm not in that big a hurry."

Unlike Wanda Meadows, John and Belle Polsgrove were better able to judge the degree of recovery Grayson had actually accomplished. And between the two of them, they agreed that the notorious bounty hunter was a far cry from his usual powerful self. He looked thin and pale from his healing wounds, much as John had been from his wounds. The couple of days first suggested turned into a week, but the results under Belle's care were evidence enough that she and her husband were right in persuading him to stay with them. Grayson, himself, could not deny the increase in his strength and his overall condition, and he credited them with perhaps preventing him from committing suicide. He could have walked into more than he could have handled, but now he felt more like he was in control of his fortune once again. When he was certain he was fit enough to do the job, he announced that he was leaving the next morning. There was no attempt on the part of John or Belle to delay him further. Belle fixed him a hearty breakfast and John wished him good hunting. He turned the gray's head to the west and bade them farewell, heading for Black Horse Creek.

"Well, there he is," Louis Reiner said, his voice low to keep from being overheard, even though Jacob Blanchard was at least forty yards away, "standing on the side of the hill like God Almighty." His wife only nodded in response. The patriarch of the notorious Blanchard clan had struck an almost regal pose in the center of the small cemetery located on the side of a steep hill. The side of the hill had been selected for use as a cemetery due to the severity of the slope, and the opinion that it was useless for anything else. On this day, when storm clouds were building up in the west and threatening to cut short the planned ceremony, the only genuine stone monument to ever be placed in the cemetery was being firmly situated in the ground. The carving of the stone just the way Jacob Blanchard wanted it had delayed the ceremony. With hands on hips, and the constant scowl on his lips, Jacob Blanchard stood glaring at a couple of his hired hands as they hurried to secure the stone before the skies opened up and drenched everyone. He occasionally looked up at the dark clouds above him, as if daring them to disrupt his ceremony honoring his son. Assembled dutifully around him were his family and hired hands.

Louis got down from the buckboard and tied up to

a fence post; then he extended his hand to help his wife down. Among the last to arrive, they moved up to the downhill side of a freshly dug grave to stand next to Shep Barnhill and his wife, Cora. The Barnhills turned to exchange quiet greetings with them, and Cora raised an eyebrow and smiled mischievously at Eunice Reiner. "Glad to see you made it to the ceremony," she whispered to Cora.

"I wouldn't have missed it for the world," Cora whispered in return. "He was such a saint."

Eunice snickered, trying to hide it with her hand, but it caught the attention of Slate Blanchard, who was standing solemnly on the upside of the grave, the Mexican woman, Maria Sanchez, standing beside him. He cast a stern frown in Eunice's direction and was about to reprimand her when his father spoke.

"All right, we'd best go ahead and put Billy's casket in the ground. It don't look like that storm is gonna hold off much longer." He turned to the pastor of the town's one church. "Go ahead, preacher, while the boys are lowerin' the casket."

It had proven quite difficult for the preacher to create a laudatory message in memory of Billy Blanchard, but he had managed to come up with some general phrases, based in most part on the forgiving nature of God and his Son, Jesus, for all sinners, no matter how great their sins. It was obvious by the rancorous expression on the old man's face that he wasn't pleased with the pastor's message. "Enough about that," Jacob interrupted. "Say more about Billy, and how he was murdered by that son of a bitch."

The first rumble of thunder came tripping across the line of hills to the west of them, and the sky darkened. In no time at all it was like night instead of midday, and the rain began to fall. Eunice Reiner commented later that night that it was a direct sign that the Lord didn't want Billy Blanchard. No one moved to get out of the rain, neither the Blanchard clan on one side of the grave, nor the small gathering of the town's merchants and their families on the other. None dared to provoke Jacob Blanchard's wrath.

It was just as the preacher ran out of words to describe the wonderful relationship between a father and son when it happened. The funeral party was suddenly startled by a sudden crash directly overhead and a jagged streak of lightning flashed across the sky. Cora Barnhill let out a shriek when all eyes were drawn by the flash to the top of the hill. There, like a dark angel of death, stood the image of the dreaded bounty hunter, Grayson. It was there for only an instant, for when the next flash of lightning split the dark cloud above the hill the image was gone.

The gathering of wet souls was cast into shocked silence. What had they seen? The image looked so ominous with the jagged bolt of lightning behind it. Was it real, or was it just imagined? But everyone had seen it—everyone but Jacob Blanchard, who was staring down into the grave, and the preacher, whose eyes were closed in prayer. Stunned almost to the point of paralysis, Slate Blanchard felt the shock of the lightning run the length of his spine. "It was him!" he gasped.

"Or his ghost!" Troy responded, for he had seen Grayson die. He looked at his brother for explanation, but there was none in the ashen face that stared back at him. Completely shaken, for now he realized that his brother had seen the same image he had seen, he blurted, "We killed him!" Having no stomach for dealing with the supernatural, he ran for his horse in a panic to leave the graveyard. Convinced that he had seen Grayson's ghost come back to haunt him, he felt he had to get away from Billy's grave and hope that Grayson's spirit was confined to the cemetery.

"Troy!" His father yelled after him. "I ain't said the service is over!" Troy ignored him and kept running, jumped on his horse and galloped off toward town. Jacob stood there perplexed for a moment by his son's failure to obey him. He turned to look at Slate. "What the hell is goin' on?" he demanded. "You look like you've seen a ghost."

"I ain't never seen one before," Slate said, "but I'm pretty sure I have now." Maria Sanchez crossed herself and moved closer to him for protection.

"What the hell are you talkin' about?" Jacob demanded again. "What's got into Troy?" He paused long enough to look at the town folk, none of them moving, all staring openmouthed toward the top of the hill. "The service is over," he announced roughly, his civility having given way to his impatience. "Get on outta here!" Only then did they move back toward their horses and wagons, drenched to the bone, and wondering if what they had just witnessed was real or imaginary.

"It was him, Pa—Grayson," Slate said, still shaken, but unlike his brother, he wasn't sure it would do any good to run. "Only it wasn't him—at least I don't see how it coulda been him."

"Grayson? You ain't makin' a damn bit of sense," Jacob bellowed. "You tryin' to tell me you saw a ghost? Where?" he demanded.

"Up there," Slate declared, and pointed, "at the top of the hill."

Jacob turned at once and looked toward the top of the hill at the empty darkness. In a moment, another flash of lightning lit the sky, revealing nothing but a dead tree that had been struck by lightning years before. "There ain't nothin' up there. You and Troy got spooked by a dead tree," he railed. Turning to the obviously frightened woman standing pressed against Slate, he demanded, "What about you, girl? Did you see anythin'?" He was growing angrier by the minute, furious that something had spoiled Billy's memorial service, and he couldn't get to the bottom of it. He glowered at Maria, waiting for an answer.

Reluctant to answer, but afraid not to, Maria responded fearfully, "There was a man standing there when the lightning came, and then he was gone."

"A tree," Jacob insisted. "You all saw a damn tree."

"No, señor," she countered timidly, "someone was standing beside the tree."

"Hogwash!" he exploded. "Come on," he ordered Slate. "We'll go up to the top and find him if there's a man up there. A ghost," he muttered in disgust. "I ain't scared of no damn ghost. If there is a man up there, I'll make a ghost out of him quick enough for spoilin' Billy's service."

Slate was still reluctant to go, torn between two fears—that of his father, and that of ghosts. He tried to convince himself that what he saw, and everybody else saw, was in fact no more than a man who had for some reason climbed to the top of the hill. In the poor light of the storm, he reasoned, and at that distance, he just looked like Grayson. *That had to be it*, he told himself, and at once felt a little sheepish for his initial reaction. His resolve strengthened, he told Maria, "You go on down to the buggy. I'll be down directly."

Jacob Blanchard didn't believe in ghosts, but he was not a careless man, so he signaled to his two hired hands to follow him and Slate up the hill to look around for the supposed intruder upon Billy's funeral. One of the hired hands, the one known as Stump, was as leery about climbing the hill as Slate had been, but he was far too timid to say so. He was one of the few people there who had actually seen Grayson up close, and he, too, was struck by the resemblance to the figure at the top of the hill. The climb up the slope, made more difficult by the falling rain, took a little time, but upon reaching the dead tree there was no one to be seen. One of his men, a rawboned man called Slim, looked around until he discovered tracks. "Over here, Mr. Blanchard," he sang out. "There was somebody up here all right." He pointed to the boot prints near the dead tree. "Probably weren't no ghost, though," he japed to Slate, "'cause ghosts don't leave no tracks."

Jacob was in no mood to appreciate Slim's humor. He regarded the footprints as a personal affront to him and Billy. "Stump," he ordered, "he musta rode up here from the other side. See if you can find some tracks."

Stump hurried down the gentle slope of the other side until he came to a level spot a quarter of the way down from the top. "Yes, sir," he called out. "He left his horses here. Looks like there was two of 'em."

"See if you can tell where he came from," Jacob said. "I wanna know what the hell he was doin' up here."

"Most likely somebody just passin' by and wanted to see what everybody was doin' on the side of the hill," Slim suggested, unable to understand all the fuss being made over somebody stopping to watch a funeral.

"Get on down there and help Stump find that trail," Jacob ordered.

After about a quarter of an hour's scout, there was little to learn from the fresh tracks, except the fact that they had evidently come from town. So the scouting party returned to the cemetery to retrieve their horses. Still determined to find the man who left the tracks on the hill, Jacob sent Stump back to the ranch with the wagon and the tools used to dig Billy's grave while he rode back to Black Horse Creek to check on any strangers who may have passed through town. "Slate," he said, "you take your little play-pretty back to the hotel and get rid of that buggy. I'll meet you at your office." There was no satisfaction in Jacob's soul after the burial of an empty box, and he needed satisfaction from some source, even if taken from some innocent stranger whose only affront to him was his curiosity to see Billy's funeral.

He had ridden into town prepared to take his bloody vengeance in the sheriff's office, or in the street if necessary, but the town was deserted. He saw no one on the street as he walked his horses boldly up to the sheriff's office and dismounted. There was no one in the office and a sign on the door said CLOSED FOR FUNERAL. He looked around at the stores, and discovered them padlocked. Thinking the saloon would surely be open, he went back to the Black Horse. It, too, was locked up tight, as was Reiner's next door. *The whole damn town closed for a funeral,* he thought. *It must be for someone pretty important.*

After trying Reiner's door, he had looked down toward the stable in time to see someone come out and look up the street at him. He was holding a shotgun. Grayson stepped off the stoop and climbed in the saddle. Burt McNally watched the stranger as he approached. As a matter of habit, he noticed the gray gelding the stranger rode, as well as the sorrel packhorse. "Howdy," he offered when Grayson pulled the gray up before the stable door and dismounted.

"Howdy," Grayson returned. "Looks like you're the only one in town that didn't go to the funeral."

"That's a fact," Burt replied, eying Grayson carefully. "Sheriff Blanchard left me to look after things here while the funeral's goin' on." He was wearing the deputy's badge Slate had given him when he and Troy had ridden to Fort Smith to get Billy.

"Who's gettin' buried? Somebody important?"

"Nobody, really," Burt replied. "It's more like a memorial service for the sheriff's brother Billy. He was shot in the back by a bounty hunter."

"Is that a fact?" Grayson responded, not surprised by the story. "They know for sure that's who shot him?"

"Sheriff Blanchard said it couldn'ta been nobody else. The bastard was bringin' Billy in to the jail, but Billy was dead when he got there."

"I reckon the fellow *was* a bastard to shoot an unarmed man," Grayson remarked. "Where's the graveyard? I might go pay my respects."

Greatly relieved that the stranger seemed to have

no evil intentions, since he had the look of someone capable of causing harm, Burt had been happy to direct him to Cemetery Hill. The weather had turned sour as Grayson rode out of town. After about half a mile he came to the hill and rode his horses about halfway up. Dismounting to finish the climb on foot, he reached the top just as the storm moved over the small gathering of people huddled on the other side. Moving up to stand behind the trunk of a dead tree, he was able to see the service going on below him. He at once identified the two men he had come to kill, and it would have been easy to shoot both of them with two quick rifle shots, but he hesitated to pull the trigger. There were too many people gathered together, innocent people, and he hesitated to execute the two murderers in front of women and children. That would not be a pleasant sight for them to see. There was also the possibility of an innocent casualty from a stray shot. He was certain he would not miss at that range, but he decided not to risk it. He would wait for a better opportunity. The decision made, he started to turn away when he was almost blinded by a brilliant flash of lightning directly overhead. It was followed almost immediately by a powerful rumble of thunder. It served as a not so subtle signal, telling him that the top of a lone hill was not a good place to stand in a violent thunderstorm. The dead tree was testimony enough to support that warning, so he started to go back down the slope to pick up his horses, but hesitated when he saw Troy Blanchard jump on his horse and race away. Slate, however, remained, so he decided he would call on the sheriff in town and worry about Troy after that was taken care of.

* * *

Slate dropped Maria Sanchez off at the hotel before taking the buggy back to the stable. "I'll be back to see you after I make sure everythin's all right," he told her. Still somewhat shaken by the image he had seen at the funeral, his preference would have been to return to her bedroom immediately after he took the buggy back. But his father had told him that he would meet him back in his office, so he had little choice but to comply.

"How'd the funeral go?" Burt McNally asked when Slate drove the buggy inside the stable doors so Burt could unhitch the horse without having to stand in the rain to do it.

"About as good as any funeral, I reckon," Slate answered. "Everythin' all right here in town?"

"Yes, sir," Burt replied. "I kept a good eye on everythin'. You know you can depend on me, Sheriff."

"Yeah, well, that's good. I didn't figure there'd be much for you to worry about," Slate said. "I'll be goin' back to my office for a spell." He planned to go see Maria as soon as his father left town, but he saw no reason to tell Burt that. "If anybody needs me for anythin', I'll most likely be in my office." He could usually count on Troy to sleep in the sheriff's office, but he wasn't sure when he'd see him again, since he took off like a stampede of longhorns. He expected that his brother was going to catch a generous amount of hell when his father caught up with him. One thing Jacob Blanchard would not tolerate in any man was cowardice, especially when it came to one of his sons.

"Say," Burt said, recalling his unusual visitor, "did that feller show up at the funeral?"

Already on his way out the door, Slate stopped. "What feller?"

"Some feller passin' through town," Burt replied, "lookin' for a drink of likker, I expect, 'cause he looked disappointed to find the saloon closed. He said he was gonna go pay his respects at the funeral. He may have been japin' me, though."

Slate thought about it before answering. *Grayson?* Maybe, but more likely a drifter just passing through like Burt said. That could explain the man standing on the hilltop at the graveyard—it had to, because Grayson was dead. Aware then of Burt waiting for his reply, he said, "Yeah, I think I saw him, but he never came down to the grave." He pulled his hat down, stepped out the door into the rain, and started toward his office. The more he thought about it, the more he castigated himself for initially thinking he had seen a ghost. He even chuckled when he pictured Troy's fearful retreat from the graveyard. *Pa's gonna take a whip to him*, he thought.

Hurrying down the muddy street, he stepped up on the short length of boardwalk before the sheriff's office to discover the door halfway open, evidently blown open by the storm. *Damn Troy*, he thought, *he was supposed to lock the damn door when he left for the funeral.* He didn't know how long his father would linger at Billy's grave, but his horse was not tied out front, so he suspected the door had been left standing open ever since the storm struck. *Why in hell didn't Burt catch it, if he was so all-fired careful about watching the town?*

He stepped inside the darkened office and closed the door behind him. Then he took his hat off and

beat it against his leg a couple of times to knock some
of the water off it. The light was so dim from the
window in front that he struck a match to light the
lamp on his desk. He turned up the wick in the lamp,
unaware of the dark shadow standing in front of
the one cell door behind him. There was not a sound,
yet something made him turn around to look, and
when he did, he dropped the lamp, stunned by the
deadly specter standing there. "Grayson!" he uttered
without conscious thought, thinking he was seeing
another ghost. Terrified, he backed away from the
desk, oblivious to the flames from the burning lamp
oil spreading in a widening circle under his desk.
Recovering somewhat from the initial shock, his
brain began to function again, and his next reaction
was to reach for his pistol. It served only to speed up
the inevitable. The sharp bark of Grayson's Winchester, already leveled at him, resonated against the
walls of the tiny room as Slate doubled over with a
bullet in his gut.

Grayson walked over to stand before the mortally
wounded man. Writhing in pain, Slate fumbled for
his six-gun again, but Grayson pinned his wrist to
the floor with his boot. "You know who I am, I
reckon," he said. "You shoulda made sure of your
kill—I am." He put a bullet in Slate's forehead, ending the wounded man's suffering. "That's one of
you," he stated, thinking now of the brother who fled
from the cemetery. He took a moment more to gaze at
the horrified eyes, still wide with fright from having
seen certain death, and the drawn face reflected in
the light of the flames still licking the pine planks of
the floor. He started for the door, then paused to
sweep a pile of papers off the desk to feed the flames

eating away at the legs of the desk. Satisfied, he eased the door open and took a look up and down the street. There was no one in sight, so he stepped out on the boardwalk. It was a Sunday, so most of the business establishments were closed. Perhaps, he thought, the old man made it an official holiday as well, in honor of his worthless son. At any rate, it made the execution much more private without a mob of bystanders.

The rain began to taper off as he walked around behind the jail where his horses were tied. Stepping up in the saddle, he rode out from behind the buildings toward the lower end of town and the road to Blanchard's ranch. As he rode past the stable, he nodded in acknowledgement of Burt McNally's wave. The young man had come out of the tack room when he thought he heard gunshots a few minutes earlier.

Billy's death had hit Jacob Blanchard hard. He had love for his other two sons, but Billy had been the one most like him. He had the fire and the "don't give a damn" that Jacob admired—and a proper streak of meanness that ensured against anybody running over him. And now Billy was gone. Slate and Troy killed the man who took Billy's life, but there was still no feeling of vengeance satisfied. It wouldn't bring Billy back.

He stayed beside the grave for a long time after everyone else had left, reluctant to leave it, seeming to forget that it was an empty grave. Then he thought of Troy thinking he had seen a ghost and running like a frightened deer, and the image disgusted him. It prompted him to end his mourning, get on his horse, and start for town with the intention of talking to Slate. He wanted to know who the stranger was who was seen looking down upon Billy's funeral. His concern was that his sons had not been as careful as they had claimed, and the man on the hill might in fact be a U.S. marshal. It would also be a good time to talk to Slate about taking a bigger role in controlling the town. His eldest son had been too content with being the sheriff and wasting his time with that Mexican woman. It was time he stepped up to help his father build the empire he envisioned. He was going to have to take the role Jacob had planned for Billy.

It was only a half a mile to town from the cemetery, so Jacob noticed the smoke almost as soon as he turned his horse toward town. Just a thin brown wisp at first, it began to take on more body as he neared the settlement and the rain began to let up. He could not tell what the source might be until he rode onto the end of the deserted main street and realized it was the sheriff's office. He kicked his horse hard and galloped the rest of the way to find Burt McNally, Roy Brown, the bartender, and Morgan Bowers, who managed the hotel, working feverishly to throw water on the blazing building. He could see that their efforts were useless. All they had to fight the fire with were buckets, and they had to run almost fifty yards to the horse trough at the stable to fill them. There was no one else to help. Those three businesses were the only ones open on a Sunday afternoon: the saloon, the hotel, and the stable.

"Where's Slate?" Jacob shouted as he rode up and pulled his horse to a skidding stop.

"Don't know, Mr. Blanchard," Burt answered. "I

ain't seen him since he brought the buggy back to the stable."

He started to run to fill his empty bucket, but Jacob grabbed him by the elbow, almost pulling him to the ground. "Did you look inside?" Jacob demanded.

"No, sir," Burt replied. "It was gettin' too hot to go in there, but I figured Sheriff Blanchard woulda come outta there when it caught on fire. He might be visitin' Maria Sanchez down at the hotel." He looked a little sheepish when he said it, thinking that he might be telling something on Slate that Slate didn't care to have known.

Jacob shot a sharp glance at Morgan Bowers, but Morgan shook his head. "I didn't see him at the hotel," he said.

"You damn fool," Jacob cursed Burt. "Slate might still be in there. Get your ass in there and make sure my son ain't in there sick, or asleep, or somethin'." He turned to Morgan and Roy and said, "You might as well quit runnin' up and down the street like a couple of idiots. That fire's too far along to put out with those buckets." He spun around to give Burt a kick in the seat of his pants. "Get in there and make sure Slate's gone."

"Yes, sir," Burt dutifully replied, although he didn't like the prospects of setting himself on fire. He walked cautiously back and forth, looking for a possible hole into the burning structure.

When Burt had hesitated past Jacob's patience, the angry old man drew his .44 revolver and threatened him. "If you don't get in there right now, I'm gonna shoot you right here in the street."

With no choice, the reluctant hero dived headfirst

through a small hole in the front wall. Unable to see more than a foot or two before him, he began to immediately choke on the heavy smoke. He would not have seen Slate had he not stumbled over his body. As soon as he realized what he had tripped on, he yelled out, "I found him!" and he started dragging the body back the way he had come. Slate was a sizable man, and his corpse was a heavy burden, but Burt had incentive enough to drag him out of the fiery trap, knowing he had only moments left, himself.

As soon as Burt emerged from the smoky jail, the others hurried to help. "Slate!" Jacob cried out in anguish. "Slate, boy, answer me!" He shucked off his coat and tried to smother the flames burning his son's clothes. Of no concern to Jacob, Morgan and Roy were frantically rolling Burt in the muddy street to extinguish the flames eating his clothes. Suddenly Jacob roared out in frustrated anger, and they turned to see him holding Slate's head up off the ground. There was a dark, round hole in the center of his forehead. Not knowing what to do, they froze when Jacob threw his head back and howled out his pain. It lasted for what seemed a long time before the old man finally laid Slate's head back on the ground. He turned to stare at them, not really seeing them, and he growled, "Grayson." He knew in his heart that it could be no other.

He then seemed to become calm, enough so that the other three men gathered around him to see if they could help in any way.

"Looks like he was gut shot, too," Burt said, pointing to the bloody shirt. He immediately regretted pointing it out when Jacob turned to fix him with eyes that seemed to accuse.

"Grayson," Jacob repeated. "I want him. I'll pay the man who brings him to me five hundred dollars, but I want him alive. He's gonna take a long time to die." He then spoke directly to Morgan. "I've got to go find Troy. That damn bounty hunter is bound to be lookin' for him now. You and Burt take Slate to the hotel and put him in a room. Then you go get the barber and tell him to get down there and fix Slate's body for buryin'. You tell him if he doesn't get down there right away, he's gonna need a coffin for himself." There was no discussion on the matter; all three of the men knew the consequences for not following Jacob Blanchard's orders. Burt ran to the stable to get a buckboard to carry Slate's body to the hotel. "Take care of my boy," Jacob ordered as he stepped up in the saddle. "I'll be back as soon as I find Troy." He wheeled his horse and reminded them, "Five hundred dollars for Grayson alive!" Then he was off, thundering down the muddy street, leaving the three frightened men to do his bidding.

Chapter 13

He returned to the same ravine that led up to a small ridge from which he had watched Jacob Blanchard's ranch house before. It was here that he had watched Stump ride out on a mule on his way to warn Billy. The recent rain had caused a little runoff that enlarged a tiny trickle that ran down the ravine to the creek. His horses were tied right at the point where it emptied into the creek. Using a pair of field glasses, he watched everyone working around the ranch, taking care to count the number of men and their whereabouts as they moved about between the barn and the corral. There were four hired hands that he could account for, but there was no sign of Troy Blanchard. If he had returned home when he fled the graveyard, he would have to be holed up inside the house. Grayson feared he would never get the open shot he had hoped for.

A woman came out of the house occasionally and

went to the pump for water—too young to be Troy's mother, he thought, perhaps a cook or housekeeper. Since he had no way to know how many hired hands Blanchard still employed at the ranch, he decided he was going to have to wait until dark to try to find out if Troy was there. For now, there was nothing to do but wait and watch, so he counseled himself to be patient.

At dusk a rider came in, and Grayson pulled the field glasses up to get a closer look. It turned out to be Jacob Blanchard. *Maybe now,* he thought, for if he had judged the patriarch of the Blanchard clan accurately, there would be some fireworks going off over Troy's hasty departure from the cemetery. Jacob pulled his weary horse up sharply before the front steps of the house and handed the reins to Stump, who had run out to meet him. Even in this dim light, looking through the field glasses Grayson could see the old man's face drawn in anger. He did not have to hear the conversation to know that Jacob was demanding to know where Troy was. Grayson waited, his rifle ready, expecting Troy to come out of the house. He had decided to take the shot as soon as Troy appeared, then take his chances on being able to escape. But Troy never showed up. Judging by Jacob's obvious gestures, Grayson suspected that Troy was not there, a fact that evidently displeased his father, and left Grayson with no idea where to look for him. *The line shack?* he wondered. For that was where Billy had gone to hide out.

Grayson knew where the line shack was, but what if Troy had gone somewhere else to hide? He was undecided whether or not to head for Rabbit Creek right away, or to wait where he was and watch the house, figuring that Troy would eventually show up.

Either way, time was a big factor, for if he made the wrong decision it could mean that Troy might be increasing his odds of escape. In the next few seconds, Jacob Blanchard made the decision for him. He yelled something out to Stump, who had almost reached the barn with Jacob's horse. Stump stopped, said something in reply, then continued on into the barn. A short time later, Stump reappeared from the barn again with a fresh, saddled horse and led it to the front steps, where he handed the reins to Jacob. Right behind Stump, another of Jacob's hired hands rode out from the barn to join them at the front steps, where the old man was still obviously giving orders. Then Jacob climbed on the fresh horse and he and the hired hand rode out toward the east.

Grayson froze, for they were coming directly toward him where he was watching from the low ridge. His first thought was that they had somehow spotted him, and he hustled to prepare for the confrontation to come. With barely fifty yards remaining, however, they turned and rode in a more northerly direction, passing the mouth of the ravine where he had tied his horses. Had either of the riders turned to look in that direction, they might surely have seen the gray and the sorrel. Grayson slid back away from the brow of the ridge and waited for the two riders to pass in front of him, all the while thinking that his horses already needed a rest. And now he was going to be forced to press them for additional miles, trailing a couple of fresh horses. He could see little choice but to follow as long as he could. He hurried back down the ravine to his horses, but instead of climbing into the saddle, he started walking, while leading the gray.

Walking as fast as he could, he felt hard-pressed to keep the two riders in sight, a task made even more difficult by the fading daylight. To make matters even harder, Jacob and his man increased their gait to an easy lope, making it harder for Grayson to keep them in sight on the horizon. When it got to the point where he lost sight of them completely, he stepped up into the saddle and pushed the gray into a lope. As soon as he caught sight of them on the horizon again, he immediately dismounted, conserving every bit of the gray's energy that he could. This routine was repeated for almost three hours before Grayson was forced to rest his horses or chance ending up on foot for good. Walking once more, he led the two horses in the darkness toward a long line of trees that he hoped indicated water, not realizing that he had caught up with Blanchard and his hired gun until he heard the shot.

"Troy!" Jacob yelled. "Dammit, it's me and Slim! Put the damn rifle down. We're comin' in." Already angry, he was now almost out of control when Troy's bullet had snapped the air between their two horses. Forced to dismount and take cover behind the horses, lest he be killed by his son, Jacob waited for a response. There was none, only quiet, but at least there was not a second shot. "Troy!" he yelled again. "Do you hear me? Answer me, boy!" Again there was quiet.

Finally, Troy called back, "I hear you, Pa. Come on in."

Jacob and Slim climbed on their horses and guided them down past a line of cottonwoods to a dilapidated board shack on the bank of a narrow creek. Troy's horse was hobbled nearby and there was a

small fire glowing in front of the shack, but there was
no sign of his son. The two riders pulled up before
the door of the shack and Jacob called out again,
"Troy! You in there?"

"I'm here, Pa." The voice came from the back corner of the shack as Troy stepped cautiously out from
behind the wooden structure, his rifle still in a ready-
to-fire position before him.

Astonished by his son's actions, Jacob demanded,
"What in the hell's wrong with you? You damn-near
shot one of us. I'm of a mind to break that damn rifle
over your back."

"I'm sorry, Pa," Troy replied, "but how was I to
know that was you, come creepin' up on me like that.
How'd I know who you were?"

"You coulda found out before you took a shot at
us," Slim commented, none too happy to have come
so close to catching a bullet.

"Shut up, Slim," Jacob snapped, then directed his
words to Troy again. "I had a feelin' you'd be up at
this old shack. You've got a helluva lot of explainin' to
do, boy. While you were hightailin' it up here to hide,
your brother's been murdered. He mighta had a
chance if you had been with him like you shoulda
been."

The news of Slate's death only served to convince
Troy that he had done the right thing when he fled.
He knew what he had seen, despite anything anyone
else said to convince him otherwise. Grayson was not
the first dead man he had ever seen, so he was certain
that they had killed him. He was also positive that it
was Grayson he had seen standing on the top of the
hill during the thunderstorm. That graveyard was
the logical place for a ghost to appear, and there was

no doubt in his mind that it had come for him and Slate. So now Slate was dead. He was not surprised. Slate should have run when he did. His mind was spinning in his head, trying to think of a safe place to hide when he realized his father was pressing him for an answer. "What?" Troy responded.

"I said your brother's dead," Jacob repeated, exasperated by Troy's reaction. "What's the matter with you?"

"I'm sorry, Pa."

"Now we gotta take care of that damn bounty hunter you and Slate said you killed," Jacob fumed. "Thanks to you and Slate's carelessness, he's killed another one of my sons." He scowled when Troy failed to respond with some show of fire or indignation. "And right now I ain't seein' the sand in you that your brothers had."

"I swear, Pa," Troy pleaded, "the man was dead when we left him in the middle of the street. It don't make no sense to go after a ghost. He's already dead. You can't kill him again."

"Horseshit!" Jacob exclaimed in disgust for his son's cowardly display in front of one of his hired hands. He saw it as a shameful affront to him personally to think he, Jacob Blanchard, could have fathered such a son. "He ain't no more ghost than that damn horse I rode in on, and by God, I'll stand up to him anytime, anywhere," he swore. "Now get on that horse. We're goin' ghost huntin', and you're gonna kill him—avenge your brothers—and this time I'll be there to make damn-sure he's dead." He stood there glowering for a few moments, smoldering in his rage. When Troy did not move, seemingly anchored to the ground before him, Jacob told Slim to remove the hobbles from Troy's horse and saddle it. Slim replied that the horse still had the saddle on it, which further riled Jacob. "Well, bring it up here with ours. We're gettin' ready to ride."

Still Troy did not move. "I'm sorry about Slate," he finally muttered. "None of this woulda happened if it wasn't for Billy shootin' that lawman over at Ed Lenta's place. Me and Slate was unlucky when we killed Grayson, and now he's come back from hell to get us."

Burning with anger and shame, Jacob suddenly lashed out at his son, backhanding him with one powerful blow that staggered Troy. "Quit that damn snivelin'," he roared. "You're makin' me sick. Now get on that damn horse."

"I ain't goin', Pa," Troy whimpered, one hand holding the side of his face where he had been struck. "I can't."

Seething now with disgust, Jacob got suddenly quiet while he continued to stare at his son. "Why, you ain't worth the powder it'd take to blow you to hell," he said. Then he deliberately pulled his pistol from his holster, aimed it at Troy's head, and pulled the trigger.

Slim, standing beside him, holding the horse's reins, jumped at the sudden discharge of Jacob's pistol. Startled, "Damn!" was all he could say as he watched Troy slump to the ground. He looked quickly at the old man, thinking he must have gone crazy.

"Tie a lead rope on to my saddle," Jacob ordered, with no more expression on his face than if he had just put down a crippled horse.

"Yes, sir," Slim responded. "You want me to load Troy's body over the saddle?"

"No. I ain't gonna disgrace my other boys by bury-in' a coward next to their graves."

"Yes, sir," Slim responded again and jumped to do his boss's bidding.

Jacob stood over his son's body for a while before reaching down and unbuckling his gun belt. When Slim finished attaching a lead line on Troy's horse, he started to step up in the saddle, unaware that Jacob had walked up behind him. He had one foot in the stirrup when the old man held his pistol up behind his head and pulled the trigger. The shot caused Slim's horse to bolt sideways, dragging Slim's body a few feet along with it. "There's been enough shame come to my house without lettin' you shoot your mouth off about Troy," he said. "I ain't got no quarrel with you, but you mighta talked about what you saw here some night when you was too likkered up to hold your tongue."

He caught Slim's horse and freed his boot from the stirrup, then tied the horse on to the lead rope with Troy's. Stepping up in the saddle, he led the horses out across the stream, heading back to Black Horse Creek. He had a burying to attend to, after which he planned to track down the demon, Grayson, who had destroyed his family.

Grayson could barely believe the executions he had just witnessed. Having worked his way close enough along the creek bank to understand enough of the conversation to realize what was going on, he had been waiting for a clear shot at Troy. Before that could happen, however, the old man did the job for him. How a man—any man—could kill his own son, even if he was a coward, Grayson could not understand.

The second execution was even more difficult to understand. He was beginning to get more insight concerning the patriarch of the Blanchard family. It could be summed up in one word—insane.

The incident that just occurred left him with uncertainty. Both Slate and Troy were dead. That was what he had come to do. What to do now left him puzzled— maybe nothing, since his mission was completed— but something should be done about the murdering old man. The best thing would probably be to put him down like the mad dog he appeared to be. Grayson wasn't sure that was his responsibility. Maybe he should have taken the shot as the old man was riding across the creek. If he was still wearing a badge, he would certainly have arrested him at the least. Someone should do something about him, he told himself, and he was the only witness to the crime. "I reckon it's up to me," he said. There was little he could do about it now, as the image of the old man faded into the darkness, because Grayson's horses were spent and in need of rest, about twelve hours' worth. He had no choice but to wait out the night and start out fresh the next day.

Before resigning himself to making his camp, he walked over to the shack to view the carnage Jacob Blanchard had left behind. Troy was wearing the shocked look of disbelief he had when his father shot him face on. The hired hand had mercifully been shot in the back of his head with nothing to warn him. Both bodies were left just as they had fallen with nothing but their weapons removed. He looked around and decided he might as well make his camp right there. Troy had started a small fire, so Grayson threw some more wood on it, then dragged the two bodies out into the brush before going to retrieve his horses. There was a lot to think about, some big decisions to make, and he hoped to have it all worked out by morning.

The solemn Creek woman prepared Jacob's breakfast, although she was not sure he would be up at the usual time. She heard him when he came in the night before, and the hour was late. She had heard him talking to his hired hands before he rode off last night, so she knew that he was going to fetch Troy. But she was sure the old man was alone when he returned. He had called young Jimmy Hicks from the bunkhouse to take care of the horses. At breakfast earlier, Jimmy told her that neither Troy nor Slim came home with Blanchard, leaving her to speculate on the reason. Knowing the old man as well as she did, it was easy to guess that something unpleasant had happened to the two missing men. With them gone, that left Jacob with only Stump and Dan Slider to run the place—plus Jimmy. Stump was not right in the head, but he could work the ranch with Jimmy's help. Both the man and the boy would give more than a full day's work every day. Slider, on the other hand, was no more than a hired gun, like Slim and Yancey and Lonnie. So the brunt of the work would fall upon Stump and Jimmy.

Her thoughts settled on the boy, and she wondered how long it would be before Jacob corrupted him to become just another horse thief and murderer like the rest of his men. She had often wondered if she should talk to Jimmy, and try to persuade him to leave Black Horse Creek before Jacob decided he was old enough to participate in the lawless activities with the crew. Jimmy was a decent boy. How long would he remain so with Jacob Blanchard's evil influence? Further thoughts were interrupted by the sound of Jacob Blanchard's footstep in the hallway. She dropped her dish towel at once and hurried to the stove to fill his cup with coffee.

"Hurry up my breakfast," he ordered. "I'm leavin' for town right away."

"Yes, sir," she responded in her broken English. "Your breakfast ready. I keep it warm in the oven." She eyed him carefully to determine his mood. Always dour, it was especially urgent this morning, so she assumed that things had not gone well the night before. She would be careful to stay out of his way, grateful that he would soon be gone.

"Holler out the door for Stump," he told her. She set his plate down on the table before him, then immediately went to the kitchen door and called out for the simple little man. Accustomed to being summoned in this fashion, Stump was on his way to the house in a matter of minutes. When Stump arrived at the kitchen door, Rachel handed him a cup of coffee, knowing that he was always grateful to get one. "We ain't got time for you to drink coffee," Jacob said, causing Stump to gulp the hot liquid as fast as he could. "You and Dan get saddled up. As soon as I've finished my breakfast, we're goin' to town. We've got some business to take care of." He studied Stump's simple features for a moment, having second thoughts about taking him with him. Stump didn't have a mean bone in his body, and that was the reason Jacob wasn't sure he could count on him when the shooting started. At least he'll make the odds three to one, he decided, and he was better at tracking than Dan.

"Jimmy can take care of things around here till we get back," Jacob said.

"Yes, sir," Stump said, and finished his coffee in several huge gulps, causing Rachel to wonder how the man kept from scalding his throat. She was glad Jacob was not taking Jimmy with him. The evil man had stolen her life. She decided to try to influence Jimmy to leave this place while he was still young enough to make a life for himself somewhere else— somewhere with no Jacob Blanchard. She often wished that she had run away from the brutal old man. But she had waited too late. When she was younger, he treated her much better, especially when she began to become a young woman. As the years and the hard work began to take a toll on her body, he started to look upon her as property, like his horse, or one of his cattle. There had never been any gentleness in the man his entire life, and as he aged, he became even more brutal toward her, deriving his greatest pleasure from abuse.

In spite of his feelings of responsibility the night before—to bring Jacob Blanchard to justice—he began to question himself again on this clear, sunny morning. There was a strong urge to ride straight to Fort Smith, bypass Black Horse Creek, and leave the chaos that was now settled upon the town to the citizens. He was sure there was no one to challenge Jacob Blanchard's authority, so consequently, life in the little community would continue on as it had—with Blanchard ruling supreme. A firm believer in "an eye for an eye" justice, he knew in his heart that Blanchard should be stopped. It just wasn't his responsibility. The people of Black

Horse Creek would have to capture their town if they thought it worth salvaging. It was much easier not to get involved. Besides, he admitted to having a hankering to return to his room in Wanda Meadows's boardinghouse. Curiosity got the best of him, however, and he decided to swing by Jacob's ranch, just for the sake of looking it over. He had little doubt that Blanchard would be looking for him to avenge his son, so he decided it might be in his best interest to see what his adversary was up to.

Returning to the same ridge from which he had scouted the Blanchard house on two previous occasions, he left his horses in the ravine while he climbed to the top of the ridge with his field glasses. It was close to noon when he arrived and all was quiet around the house and barn. There appeared to be no one working near the corral or the smokehouse. If Blanchard was there, he was inside. While he lay there watching, the woman came out the back door and banged on an iron triangle with a piece of iron rod hanging there. *Dinner time*, Grayson thought and watched to see how many answered the call. He looked toward the bunkhouse, expecting to see someone turn out. No one did. One hand came out of the barn, a boy, and hurried up to the house where the woman exchanged a few words with him before they both went inside the kitchen. *There's nobody here!* The thought occurred to him. *He's left no one here but the woman and a young boy while he's taken the rest of his men and probably gone looking for me.* He started to head for town, himself, then decided it would be his best opportunity to know for sure exactly how many guns he was likely to face if he went after Blanchard.

*   *   *

Rachel paused, the coffeepot in her hand, having just refilled Jimmy Hicks's cup. "Somebody's coming," she said. Jimmy, seated at the table, paused also, but only for a moment when Rachel put the coffeepot back on the stove and went to the door to see who it was. "Stranger," she announced. "I never see him before."

Curious, Jimmy got up from the table and joined her by the door. "Me neither," he said. Assuming it was someone who had come to see Blanchard, he stepped outside to greet their visitor. "Howdy," he greeted the rider. "If you're lookin' for Mr. Blanchard, he ain't here right now."

"Is that so?" Grayson returned. "Well, I'm sorry I missed him." He stepped down, and seeing Rachel standing in the door, nodded. "Ma'am." She made no response. Grayson continued. "Yep, I'm sorry he ain't here. I heard he might be lookin' for some extra hands, so I thought I'd come talk to him about a job."

"You ain't from around here," Jimmy stated.

"That's a fact," Grayson said. "I just rode up from Texas." He looked toward the barn and the bunkhouse, then asked, "Is there anybody else around I could talk to? A foreman or somebody?"

"No, sir," Jimmy replied. "There ain't nobody here right now but me and Rachel. But I reckon you heard right, Mr. Blanchard will most likely be lookin' for some more men."

"You expect Mr. Blanchard back anytime soon?"

"Not likely," Jimmy answered, "maybe later tonight. He rode into town."

"Much obliged," Grayson said. He had the confirmation he had sought. Blanchard's crew was reduced to himself and possibly some other men who may be with him, plus this young boy. And Jimmy didn't impress him as a real gun hand, although he didn't discount the possibility altogether. After all, Billy Blanchard wasn't much older than this boy when he established himself as a hardened killer. He turned and prepared to step up in the saddle.

Rachel had remained in the doorway, silently listening to the conversation between Jimmy and the stranger. Studying the man intently as he questioned Jimmy, she now spoke. "We're eating dinner. We have plenty of food if you're hungry."

Surprised, for he hadn't even thought of that possibility, Grayson hesitated a moment to think the invitation over. It didn't seem like the right thing to do since he had come with the intent of possibly shooting her boss. *Why not?* he thought. *No sense in letting good food go to waste—might be a good cook.* It also occurred to him that if she wasn't, it might be one of the reasons the Blanchard clan was so damn mean. "Why, that's mighty nice of you, ma'am. I guess I could take dinner with you. It's been a while since I've sat down to a lady's cookin'."

"Want me to pull the saddle off your horse?" Jimmy asked.

"No, thanks just the same," Grayson replied. "I won't be here that long. Soon as I eat, I reckon I'll be on my way—see if I can catch up with Mr. Blanchard in town."

It seemed more than a little strange, sitting down to a meal, just the three of them in the middle of a huge working ranch. It was a lot of responsibility to leave on the shoulders of the young boy. As far as the quality of Rachel's cooking was concerned, he had to admit that it was some of the best he'd had, even compared to Wanda Meadows's. It was a cordial dinner with Grayson able to fabricate enough stories to answer Jimmy's many questions about raising cattle in Texas. By the time the meal was finished, he had come to the opinion that the woman and the boy were involved only in working the ranch and had nothing to do with Blanchard's darker business. With sincere thanks to the Creek woman for her hospitality, he bade them farewell, and stepped up on the gray gelding.

"Maybe we'll see you again, soon," Jimmy called out after him.

"Maybe so," Grayson replied.

Rachel had said very little during the entire meal, as was her custom, but she listened carefully to all that was said. Most of it was idle conversation about the weather, the season, and trail drives up from Texas. She was an intelligent woman and able to think for herself. She watched the stranger ride off toward the gate by the path and thought to herself, *Grayson.* She decided it best not to share the thought with Jimmy.

A meeting had been called of the small group of citizens who were secretly seeking to free the merchants from the costly yoke of Jacob Blanchard. The recent killings and the burning of the town's jail had been signal enough that their little town was on the verge of destroying itself. There was still no word from Henry Farmer's son, Bob, and no contact from anyone in Governor Anthony's office. "I'm bettin' that boy's dead—lyin' in some gully between here and Topeka," Shep Barnhill said. "Jacob Blanchard wasn't about to let somebody go up there and tell those people what's goin' on in Black Horse Creek." His comment triggered a wave of grumbled responses.

"If that's so," Earl Dickens asked, "who told him Bob was on his way to see the governor?"

"If I had to guess, I'd say it was most likely Roy Brown," Shep commented. The bartender next door at the saloon was an easy suspect since he worked directly for Jacob Blanchard, who owned the Black Horse Saloon. Looking around the room at those gathered, it was difficult to believe any of the others would have told Blanchard.

"Well, then," Dickens countered, "who told Roy?"

"I doubt anybody did," Louis Reiner said. "There ain't any use to jump to hasty conclusions. We don't know for sure that Bob Farmer didn't get to Topeka. Maybe he got to see the governor and maybe not. We haven't heard from him one way or the other—and that's all we really know for sure. So we might as well decide what we're gonna do without government help. There ain't gonna be a better time for us to take over this town than right now," he suggested. "Slate Blanchard's dead and Troy hasn't been seen since the funeral. We don't have a sheriff or deputy. We don't have a mayor or city council. We're just a bunch of dumb merchants who got hoodwinked into paying Jacob Blanchard taxes for trying to run a business on land that doesn't really belong to him."

"Hold on!" Morgan Bowers called out from his position by the window. "Quiet down! Here comes Burt McNally. He looks like he's coming here."

"It's all right," Reiner said. "He *is* coming here. Burt's in this with us. I'll vouch for him."

"Are you sure he ain't comin' here just to take

names?" Shep asked. "Every time Slate and Troy ain't around, Burt's the actin' sheriff." He looked around him, looking for support for his suspicions. "There's liable to be hell to pay if ol' Blanchard finds out what we've been talkin' about. He ain't in too good a mood as it is, ever since Slate got killed."

"I'm sure he's all right," Reiner insisted. "He doesn't like Blanchard any better than the rest of us. He and I have had several talks about what we could do to run our own town."

"You coulda fooled me," Bowers said. "I was working right beside him when we were trying to put out the fire in the sheriff's office. He never said a word about it, even when Blanchard made him jump in that burning building to drag Slate out."

"I expect he wasn't sure he could trust you," Reiner replied.

Further discussion on the matter was halted when Burt stepped up on the walk and opened the door. He paused momentarily to look around at his neighbors, nodding to each in turn. "I think you might wanna know that Mr. Blanchard just rode into town. Stump Haskell and Dan Slider are with him, but not Troy. They're over at the barbershop talkin' to Percy about Slate's body, I reckon."

"Well, I guess that's the reason Percy didn't show up," Reiner said. "He said he was going to be here."

"Oh, hell," Morgan Bowers swore. "I hope Percy ain't in any trouble. Blanchard told him to take Slate's body to my hotel and lay him out in one of my best rooms. Percy told me he couldn't work on Slate there, so he moved him to his place. Blanchard might not like that."

"Maybe he'll understand that Percy's got all his tools and stuff back of the barbershop," Reiner said.

"Huh!" Shep blurted. "When have you ever seen Blanchard understandin' anything that's against his orders?" The question was barely out of his mouth when it was punctuated by the sound of a gunshot in the direction of the barbershop. The room was immediately immersed in silence as everyone froze in place for a long moment, listening.

"That don't sound good," Earl Dickens blurted.

"We mighta just lost us a barber," Shep said.

"Maybe it'd be a good idea if we broke this meeting up," Louis Reiner suggested. "It wouldn't be too good if Blanchard came down here and found all of us together—might make him suspicious." Everyone agreed. "Best get back to your establishments," Reiner went on. "File outta here one or two at a time. Some of you can slip out the back. Now is not a good time to get him to thinking we're up to something."

"I wonder if I oughta go over to Percy's to check on him?" Burt questioned. "I guess I'm the actin' sheriff with Slate dead, and Troy gone."

"That's up to you," Earl Dickens said, "but damned if I'd go near his place right now."

As fearful as most of them were, Shep couldn't resist making a joke. "I reckon ol' Blanchard is plannin' to have another funeral—this one for good ol' Slate. I hope it's as big a circus as the one for that empty box we all prayed over."

"I think it would be a good idea for you to get back down to the stable," Earl Dickens told Burt. "He's gonna want to put his horses up if he's planning on staying in town."

"Right," Burt replied. "You'll be at the house?"

"Yes, Mary Agnes is ailing lately, and I think it best if I stay close by her," Earl said.

Burt was not surprised. His boss was never anxious to be around his stables whenever Jacob Blanchard was in town. And Mary Agnes seemed to time her ailing spells pretty much on Blanchard's schedule. "I'll take care of things," Burt assured him. He started to head out the door, but stopped to make one additional comment. "What we need is that feller, Grayson, to pay the town another visit. Damned if he don't match Blanchard for meanness."

"Be careful what you wish for," Louis Reiner said. "That man might burn the whole town down. We'd best wait until we see what Blanchard is gonna do before we have another meeting. Maybe he'll bury Slate, then head out to look for Grayson." He stood at the door until all members of the secret citizens council had filed out the door; then he turned his CLOSED sign outward, locked up for the night, and hurried across the alley to his house on the one side street in town. Maybe things would look a little more peaceful in the morning, and if he was lucky, he wouldn't have any contact with Blanchard at all.

Yours is the closest house to my saloon, so I reckon you can help that Mexican woman get Slate ready for his funeral."

Astonished by the request, Louis could not respond at first. He looked at the fearsome man, whose huge body seemed to hover over his front door, then took a couple of frightened glances back at his wife, who was now standing in the front hall, their two young children peering around her skirt. "I'm sorry, Mr. Blanchard, but I don't really know anything about that sort of thing. Percy Edwards usually takes care of that." His response obviously did not please the angry man.

"Percy Edwards ain't with us no more," Blanchard stated, his tone deadly calm. "He passed away unexpectedly." He waited for the impact to set in with Reiner. "So now, I'm askin' you to do me the favor of takin' care of my boy. Are you gonna help me?"

The question was easily interpreted by Reiner to mean, *Or do you want the same as Percy?* "Wh-why of course I'm willing to try to lend a hand if I can," he stammered. He glanced again at Eunice, then back at Blanchard. "We were just in the middle of our supper . . ." Louis started, but was not allowed to finish.

"Right now, Reiner," Blanchard ordered. "I've got a lot of things to do, and my boy's waitin' in that damn toolshed Edwards called a funeral home."

"Of c-course," Louis stammered again. "I'll get my coat." He started to turn away, but collided with Eunice, who had hurried to bring his coat. "You and the kids finish your supper. I'll be back as soon as I can," he told her. Out the door then, he stood on the porch for a moment, not sure if he was to lead or follow.

Blanchard climbed in the saddle and said, "Climb up behind Stump. I ain't got time to wait for you to walk over there."

Stump edged his mule up to the porch to make it easier for Louis to get on. "Evenin', Mr. Reiner," the simpleminded ranch hand offered cheerfully. "Too bad we had to interrupt your supper."

Reiner didn't answer as he scrambled up behind Stump. Feeling completely helpless and out of place, he looked back to give his wife a forlorn glance as he bounced along on the back of the mule. He was ashamed of the fact that he didn't have the starch to tell Blanchard that he was not a servant to be ordered around, and that he was not a mortician at any rate. He could not see that he had any other choice, however, for it appeared that Blanchard's true colors were coming to the surface. He had been uncompromising in the past, but now he was practicing his cruel and crude solutions in the open, punishing any who opposed his rule. How Reiner and his fellow citizens were going to overcome this tyrant's rule seemed an impossibility to him at this moment. But it was plain enough that it was past time when they must unite to move against Blanchard. It was difficult to think of revolution while bouncing up and down on the hind quarters of a mule, however.

When they pulled up before Percy Edwards's shop, Louis slid off the mule and went inside while the others were still dismounting. Going through the door, he stopped to drag Percy's body aside when he found it lying directly in front of him. "Leave him be," Blanchard instructed. "He ain't goin' nowhere." He pointed toward the door leading from the barbershop to the rooms behind. "Slate's in there."

Reiner opened the door to find Maria Sanchez bending over the badly burned body of the late Slate Blanchard. She visibly cringed when she looked around to
find Jacob back again. "I've fix Slate up good as I can,"
she pleaded as if expecting to be told it was not good
enough. Louis noticed a fresh bruise on one side of her
face, a souvenir no doubt from a discussion with Jacob
Blanchard. "All his clothes got burnt up," she explained
when she saw Reiner's quizzical expression upon seeing the calico shirt she had dressed him in.

"It don't make no difference now," Blanchard said.
"We'll find him a proper coat over at the hotel." He
turned to scowl at Maria. "Did you get him all sewed
up in the back?"

"Si, señor. I made one shirt out of two. I sewed the
pants together in the leg."

"All right, then," Blanchard directed, "you two get
him by the shoulders, and you, girl, help Reiner take
his feet—and we'll carry him over to the hotel." He
stood back to oversee the operation. "Easy now, goin'
through the door."

So the four of them carried Slate's body across the
street to the hotel, where Morgan Bowers had a room
waiting. Reiner was perturbed to have been recruited
for the purpose of carrying one of Slate's feet when
Blanchard could have done it himself. When they
took Slate into the hotel room, however, he learned
the real reason the old man had picked him to help.
He mumbled something about hurrying along home
now that Slate was settled in an appropriate place to
await his funeral, but Jacob detained him a bit further. "Let's you and me go into the parlor and talk a
little," he said. "Dan, you and Stump wait for me out

on the porch where you can keep an eye on the street." He motioned Reiner toward the hotel parlor.

When Reiner walked in the room he found Morgan Bowers standing there by the fireplace, looking extremely uncomfortable. When Reiner met his gaze, Bowers looked quickly away and started for the door. But Blanchard stopped him before he reached it. "Why don't you stick around, Bowers," he said. Bowers returned to his place by the fire, but for only a moment before Blanchard spoke again. "Have a seat over there on that settee," he told him, then motioned for Reiner to sit down beside him. The old man was well aware of his intimidating presence, and he knew how to use it. The two nervous proprietors sat side by side on the sofa like two mischievous schoolboys called to the headmaster's office, while the fierce old man hovered over them like a dark thundercloud.

"I think it's time we had a little talk," Blanchard began. "Things ain't goin' so good around here of late. I'm a grievin' man—all my sons killed within the last couple of months—two of 'em in the last couple of days." The comment did not slip by Reiner unnoticed, and he then realized that Troy had been killed also. "That ain't your fault," Blanchard went on. "I know that ain't none of your doin'. An outsider— a damn back-shootin' murderer—came in our town to kill my boys." His voice reflected a hint of anger then, but he quickly reverted back to the calm tone he was attempting to maintain. "Now, you two fellers are the first two I set up in business here, so that's why I'm talkin' to you, instead of any of the others. I think most of the others kinda look at you men to run the town, especially you, Reiner. Sometimes they might even have meetin's at your store to talk over problems and such."

Reiner blanched white at the remark. He risked a quick accusing glance in Bowers's direction, but Bowers refused to meet it. It was confirmation enough for Reiner to suspect that Bowers had sold them out. Turning back to Blanchard, he replied weakly, "I wouldn't say we have formal meetings in my store—just sometimes several of the others might stop by to talk about the town and business in general—just visiting."

"Yeah, that's what I figured," Blanchard said. There was a smile on his lips, but a dark frown knotted his heavy gray eyebrows as he gazed steadily at Reiner. "I might like to be there for one of your little get-togethers, myself. You know, I've put up a helluva lot of money to keep you boys in business, so I figure I oughta be in on anythin' that's happenin' in our town. We're kinda like a family. Don't you think, Bowers?" He shot Bowers a quick glance and Morgan nodded his head vigorously. Turning back to Reiner, Blanchard continued. "Even in a family, if one of the members of the family is doin' wrong, and makin' it hard on the rest, you have to punish him—sometimes just a little—sometimes if it's a big thing he's done wrong, then you have to come down hard on him. Ain't that right, Reiner?"

"Well, I suppose so," Reiner stammered, "but I don't know . . ."

Blanchard cut him off. "Now, you take Henry Farmer. He didn't wanna play by the rules—didn't wanna keep the bargain we agreed on when I set him up in business. He didn't get but a little bit of punishment, and it wasn't by me. He was just unlucky when his place caught fire and burnt up everythin' he owned. Lady Luck seems to take care of things like that, and keeps the scales in balance. Same thing happened with Percy Edwards. He didn't do right by my boy Slate, and he started foolin' around with a .44 handgun, just like the one I carry, and the damn thing accidentally went off and killed him." He let that sink in for a few moments before continuing. "So I guess what I'm sayin' to you two upstandin' citizens of our town is Black Horse Creek don't need no mayor and no city council. If you have any problems, you come to me and I'll take care of 'em. And I'll take care of hirin' a new sheriff—save you the trouble of tryin' to elect one. Now, are there any problems we need to talk about tonight?"

"Why, no," Reiner answered. "I don't think so." He couldn't help worrying about what else Bowers had told him. *Surely*, he prayed, *not the fact that Bob Farmer had gone to Topeka to talk to the governor.*

"All right, then, I reckon you're anxious to get back to finish your supper, but there's just one more thing we need to talk about. The murderin' son of a bitch that killed my boy might still be slinkin' around here. I'll hunt him down, and I'll kill him like the dog he is, but my advice to you and everybody else in town is, if he shows up before I catch him, kill him. My five hundred dollar reward still stands for any man who kills him." He paused to make sure they understood. "That's a helluva lot of money, but he can cause this town one helluva lot of trouble." He stepped back, symbolically releasing them from the sofa. As both men headed for the door without delay, Blanchard remarked to Bowers. "Send somebody over to the barbershop to dig a hole and bury that son of a bitch before he starts stinkin'."

"Right," Bowers answered. When they left the parlor, he followed Reiner out the front door of the hotel. "Where the hell am I gonna find somebody to dig a grave this time of night?"

Reiner didn't bother to answer his question. He had several of his own. "What the hell did you tell Blanchard? How much did you tell him? And why? Dammit, man, you might have put all our necks in a noose."

"No, no, Louis." Bowers was quick to object. "I swear, I didn't tell him much of anything. He just put two and two together—most of it guesses. I think maybe Roy told him we were in your store today. When he hit me with it, I might have admitted that we were there. I mean, if Roy already told him, then there wasn't much sense in lying. I told him it was just a few of us town folk visiting."

Reiner shook his head slowly, wondering how much Bowers had really confessed to Blanchard, and wondering also if he needed to be on the alert for any accidental fires at his home or store. *What's done is done*, he thought. There was nothing he could do about it now. "I'm going home," he said abruptly and left Bowers standing there trying to figure out how he was going to get a grave dug.

Much to Bowers's relief, he was spared the physical labor of digging Percy Edwards's final resting place. With the sheriff's office no more than a pile of burnt timbers now, Blanchard decided he needed to establish a new center of operations from which to control the town. The now empty barbershop was the logical choice, so he told Stump to find a shovel and plant Percy behind the building. Bowers was quick to reassure him that he would stay close to the hotel to make sure Slate's body was not disturbed. Of course, a new grave would be necessary in the cemetery, so he volunteered to send someone to get the two young farm boys who had served that purpose for Billy.

"We'll hold the service for Slate tomorrow," Blanchard told him. "You spread the word around town to everybody. We'll see how many folks show up to pay their respects. I need to know the ones who don't."

When Bowers finally had the opportunity to remove himself from the presence of the vengeful tyrant, it was already in the wee hours of the night. Although the hour was late, he found his wife waiting up for him back at the hotel. Relieved to see him come plodding into their first floor living accommodations, she could not think of sleep until he had told her everything that had happened. "I was afraid that insane man might decide to shoot you like he shot poor Percy," she fretted.

"I'm wondering if that might have been easier on me in the long run." He sighed as he sat on the edge of the bed to remove his shoes.

"Don't say such a thing," she scolded. "It's bad enough that old demon took our best room and turned it into a funeral parlor—with that poor excuse for a human being, Slate Blanchard, lying on our clean sheets like the king of Kansas."

Bowers shook his head slowly as he thought about all that had happened that day. "I just don't understand how I got to be his servant," he complained. "Everything he thinks of, he looks at me to get it done, and I just want to be finished with the man."

He paused a moment while he continued to think about it, still holding one shoe in his hand.

Watching him intently, his wife asked, "What are we going to do, Morgan?"

"I don't know," he replied truthfully. The two of them had had many discussions during the past year as to whether or not they should just abandon the hotel and pull out in the middle of the night without telling anyone where they were going. The thing that had prevented them from doing so was the fact that they would be sacrificing everything they had managed to accumulate since they sank all their resources into the operation of the hotel. Blanchard would never allow them to escape the town with a couple of wagons of furniture, leaving the hotel empty of furnishings. Bowers looked up to see his wife waiting for an answer, one she knew he didn't have. "I don't know," he said again. "I guess the only thing we can do is to hope the town can somehow band together and drive Blanchard out." He looked at her helplessly, knowing the chances of that happening were practically nil. "We'll have to see what everybody else has to say about it whenever Blanchard leaves us to go hunting for that man, Grayson." He shook his head in disgust and added, "Of course, we'll have to have a memorial service for that piece of cow dung in the front bedroom first."

The morning broke cool and cloudy with just a hint that rain might not be far off. Jacob Blanchard stepped out on the small stoop of the barbershop and looked up and down the street. A farm wagon on its way to Reiner's store was the only sign of life in the small town. The smell of burnt timbers from the ruins of the sheriff's office was still on the morning breeze, and Blanchard wrinkled his nose in disgust as he sniffed it, for it prompted him to think about the circumstances that caused the fire. Snorting angrily in an attempt to expel the taunting reminder from his nostrils, he stepped onto the street and headed for the hotel dining room to eat breakfast, followed a few minutes later by Stump and Slider.

He had a lot on his mind—a lot of decisions to make. For he felt he was losing control over the lives of the citizens of Black Horse Creek. It was definitely a warning sign when the people were having secret meetings. He was convinced that the key to reclaiming complete control was the elimination of Grayson. He was responsible for the deaths of two of his three sons, but more than this, he showed the people of the town that someone could come in and kill the sheriff. It was imperative that he was made to pay the price and his body must be displayed like Billy's body in Fort Smith. It was the first time he had been so short of men working for him, and that would have to be corrected as soon as possible. But first, Grayson must be hunted down and killed. The more thought he had given the notorious ex-lawman, the more he was convinced that Grayson was not on the run after killing Slate, for if he had come to kill Slate, then he had come to kill Troy, too. *If he doesn't know Troy's dead*, he thought, *then he'll be slipping around waiting for a chance to get a shot at him*. He didn't see any way that Grayson could know about Troy's death, so he felt certain he was still lurking around the outskirts of town, watching—maybe watching him right now as he entered the side door of the hotel. He couldn't help but pause and look around behind him, as if feeling the bounty hunter's eyes on him. All he saw was the thin grim face of Dan Slider and the eager glow of anticipation for the breakfast about to be consumed on Stump's whiskered face. The sight further disgusted him. It reminded him of his present vulnerability without a sizable gang to enforce his bidding.

At the far end of the street, a lone rider slow-walked his horses into the back door of Earl Dickens's stable. Young Burt McNally was busy forking hay over the stalls near the front of the building and failed to notice until he turned and found Grayson standing a dozen feet behind him. Startled, Burt could not react at once, not knowing if he was in danger or not. Undecided if he should reach for his pistol or not, he remained frozen for a long moment before deciding it would be a useless attempt to beat the rifle casually held by the somber Grayson. When his mind began to function normally again, he remembered that his gun belt was hanging on a nail in the tack room, which explained why there was no sign of urgency in the stoic face watching him. "I need to leave my horses here for a little while," Grayson said. "They need some grain. They ain't had none in a spell."

"Damn, you scared the hell outta me," Burt finally confessed. "I thought my time was up."

Genuinely surprised by the statement, Grayson asked, "Why would you think that?"

"'Cause of what happened to the sheriff," Burt answered. "Jacob Blanchard put a five hundred dollar price on your head—to anybody that shoots you."

"Is that a fact?" Grayson replied calmly. "You thinkin' about collectin' it?"

"Hell no," Burt was quick to assure him, as he filled a bucket with oats for Grayson's horses, "and nobody else is, either, except maybe Dan Slider and Stump. If you're lookin' for Troy, he took off. He ain't here in town."

"Troy's dead," Grayson said.

"You got Troy?" Burt blurted.

"I didn't. His father did—shot him and another fellow that worked for him."

"His father?" Burt exclaimed "Why? Because of you?" Aware then that he still held the pitchfork, he threw it aside in case Grayson might think he had ideas about using it. "Damn," he swore, amazed. "The old man shot his own son?"

Grayson nodded. "So now, I reckon that leaves the job of sheriff up to you. I think you told me you had the job when both of the Blanchard boys were gone."

"Well, yeah, I—I reckon," Burt stammered, not sure he wanted it. He wasn't sure he could believe Grayson. It seemed more likely that Grayson had killed Troy, if Troy really was dead. "What are you fixin' to do?" he asked anxiously, afraid the menacing assassin might have plans to destroy the entire town.

"I've been thinkin' about that," Grayson replied. "I came after Slate and Troy because they ambushed me in Fort Smith, rode off and left me for dead. They're both dead now, so I reckon that settles my debt. Looks to me like you and the other folks in this town have to decide what you're gonna do about the old man. I just have an idea about how he's been runnin' the town, but I know for a fact that he killed his son and one other man."

"That ain't all," Burt declared. "He killed Percy

Edwards yesterday, shot him down because he took Slate's body back to his shop to get it ready to bury."

"Sounds like the folks in this town are ready for a hangin'. Maybe it's about time you thought about some honest-to-God law and order in your town. So I reckon the first thing you've gotta decide is if you're man enough to take on the job of sheriff." He paused to watch Burt's reaction. It was obvious that the young man was busy turning it over in his mind. After another moment, Grayson said, "I'll help you arrest Jacob Blanchard. You might need a hand, since he's got two men with him."

Grayson's offer was enough to help Burt make up his mind. "I'll do it. I'm man enough to take on the job." Grayson nodded his approval. "I need to tell a couple of the others what I'm fixin' to do," Burt went on. "Louis Reiner and Morgan Bowers oughta be told what's gonna happen—and my boss, Earl Dickens, I reckon."

"Let's get started, then," Grayson said. "Do you know where Blanchard is now?"

"Him and those two hired guns of his spent the night in Percy's place last night. He ain't plannin' on leavin' town anytime soon, 'cause his horse is in the corral. Anyway, I know he's gonna hang around till he buries Slate. And I talked to Reiner this mornin'. He said Blanchard told him he was gonna stay in town to have a talk with all of us about the things he ain't happy with in town. So he's either at the barbershop or the hotel, maybe the saloon." He paused a moment to recall. "Stump and Slider came and got their horses early this mornin', but they're still in town."

"Let's get to it, Sheriff," Grayson said.

* * *

Louis Reiner had much the same reaction as Burt when he turned to see who had just walked into his store and discovered the solid form standing behind Burt McNally. He was so startled that he dropped the broom he had been sweeping with. Embarrassed by his nervous fumbling, he quickly picked up the broom and stood there speechless, waiting for Burt to speak.

"It's time we took some action to free our town from Jacob Blanchard," Burt announced in a new-found voice of authority. "I'm fixin' to arrest him for the murders of Percy Edwards and Troy Blanchard." He paused to remember. "And one other feller that worked for him."

Reiner was not certain he could trust his own ears. Burt sure spoke with confidence, but Reiner could not take his eyes off the menacing figure behind him. Grayson saw the uncertainty in the storekeeper's gaze, so he offered a suggestion. "I reckon what the sheriff is tellin' you is that you're gonna want to appoint a judge and jury, so you can give Blanchard a fair trial before you hang him."

It was still not enough to shake Reiner from the paralysis caused by Burt's call to action. For more than a year the small group of concerned citizens had talked about rescuing their town, but he had wondered if it would ever amount to anything more than talk. "You're going now to arrest Jacob Blanchard?" he asked, not sure he had heard correctly.

"That's a fact," Burt replied confidently.

"That might not be so easy, Burt," Reiner cautioned. "The old man's got two of his gun hands with him. Maybe we oughta think about this before you go getting yourself killed."

"We've done enough talkin'," Burt returned. "It's time to do somethin'. Grayson, here, said he'd back me up."

Suddenly, Reiner felt a surge of excitement race through his veins when he realized that it was no longer just talk. It was real. This day in late summer would be remembered as the day the citizens of Black Horse Creek rose up and took possession of their town. "All right!" he exclaimed. "It's time! I'll run over and tell Shep. We'll use Percy's shop for a jail." He paused when he thought about it, then grinned and said, "Blanchard said he was making that the jail. He can be the first customer."

Grayson could understand their excitement, but he felt he needed to remind them of the danger involved in arresting Jacob Blanchard. "You'd best let the sheriff and me make the arrest before you round up your jury. There's liable to be some shootin', and we don't want any bystanders gettin' shot."

"Right!" Reiner quickly agreed. "We'll stay back out of the way, but we'll round up as many as we can find for when you have him arrested."

"You know where he is right now?" Grayson asked.

"The hotel," Reiner blurted. "Morgan Bowers was in here a little while ago, and said Blanchard was in the hotel, in to visit Slate."

Grayson looked at Burt and nodded. "Right," the new sheriff said. "Let's go!"

Stump Haskell took his feet off the porch railing and let the front legs of his chair drop back to the floor. "Damn! Look comin' yonder."

Dan Slider opened his eyes, annoyed by Stump's

intrusion on his short nap in the warm afternoon sunshine of the hotel porch. "Who the hell's that?" He recognized Burt McNally, who worked in the stable, but he had never seen the big fellow walking with him.

"Grayson," Stump answered. "That's Grayson with him. I'd best go tell Mr. Blanchard." He got up at once and went inside the hotel.

"Yeah, you do that," Slider called after him. "I'll take care of Mr. Grayson." He looked forward to the confrontation. He'd heard about Grayson until he was sick of it. Knowing that the man who took Grayson down would gain a hell of a reputation for himself, he didn't intend to miss his opportunity. He was confident in his knowledge that he was faster with a gun than any man he had ever met, and that included Yancey Brooks. Blanchard had often voiced regret that Yancey and Lonnie Jenkins had never returned from their attempt to track Grayson down. He would find out today that he had sent the wrong man to do the job. He got up from his chair, reached down to make sure his .44 was riding easy in its holster. Then he walked over to stand squarely at the top of the porch steps to wait for Burt and Grayson.

"Where you headed, Burt?" Slider asked, his tone one of obvious contempt.

"This is sheriff's business, Slider," Burt answered. "I'm lookin' for Blanchard, and it ain't no concern of yours."

Slider dropped his hand to rest on the handle of his pistol. "Anythin' that's got to do with Mr. Blanchard is my business. I'm the one who says whether you can bother him or not, so you'd best tell me what you're about."

Burt hesitated a few moments, so Grayson spoke for him. "You're talkin' to the new sheriff, so you'd be wise to step aside and let him get on with his business."

"The new sheriff?" Slider scoffed. "That's a sure-nuff joke if I ever heard one. Mr. Blanchard will be the one decidin' who's sheriff." He then turned his full attention to Grayson. "I reckon you'd be the big stud hoss name of Grayson. Well, you're lookin' at the big stud hoss of this town, so you can just turn your sorry ass around before I give you a bellyful of lead." Slider felt certain that if he was anything like his reputation, Grayson would find it hard to back down from his challenge. He stood poised, his hand still resting on the handle of the Colt, the smile spread across his thin features signaling the pleasure he anticipated.

"You sayin' you intend to stand in the way of the law?" Grayson asked calmly.

"That's right, stud," Slider replied.

"All right, then," Grayson said, and calmly pulled up the rifle he had been holding casually before him. Before the startled man could react, he pumped a .44 slug into his gut. As Slider doubled over in pain, still trying to draw his weapon, Grayson ejected the spent cartridge and finished him off with a second shot. He cocked the Winchester again and looked at Burt, who was as stunned as Slider had been. "Let's go. We're wastin' time."

Upstairs, watching from the front bedroom window, Jacob Blanchard was a witness to the elimination of another of his men at the hands of the relentless stalker. Thinking Slider would stop the ex-lawman, he cursed himself for not taking the shot from the window when he had the chance. Now it was too late, for Grayson was under the cover of the porch roof. Suddenly his anger turned to a feeling of sheer panic when he realized that Grayson was actually coming for him. He was no longer the hunter, he was the prey. It was a feeling he had never dealt with, because he had never before felt fear of any man. At that moment, he decided he was trapped there in the hotel room, and his only thoughts turned to those of escape.

He moved away from the window to confront a confused disciple in the person of Stump Haskell, waiting to be told what he should do. "Get to the stairs and stop them from coming up here!" Blanchard commanded. The dutiful Stump jumped to obey. Blanchard followed him out into the hall and directed him to a position at the top of the steps. Then he ran down to the end of the hall to the back stairs. Almost stumbling due to his haste, he nevertheless made it to the bottom of the stairs, and out the back door, to where Stump and Slider had tied their mounts. Pushing Stump's mule aside, he climbed up on Slider's horse, and flailed the sorrel mercilessly in his panic to escape. Down across the creek, he galloped behind the buildings, his one thought to make it to his ranch where he could hole up in his house.

Unaware their intended target was away and galloping toward home, Grayson and Burt walked through the hotel parlor to the foot of the front stairs, only to find themselves facing Stump looking down at them. The simple man was obviously befuddled by the situation he found himself in. "I—I don't think Mr. Blanchard wants you up here," he stammered, unaware, as they were, that his boss had fled. "He don't want nobody botherin' Slate's body," he offered, unable to think of something better to tell them.

"Stump," Burt said as calmly as he could manage, "you need to step aside and let us pass." He placed a foot on the bottom step. Stump dropped his hand to hover over his revolver, trying to decide whether to pull it or not. "We're on official business, Stump. Mr. Blanchard's wanted for murder, and we need to arrest him. So you don't want to get in the way of that."

Stump's brain was whirling out of control as he stared glassy-eyed at the ominous form of Grayson. He had never been forced to face a showdown like this one before. He knew Blanchard expected him to stop them, but Burt McNally had never done him any harm. In fact, Burt had always treated him kindly. But Mr. Blanchard would be extremely angry if he didn't follow his orders. In the final moments, Stump couldn't shoot Burt. He shook his head sorrowfully as if he had failed in his duty, and stepped aside.

"Good man, Stump," Burt said. "You did the right thing." He hurried up the stairs then with Grayson close behind him.

"Careful," Grayson warned, while keeping a cautious eye on Stump in case he had a change of heart. "Don't walk into an ambush. I wanna see you as sheriff for longer than half a day." Nearing the front of the hall, they could see the bedroom door standing wide open and the body of Slate Blanchard on the bed. Grayson moved ahead and slid up beside the door where he could take a quick look through the crack behind the door. "He ain't in there," he announced, and they both turned right away to make sure he wasn't behind them. There was no one there but a bewildered Stump Haskell.

A careful search of the other rooms on the floor came up empty before they went down the back stairs and discovered Stump's mule standing alone. Fresh tracks told an obvious story. "He's hightailin' it for home," Stump announced. At that point, Morgan Bowers and Maria Sanchez joined them, finally emerging from the refuge they had taken in the kitchen.

"Are you willin' to finish this thing?" Grayson asked Burt.

"I reckon," Burt replied.

The Creek woman went to the kitchen door and looked out across the yard toward the barn where Jimmy was busy replacing a couple of poles in the corral. He was working as hard as a man could, but the place was much more than one man could manage. Jacob was going to have to hire a crew to maintain the ranch, and he was going to have to do it soon, she thought. The crew of gunmen he had hired before were not inclined to work hard on the mundane chores of a ranch. They were more suited to murder and rustling, but they had been of some help when it came time for the fall roundup and branding. But now they were all gone, killed or run off, except for Stump and Dan Slider. She had to believe that it was a case of good riddance. Summer was nearing an end. Soon it would be time for roundup, and Jimmy said that Jacob's cattle were scattered all over the prairie. He needed help, but she told herself that it was Jacob's problem, not hers or Jimmy's.

She watched the young boy for a moment more before returning to her oven to check on her biscuits. Finding them ready to take out, she took her dish towel and pulled the pan from the oven. Thinking again of Jimmy, she placed a couple of the hot biscuits on the towel and used it to carry them out to the hardworking young man. He grinned when he saw her coming, having also spotted the dish towel in her hand. He had a special place in his heart for Rachel. She was the closest thing to a mother he could claim, his real mother having died giving birth to him. He only wished she had a better lot in life than being the slave to Jacob Blanchard.

"I thought maybe you like a hot biscuit," she said in her broken English. "Still little while to supper. Maybe you hungry."

"I'm always hungry for your biscuits," he said cheerfully.

"You work hard," she said, after watching him attack the hot biscuits.

"Yeah, and I ain't gettin' it done," he replied. "I need Stump to get back here."

She started to return to the house when a rider topped the east ridge and rode down toward the gate. They both paused to identify their visitor. After a moment, Jimmy said, "It's Mr. Blanchard, and from the looks of that horse, he must be in a hurry." They stood there watching, and when he got to the open gate, Jimmy said, "He ain't ridin' his bay. That's Slider's horse." Neither expressed it, but both wondered why the old man was alone, although it would not be the first time he had ridden off with one of the men and returned alone. They waited until he pulled the exhausted horse to a stop before the corral.

"What the hell are you two standin' out here doin' nothin' for?" Blanchard demanded angrily as he came out of the saddle. "Can't nobody do what I pay 'em for?" Obviously in a panic, he released the horse's reins and began to shout orders. "To hell with that horse!" he yelled at Jimmy when the boy took the reins and started to lead it toward the barn. "We ain't got time for that."

"Don't you want me to unsaddle him?" Jimmy asked. "He looks pretty much wore out."

"Leave the damn horse alone," Blanchard ordered. "Go to the bunkhouse and get your rifle and plenty of cartridges." He then turned to Rachel and pointed toward the kitchen door. "You go to the house and get my shotgun and all the shells you can carry."

She did not have to be told. "Grayson," she said. "He's coming."

"Yes, dammit!" Blanchard responded. "He's comin' and we're gonna be ready when he gets here. We'll have three guns waitin' for him and that damn young pup of a sheriff they picked for themselves. Now get to the house like I told you!" He gave her a sharp backhand on her behind to emphasize his command.

Jimmy winced when the old man struck her. It was uncalled for, but the long-suffering woman had learned to live with his harsh treatment. Thinking he might be on the receiving end of the same treatment, he dropped the horse's reins and ran to the bunkhouse to get his rifle. He was confused by Blanchard's ranting, and not at all certain he was ready to fight Grayson and the new sheriff, whoever that was. At the same time, he was reluctant to question Blanchard's orders. Jacob, in the meantime, stood there by the corner of the corral looking around, trying to decide where best to set up his defense—the house might be too big to defend with only the three of them, the barn too open. *The bunkhouse*, he decided. It was a solid structure of logs that would give the best protection. *The son of a bitch won't be expecting us to be holed up there*, he thought, *and we can catch him by surprise between the bunkhouse and the main house.*

In a very few minutes, Rachel came from the house, carrying the shotgun at about the same time Jimmy returned from the bunkhouse. Blanchard told them of his plan. "We're gonna wait for 'em in the bunkhouse. When they ride up to the house lookin' for me, we'll shoot 'em down like sittin' ducks on a pond. It'll be three of us against two of them." He glared at them and gave an emphatic nod of his chin. "They'll find out who runs my town, by God."

"Who did you say was the new sheriff?" Jimmy asked.

"That young pup that works for Earl Dickens," Blanchard snorted. "He's got a little too big for his britches. The whole damn town has got a hard lesson to learn. Well, they'll get my message when they see Grayson's corpse hangin' at one end of town, and Burt McNally's hangin' at the other."

The more the infuriated man ranted, the more uncertain Jimmy became. He knew Burt McNally. He didn't want to kill him—or Grayson either. He had stayed on working for Blanchard because he needed the job. He had never wanted to take part in any of Blanchard's lawless activities, and now he was afraid to say so. Rachel, however, was not.

"I not shoot anybody," she calmly announced. "I fix food for you. That's my job. These people are your enemies, not mine." She paused only a moment when she saw the fury in his face. Knowing the damage was already done, she added, "Jimmy should not shoot, too. He's no gunman."

"Why, you sassy-mouth Injun bitch!" Jacob roared, and struck out at her with his pistol, but she ducked away from him in time to avoid taking the blow on her head.

"No more you hit me," she cried, and started to raise the shotgun she held.

Blanchard grabbed the barrel of the weapon and easily wrenched it from her hands. "No more I hit you, hell," he mocked. "You was thinkin' you was gonna shoot me with this shotgun? I'll beat the livin' hell outta you." He threw her on the ground and stood over her, holding the shotgun like a club.

Jimmy was frozen in a paralysis of indecision, a witness to the horrible beating about to be administered to one who was always kind to him. He could no longer think because of the thunderous pounding of his heartbeat in his ears as Blanchard raised the shotgun to strike. He didn't remember pulling the trigger, and was nearly as startled as Blanchard when the rifle suddenly fired, sending a bullet ripping into the old man's side. Jacob staggered with the impact, and tried to turn the shotgun on Jimmy, only to be stopped by the solid impact of Jimmy's next shot in his chest. The shotgun fell from Blanchard's hands, but he remained on his feet, his body bent forward like a great ape as he stared at Jimmy with unbelieving eyes. Both the young boy and the Creek woman, Rachel, seemed stunned as they watched the old man fearfully. After a long moment, Blanchard sank to his knees, where he remained for several moments more, before finally falling face-first in the dirt.

Barely able to believe she was still alive, Rachel quickly looked to Jimmy. Seeing the stark bewilderment in his eyes, she scrambled to her feet and quickly went to him. "Everything all right," she gently told him. "You done the right thing. He not hurt nobody no more." She could see that he was still not sure what he had done, so she told him. "You save my life. I thank you." She then took his elbow and started him toward the house. "We best sit down now—talk, maybe drink coffee, decide what to do." She could not help a feeling that she had just been released from a terrible bondage, at the same time wondering what would become of her now that her master was gone. It was far too late to think about possibly returning to her village. There was nothing they could do now but calmly wait for Grayson, so they left Blanchard's body where it lay, and went into the house.

It was almost dark when Grayson and Burt crossed the east ridge and rode down into the river valley. They pulled up short of the gate to look things over before riding in, halfway expecting a rifle shot from the house. But there was none. Then Grayson noticed the two people sitting in rocking chairs on the front porch. It was difficult to tell in the half light, but it appeared to be Rachel and the boy—he had forgotten his name. "Over there!" Burt said, calling his attention to what looked to be a body lying near the corral.

"Why don't you go over and take a look," Grayson suggested, gesturing toward the body. "Might not be a bad idea to step down and keep your horse between you and the house." He then followed his own advice and dismounted, pulling his rifle from the saddle sling as he did. There was no sense in taking a chance on Jacob Blanchard hiding behind the two on the porch, with a rifle trained on him. They parted and Grayson walked his horse toward the front porch, taking care to walk even with the gray's withers, his rifle resting across them.

"Mr. Blanchard's dead," Jimmy called out when Grayson was within a few yards of the front steps. "That's him over yonder by the corral."

At almost the same time, Burt called out, "It's Blanchard! He's dead."

"Who killed him?" Grayson asked Rachel.

"I did," Jimmy immediately volunteered.

"He save my life," Rachel quickly interjected. "Blanchard was gonna kill me if Jimmy don't shoot him."

It was obvious by the woman's tone that she was afraid Jimmy might be hauled off to jail, so Grayson was quick to assure her that Jimmy had nothing to fear. "I'll surely accept your word on that," he told her, "and I don't reckon Sheriff McNally will see it any differently. He was set for a hangin' anyway. And to tell you the truth, I didn't expect he'd come peacefully." He turned to Jimmy. "So I reckon you just did the sheriff's job for him."

it was not really that far from Dodge City and the railroad, and there was plenty of good grassland for herds being driven up from Texas. As Mayor Reiner said, "The sky's the limit. We can build our town into one of the busiest towns in the state of Kansas."

As far as Jacob Blanchard's ranch was concerned, the city council thought it only fair to cut out five hundred acres and award that, the house, and the outbuildings, to Rachel, with Jimmy and Stump as share owners. Stump was forgiven for having worked for Blanchard, since he had never actually harmed anyone, and he had refused to shoot Burt McNally. There was generally a bright cloud of optimism over the entire town.

Standing apart from the suddenly busy rebirth of Black Horse Creek, the one man who had more to do with the town's revolution than any other, Grayson silently witnessed the scurrying about of the town's leading citizens. From one quickly called meeting to the next, they seemed to be constantly running up and down the street, from the hotel to the saloon, to Reiner's store in their enthusiastic quest to establish themselves as a community of promise.

Amid all the activity, he was no more than a bystander, no longer the sinister bounty hunter sent to destroy the Blanchard dynasty. No longer a figure of mystery and fear, he was greeted courteously, but he was not one of them. The only person who expressed his appreciation was Burt McNally, and that surprised Grayson, for he never expected appreciation. From the beginning, his sole purpose had been to seek revenge for his attempted murder by Slate and Troy Blanchard. And he didn't give a damn

about the future of Black Horse Creek. Seeing all the
joyous activity now, however, he was moved to regret
not being a part of it—or at least a part of some positive and useful future. The more he thought about it,
the more resigned he became to make something of
his life other than a hunter of felons. His thoughts
drifted automatically to a handsome widow in Fort
Smith, and he decided that he needed to get back to
Wanda Meadows's boardinghouse as quickly as he
could. When he had left her, she made him promise
to be careful. That wasn't much, but it might mean
that she cared what happened to him. "Worth lookin'
into," he stated.

   "Did you say somethin'?" Burt asked.

   "Yeah," Grayson replied, "I said so long."

Please read on for a look at
another exciting historical novel
from Charles G. West

WAY OF THE GUN

Available from Signet.

Looks like I might have company, young Carson Ryan thought as he watched the two riders approaching the North Platte River. Always one to exercise caution, he remained in the cover of the cottonwoods on the north bank until he could see what they were about. *Cow punchers from the look of them,* he decided. They had no packhorses that would indicate it was just the two of them on their way somewhere; maybe they were scouts for a wagon train of some kind. As he watched, the two separated to inspect the banks up and down the river, almost as far as Carson's camp. It was obvious to him then that they were selecting a crossing. Unable to contain his curiosity any longer, he led his horse over beside a tall cottonwood and pulled off his boots. Then he stood on the buckskin's back to reach a stout limb. Climbing up in the tree, he looked back to the south, and soon got the answer to his question. A faint cloud of brown dust in the distance announced the approach of a cattle herd. He remained up in the

tree until he saw the first steers. With no further concern for caution, he descended the tree to drop down
onto the ground. When the two point men rode back
to meet the herd, he sat down and pulled his boots
back on.

It's getting a little late in the day to cross the river, he
thought. *They'll most likely hold them on the other side
tonight and cross them over in the morning.* He knew from
experience that cows weren't fond of river crossings.
Although only seventeen years of age, he had worked
with cattle for most of those years, and he guessed it
would always be in his blood. He was hoping to catch
on with a herd heading for Montana, where there were
already some big outfits grazing their cattle on the
vast open bunch grass prairies. He had come up from
Texas with a herd of twenty-five hundred head belonging to Mr. Bob Patterson. Starting on the Western Trail
at Doan's Crossing near Vernon, Texas, they went only
as far as Ogallala. Mr. Patterson tried to persuade him
to return to Texas with him to pick up another herd,
but Carson wanted to see Montana. Patterson wished
him well, and Carson set out for Fort Laramie, thinking it a possibility to catch a herd stopping there for
supplies. It was a long shot, but at seventeen, a boy
can wait out the winter and hope for something in
the spring.

Carson was thinking now that he must have luck
riding with him, because he had decided to make
camp earlier than usual—when along came a herd.
Maybe they could use another hand. One thing for
sure, they weren't looking to buy any supplies at Fort
Laramie, because if they were, they missed the fort
by a good forty miles. "We'll just sit right here and
see what kinda outfit they are," he told the buckskin

gelding. On second thought, he decided it would be better to cross over to the south side, since that was more likely to be where the herd would be bedded down for the night. While he waited, he decided he would inspect the river to find the place he would pick to cross a herd.

"Well, now, who the hell is that?" Duke Slayton asked when he sighted the lone rider waiting by the river.

Johnny Briggs turned in the saddle and looked where Duke pointed. "Damned if I know," he replied. "He weren't there when me and Marvin scouted the banks."

"Well, he's sure as hell there now," Duke came back. "You and Marvin go on up ahead and make sure he ain't got no friends layin' below that river-bank, waitin' to pop up, too."

Johnny wheeled his horse around a couple of times, straining to get a better look at the man before he complied with Duke's order. He had his suspicions the same as Duke, and he wasn't anxious to become the sacrificial lamb in the event there might be a wel-coming party waiting to gain a herd of cattle. "He don't look to be much more'n a kid," he finally decided. "He might just be a stray, lookin' for a job. And we're damn sure short of men," he added.

"Or lookin' for a meal," Duke said, although he noticed that the young man was riding a stout-looking buckskin and was leading a packhorse. "You goin' or not?"

"I'm goin'," Johnny replied and wheeled his horse once again. "Come on, Marvin." The two of them were off at a fast lope while Duke turned back to meet Rufus Jones, who was riding forward to meet him.

"I'm thinkin' 'bout beddin' 'em down in the mouth of this shallow valley, where they can get to the water, and there's plenty of good grass," Rufus called out as he pulled his horse to a stop. "That all right with you?"

"Yeah, hell, I don't see why not. I ain't wantin' to try to push 'em across tonight, and that's a fact," Duke replied. They were driving close to two thousand head of cattle, and by the time the boys riding drag caught up, it would most likely be approaching dusk. The herd had been strung out for about two miles since the noontime rest.

Up ahead, Johnny and Marvin slowed their horses to a walk while both men scanned the brush and trees behind the lone stranger, alert to anything that didn't look right. With nothing to suggest that foul play was afoot, they walked their horses up to the rider awaiting them. Johnny was the first to speak. "Well, young feller, what are you doin' out here all by your lonesome?"

"I was campin' down the river a'ways," Carson replied, "and I saw you ride up. So I thought I'd say howdy—maybe visit awhile if you're fixin' to bed that herd down here."

Johnny studied the young man carefully. He was young, right enough, but he was a husky fellow and fairly tall, judging by the length of his stirrups. He could see no deceit in the deep blue eyes that gazed out at him. "Why, sure," Johnny responded. "Right, Marvin?" He didn't wait for Marvin's answer. "We're always glad to share our campfire with strangers. Where you headed, anyway?"

"Well, I was thinkin' about ridin' up to Fort Laramie and maybe catching on with a herd movin' on through to Montana Territory."

"Is that a fact?" Marvin asked. "Maybe you should talk to the boss." He nodded toward Duke Slayton, who was riding up behind them now. "'Cause that's where we're pushin' this herd—up Montana way."

Maybe Lady Luck *was* following him, he thought, as a sturdy-looking man with a full face of gray whiskers rode up to join them. Like the two before him, he cast a sharp eye back and forth along the line of the bank behind Carson. Figuring that if there was any funny business planned, it would have already been happening, he nodded to the young man. "Howdy, young feller," he remarked. "Where are you headed?"

Marvin answered before Carson had a chance. "He's on his way to Fort Laramie, lookin' to catch on with a herd goin' to Montana."

That brought a look of interest to Duke's face. "Well, now, is that so? You ever work cattle before?"

"Yes, sir. I just came up from Texas with a herd that belonged to Mr. Bob Patterson, but he only took 'em as far as Ogallala."

"How come you wanna go to Montana?" Duke asked.

"'Cause I ain't ever been there," Carson replied.

Duke grinned. "I reckon that's reason enough. Reminds me of myself when I was about your age." He paused to think about it a moment longer before deciding. "We are short a man." He glanced at Johnny and shrugged. "Hell, we could use about two more men than we've got, but one more would make a heap of difference. Wouldn't it, Johnny?"

Johnny responded with a grin of his own. "I reckon that's the truth, all right."

"I guess we could give you a try," Duke went on.

"This feller, Patterson, I reckon he was payin' you about twenty dollars a month. Right?"

"No, sir," Carson replied. "He was payin' me thirty dollars."

"That's the goin' rate for an experienced cowhand," Duke came back. "And right now you're a pig in a poke." Carson shrugged indifferently, and Duke continued. "I'll tell you what I'll do. I'll give you a try at twenty until you show me you can cowboy with the rest of us. Whaddaya say?" Carson started to reply, but Duke interrupted when a thought occurred. "You ain't wanted by the law, are you?"

"No, sir," Carson answered. "I ain't." He hesitated for a moment, then said, "I reckon I'll go to Montana with you." He knew he was worth more than the twenty dollars offered, but he didn't blame the man. Besides, he figured, he was bound for Montana one way or another, so he might as well go with this outfit. It might be a better bet than looking for one passing near Fort Laramie this late in the summer. He didn't know where in Montana they were taking the cattle, but if he had to guess, he'd say they had over three hundred miles to go. So they were cutting it pretty close as far as the weather was concerned. It was going to get pretty cold in a month or so.

"Fine," Duke said. "My name's Duke Slayton. This is Johnny Briggs and Marvin Snead. What's your name?"

"Carson Ryan."

"All right, Carson, you can meet the rest of the boys at supper. Might as well just wait around till the drags come in and we settle the herd in this valley. You can dump your bedroll and other stuff in the chuck wagon and talk to Skinny Wills—he's the wrangler—about a string of horses." He turned to Johnny then. "You and Marvin pick the best place to cross in the mornin'?"

"Right here where we're sittin' is about as good as any, I reckon," Johnny said. "There ain't much bank to climb on the other side."

Duke turned to Carson then, in a spirit to playfully test the new man. "What do you say, Carson? This look like a good place to push 'em across?"

"No, sir," Carson replied stoically. "If it was me, I'd try it upstream a couple hundred feet, maybe on the other side of that tallest cottonwood." He pointed to the tree.

All three men looked genuinely surprised to hear his reply. "Is that so?" Duke responded. "And why would you do that? The banks are good and low on both sides right here."

"Quicksand," Carson answered matter-of-factly.

"Quicksand!" Johnny exclaimed. "How do you know that?"

Carson shrugged. "Well, I don't know for sure, but I noticed a couple of places toward the other side where the water looked like it was makin' little whirlpools. And it wasn't flowin' around any tree roots or rocks or anything, and that's what the water looks like when there's quicksand under it."

Duke couldn't contain the laugh. He threw his head back and roared. "Whaddaya think, Johnny? Maybe we oughta go ahead and give him the thirty dollars."

"I'm just sayin' that's what the water looked like when we got into some quicksand on a drive two years ago crossin' the Red River," Carson quickly offered, afraid he might have made an enemy of Johnny. "Might not be quicksand here at all."

"Ain't worth takin' the chance," Johnny said, apparently not offended. "That stuff can cause a lot of trouble that I'd just as soon be without."

"All right, we'll cross 'em up above the big cottonwood," Duke said cheerfully. "And if we get into any quicksand, we'll hang Carson in the damn tree. Does that suit everybody?" Everyone grunted in approval, including the new hire. "Now, let's get them cows watered. Come on, Carson, I'll take you to see Bad Eye—he's the cook."

Also available from
Charles G. West

"THE WEST AS IT REALLY WAS."
—RALPH COMPTON

Way of the Gun
(Coming March 2013)

Even at seventeen years old, Carson Ryan knows
enough about cow herding to realize the crew he's
with is about the worst he's ever seen. They're
taking the long way around to the Montana prairies,
and they're seriously undermanned. They're also a
bunch of murdering cattle rustlers—and now the law
thinks he's one of them...